"SO I JUST RAN WITHOUT A SHIRT...

...for a quarter mile and would've gotten to go anyway?"

"Not really. But I wanted to make you feel bad. By the way, has anyone ever told you you're completely mad?"

I laughed and turned around to unravel my tank top and slip it over my head, a huge smile on my face. "So, what time do we leave for the air—"

I suddenly felt his hot sweaty body pressed up against my back, his one hand on my bare waist, the other sweeping my long hair to one side. "No need to put that back on."

My breath caught in my throat. "Wha-wha-what are you doing?" I whispered, feeling his hands slide up the front of my body and begin touching my breasts over my bra. He was hard. Really, really hard, and straining against my lower back.

"I think that's fairly obvious; keeping our deal," he said, his hot breath tickling my neck.

I was about to say something to explain how I didn't really want him to do what he was doing, but it would've been a lie. The heat of his skin on my back, his hard cock pressing into me while his hands massaged my breasts felt better than anything I'd ever experienced.

His lips trailed down the side of my neck and stopped right on the little spot where my shoulder started.

How was this happening? Because wasn't he...didn't he have that problem with...?

other works by mimi jean pamfiloff

IMMORTAL MATCHMAKERS, Inc.
(Book 1/Paranormal Romance/Humor)

FATE BOOK (New Adult Suspense/Humor)

FATE BOOK TWO (New Adult Suspense/Humor)

THE HAPPY PANTS CAFÉ (Prequel/Romantic Comedy)

THE MERMEN TRILOGY (Dark Fantasy)

Mermen (Book 1)

MerMadmen (Book 2)

THE KING TRILOGY (Dark Fantasy)

King's (Book 1)

King for a Day (Book 2)

King of Me (Book 3)

THE ACCIDENTALLY YOURS SERIES
(Paranormal Romance/Humor)

Accidentally in Love with...a God?

Accidentally Married to...a Vampire? Sun God Seeks...Surrogate?

Accidentally...Evil? (a Novella)

Vampires Need Not...Apply?

Accidentally...Cimil? (a Novella)

Accidentally...Over? (Series Finale)

COMING SOON

MERCILESS (Book 3, the Mermen Trilogy)

MACK (Book 4, the King Series)

TOMMASO (Immortal Matchmakers Series, Book 2)

BRUTUS (Immortal Matchmakers Series, Book 3)

GOD OF WINE (Immortal Matchmakers Series, Book 4)

TAILORED FOR TROUBLE
(THE HAPPY PANTS SERIES Book 1) (Romantic Comedy)

fugly

Mimi Jean Pamfiloff

a Mimi Boutique Novel

Copyright © 2015 by Mimi Jean Pamfiloff

All rights reserved. No part of this publication may be reproduced, distributed, or transmitted in any form or by any means, including photocopying, recording, or other electronic or mechanical methods, without the prior written permission of the writer, except in the case of brief quotations embodied in critical reviews and certain other noncommercial uses permitted by copyright law.

This is a work of fiction. Names, characters, places, brands, media, and incidents are either the product of the author's imagination or are used fictitiously. The author acknowledges the trademarked status and trademark owners of various products referenced in this work of fiction, which have been used without permission. The publication/use of these trademarks are not authorized, associated with, or sponsored by the trademark owners.

ISBN-10:0-9962504-4-1
ISBN-13:978-0-9962504-4-3

Cover Design by EarthlyCharms.com
Editing by Latoya C. Smith and Pauline Nolet
Interior design by WriteIntoPrint.com

Like "FREE" Pirated Books?
Then Ask Yourself This Question:
WHO ARE THESE PEOPLE I'M HELPING?

What sort of person or organization would put up a website that uses stolen work (or encourages its users to share stolen work) in order to make money for themselves, either through website traffic or direct sales?

Haven't you ever wondered?

Putting up thousands of pirated books onto a website or creating those anonymous ebook file sharing sites takes time and resources. Quite a lot, actually.

So who are these people? Do you think they're decent, ethical people with good intentions? Why do they set up camp anonymously in countries where they can't easily be touched? And the money they make from advertising every time you go to their website, or through selling stolen work, **what are they using it for?**

The answer is you don't know.

They could be terrorists, organized criminals, or just greedy bastards. But one thing we DO know is that **THEY ARE CRIMINALS** who don't care about you, your family, or me and mine.

And their intentions can't be good.

And every time you illegally share or download a book, YOU ARE HELPING these people. Meanwhile, people like me, who work to support a family and children, are left wondering why anyone would condone this.

So please, please ask yourself who YOU are HELPING when you support ebook piracy and then ask yourself who you are HURTING.

And for those who legally purchased or borrowed or obtained my work from a reputable retailer (not sure, just ask me!) muchas thank yous! You rock.

The unauthorized reproduction or distribution of a copyrighted work is illegal. Criminal copyright infringement, including infringement without monetary gain, is investigated by the FBI and is punishable by fines and federal imprisonment.

dedication

To Cassie.

Because you always know just what to say when everyone is having a fucking ugly day.

fugly

chapter one

They say that beauty is in the eye of the beholder. And while I can't argue with that, I can say the same holds true for ugly. Especially in my case.

I used to think I was beautiful—on the inside, anyway—and he was the monster. A horrible, unscrupulous, arrogant prick hiding behind the face of a bona fide, modern-day sex god. CEO, model, a man who had everything.

I was wrong. About both of us. And my blindness has led us to the edge. A pivotal cluster fuck.

My name is Lily Snow. I am twenty-five years old, five foot six, weigh one hundred and twenty pounds, and I have just fucked up my life. Along with his.

Good God, I never should have put him in a position like this. But what else could I do? I'm just an ugly girl in love with a beautiful man.

I'm so sorry, Max. I'm so, so sorry.

Two months earlier.

Do not be afraid. He's just a person. Do not be afraid. He's just a person. As I fidgeted on the white couch in the middle of the minimally decorated lobby—bright white walls, floors, and furniture with a few oversized photos of red juicy lips on the walls—I quietly prepared for the most important interview of my life: a role as junior sales manager at Cole Cosmetics—aka C.C.—in Chicago where I now lived. Getting this job would symbolize walking through a door people said would never be open to someone like me. And once I got in, it would serve as a stepping-stone for everything I wanted in life, mainly starting my own cosmetics company.

Someday.

In the meantime, I needed this—the experience, the prestige—and to prove to myself I had what it took to work at the world's most edgy, glamorous cosmetics company that had set every trend for the last six years. One whisper from C.C., and the stylish masses of A-list actresses, pop divas, and fashion designers scrambled to catch up. This summer, sea-foam-green eyeshadow and orange lips were God, but I didn't dare wear anything so bold. Calling attention to my face was not a smart move.

"Lily Snow?" I heard a woman call my name.

I looked over at the slender, gorgeous redhead,

not much older than me, wearing a fitted blue dress and strappy blue heels. Her smoky, mascara-caked eyes scanned the nearly empty lobby, looking right over my head.

"Hi. I'm Lily Snow."

Her eyes fell on my face with a spark of shock she quickly tried to conceal. "You're…Miss Snow?"

I gave her a quick nod.

"Oh," she said stiffly. "Don't you have lovely hair."

Her comment was what I liked to call a "conscience clearer." It was when someone realized they just acted like a coldhearted ass and then quickly tried to make it up to me with a compliment. Usually about my long, wavy blonde hair or my "cute little body."

I stood from my chair and extended my hand. "Thanks. I'll trade my hair for your shoes. Your Manolos are to die for." They were a limited release made just for Oscar season. Very expensive.

My shoes, for the record, were Franco Sarto heels I'd found on clearance at The Rack, black and simple, just like my pencil skirt and blouse. I would've loved to wear something more expensive, but the job I'd been in—a one-year consulting project at B&H Cosmetics—was for the experience rather than a big paycheck. I could've done better, but I'd had my sights on C.C., and I knew Mr. Cole, the owner, worked at B&H right after college.

I'm on your heels, big man.

A little smile popped on the redhead's face. "My boyfriend got them for me," she said, doing a little pivot to show off the shoes. "He works for Babs Levine."

Uh. Wow. Babs was the world's top formal dress designer, who once worked for some of the biggest names in fashion before going out on her own. She practically owned the red carpet this last season.

"Well," I smiled, "if you ever get tired of your boyfriend, I'm single."

She laughed so loud her voice echoed off the sterile-looking walls of the lobby. "I don't think so."

I wasn't sure if she'd meant she'd never give the guy up or that he'd never go for me in a million years.

Both. Definitely both. I didn't take offense, though. I'd made the comment to break the ice, and it worked. She introduced herself as Keri and became all smiles and warm chatter on the elevator ride up. I liked her immediately.

"So what's it like having Maxwell Cole as your boss?" I asked.

The stainless steel doors slid open, and we entered the executive lobby on the top floor of the Chicago high-rise. *Holycrap.* Everything had an epic, larger-than-life feel—the floor-to-ceiling glass windows, sleek black furniture, and five pairs of red lips with the C.C. logo etched onto the cement floor. I half expected angels to come fluttering from the walls, blowing their horns. *It's like meeting a real live god.*

And a god I would meet.

Maxwell Cole, the founder and CEO, was thirty-three, a marketing genius, Stanford grad, and handsome as hell. And he had morals. No, I'd never met the man, but I did my thesis on his company's business model, and he was the heart and soul of the place, which was why he handpicked his corporate office salespeople even if they'd report to someone else. Which I would. Something like three levels down.

Still, I wanted to know everything about working for the man. I was ready to please him, bow to him, and make little origami shrines at his feet while he sat in meetings. The chance to work with a legend like this, even from afar, was a dream come true. And exactly what I needed if I were to run my own cosmetics company—one that I'd dedicate to making women feel beautiful and special no matter what they looked like.

Someday.

Keri's smile melted away into something I'd describe as a polite smirk—like she knew something I didn't. "Working for Mr. Cole is...great. Demanding, but great."

For some reason, the only part of her comment I bought was the word "demanding." I found that strange.

She added, "But you'll get to see for yourself in

two minutes." She showed me into a small conference room in the corner, just big enough to seat four around the tiny orange table. The room, though it had an amazing view of Chicago and Lake Michigan, felt far too cozy and instantly put me on edge. I realized how close I'd have to sit to Maxwell Cole. And while I wasn't ashamed of myself, I wanted him to focus on my words and my résumé, not on my face.

It's Maxwell Cole. He'd never judge you like that. How'd I know? In an interview he'd done for *Money Magazine*, Maxwell Cole talked about how he only dated women whose "souls turned him on." Anyone who followed celebrity gossip knew he'd meant it, too. That man had been seen dating some of the least attractive women in Hollywood. Okay, some pretty ones, too. But he didn't seem to care one way or another. More importantly, he'd built his entire company on one philosophy: "When it comes to your looks, the only opinion in this world that matters is yours." C.C.'s in-your-face, anti-idealization of women went as far as frequently featuring some pretty imperfect models in their ads. Definitely not your standard Victoria's Secret gals. Of course, the C.C. women—wrinkles, gapped teeth, very average looking—were all runway beauties compared to me. But that was something I'd come to grips with years ago.

"Thank you," I said to Keri and took the seat that put my back to the view of the city so I wouldn't get distracted during the interview.

"Can I get you anything, a water or coffee?" Keri asked with a warm smile before taking her leave.

She seemed like a genuinely sweet person, which felt encouraging. I wanted to work with nice people. It was why I came here.

"Thanks," I replied. "Water would be great."

"I'll be right back, then." She left, and I looked up at the clock above the doorway. Four o'clock on the dot. Interview time. *Okay, stay calm. You are smart, overqualified for this role, and have a perfect résumé. And you're nice.*

As I gave myself a pep talk, I noticed a large figure looming in the doorway, and then, just like in the movies, everything around me dissolved into nothing. There was just him.

Holy shit.

His beauty was pure male magnificence—high cheekbones and strong jaw that gave his face a masculine sculpted look; and lips that were full and sensual, surrounded by a wash of dark brown even though I could tell he'd shaved this morning.

Mr. Cole was so goddamned beautiful it hurt to look at him. *But how the hell is it possible he's better looking in person?* And his cologne was…was…I never knew a man could smell that good.

It's really him. Then my blasted brain kicked on and urged me to mentally strip away that perfectly tailored, navy-blue power suit covering his lean, muscular, exquisite body—the one he'd shown the world last season in the "Get Naked. Get Real" campaign for their new Nude and Natural makeup line. With the exception of his penis, which had been tragically blocked by his large hands, he'd displayed every ripped inch of his abs, chiseled pectorals, bulging arms, and tats.

He is un. Real. I mentally sighed. *And those eyes...*

As I basked in their hazel beauty, his eyes met mine, and it felt like a cold slap. I saw that same look on everyone's faces the first time they saw me. Pity or revulsion. Luckily, most tried to mask it once the first wave of shock passed. Then they got to know me, and I won them over.

However, before I could utter a word, his superbly masculine face went from having a subtly sickened expression to a displeased one—a slight hardness in his eyes and firmness of his lips. Body language says a lot, too, and the tension in his tall frame said he didn't want to waste his time with me.

But wait. Why is he put off by my looks? That didn't make sense given who this was. Had I imagined it?

"You must be Lily Snow," he said, still standing in the doorway, his voice cold, hypnotically deep, and authoritative.

I smiled nervously and stood, extending my trembling hand. "Mr. Cole, it's an honor to meet you. I did my master's thesis on your company."

His hand reminded me of an old, rusted-out clunker with a stalling engine, painfully chugging its way to meet my awaiting handshake. When his reluctant palm finally made contact, I couldn't help wanting to interpret the human warmth of his skin as reassurance I had imagined his reaction to me.

Yes, he's an important man with a lot going on. With a company this large and billions on the line, it was very possible he had a few fires on his plate. His mood had nothing to do with me. It couldn't.

I shoved my nerves down a deep dark hole and gave his hand a firm, confident squeeze to demonstrate my assertive nature.

He jerked his hand away.

What in the...? My mind scrambled, reaching for an explanation, any at all, as I sat and laced my fingers together in my lap. I couldn't make sense of this.

"So." He took his seat and scooted back against the wall. He'd put himself only a few feet away, but it was an unnatural distance that left a space between the table and his long legs. "You are interviewing for the junior sales position."

"Yes," I replied, trying to hold it together and hoping to God I was wrong about what was happening. Perhaps he was a germophobe or one of those people who hated to be touched?

With an unsteady hand, I slid my résumé from my black leather portfolio and passed it to him. I'd sent a copy of my CV to his HR person, but who knew if he'd had time to read it.

Nope. I guess not.

His intense hazel eyes began skimming while I sat there staring, mortified and unsure of what to say or do.

"You're not qualified." He threw the sheet of paper on the table and shot me a harsh look before abruptly standing.

"But I—"

"Thank you for coming," he said in a tone that told me he wasn't thankful at all. More like put out, annoyed, maybe pissed off.

My mouth hung open as he walked out of the tiny conference room, not bothering to shake my hand or look at me or hear anything I had to say.

My emotions fell somewhere between epic rage and heartbreak. He'd treated me like a leper or some mangy dog with rabies. And as my mind quickly digested everything that happened in the last sixty seconds, I could only come up with one reason for his behavior: my looks. And, hell no, I wasn't crazy or making it up. That expression on his face when he'd walked in the door? The way he'd shaken my hand?

I covered my face and let out a shaky breath. *This can't be happening.* I expected this sort of behavior from a shallow, pompous asshole that only valued women for their beauty, but from Maxwell Cole?

My mind went into a tailspin of anger, despite my conscience urging me to take the high road—a road I knew like the back of my hand. After all, I was a nice, caring person. I didn't yell at people—or hadn't in years. But that had been back in school, and only when some jerk decided to mess with one of my painfully shy friends or my disabled brother.

But you can't let Maxwell Cole do this, Lily. I'd worked my ass off to have the right experience for a job like this. Okay, yes, I had other options besides C.C.—I wasn't stupid or naïve enough to put all my eggs in one basket—but those other companies weren't Cole Cosmetics. They weren't companies I related to and believed in. Those other companies didn't tell the world you were beautiful for who you were on the inside and to buy their products simply because you enjoyed pampering yourself. Cole Cosmetics didn't believe in making women feel ugly to sell makeup. And that's exactly what inspired me to work in this industry. We all deserved to feel beautiful and have nice things regardless of what others thought about our looks.

Only that prick has been lying to the world.

I grabbed my résumé from the table and stormed after Mr. Cole, quickly spotting him disappearing into a room in the opposite corner. Probably his private office.

So what? Let them drag me out. First, he was going to hear what I had to say.

When I stormed through the doorway, Maxwell Cole already sat at his fancy-shmancy, black-cherry desk, talking on the phone in all his handsome asshole glory, looking perfectly unruffled, acting like *that* hadn't just happened.

His eyes locked on mine, and he seemed unfazed as I approached his glorious fucking desk, where a glorious fucking built-in display case behind him exhibited his multitude of shiny plaques and awards like a shrine to himself. A giant whiteboard on the wall to his side had the words "I'm a Take What's Mine Kind of Woman" written on it, and the floor-to-ceiling glass on the other side of the room gave him an amazing view of the city. One he probably didn't appreciate.

Oh. I'm takin' what's mine, buddy. And I was after my pride.

"You're a f-fucking asshole." I threw my résumé in front of him, my hands shaking half with fear, half with anger, and half with adrenaline. *That's right. Three halves! I'm a dangerous woman!*

His hazel eyes shot up at me with extreme irritation. "I'll call you right back, Chuck." He hung up the phone, not taking his eyes away.

"You didn't even read my résumé," I spat, my heart pounding. I couldn't believe I was doing this, yet I couldn't help myself. Maxwell Cole suddenly represented every person who'd ever done me wrong, and I was tired of taking that stupid high road. I was tired of shrugging it off. I deserved a fair fucking shake, goddammit!

"I read your résumé," he said with a deep smug voice, lacing his fingers together over his stomach and leaning back in his shitty, black-leather exec chair like the huge dick that he was. "You're not a fit. Now get the hell out of my office."

"No. You didn't," I argued, "because if you had, you'd see that I have an MBA from Stanford, just like you, and I have two years of sales experience, which includes one year at B&H Cosmetics. You'd also note that I graduated top of my class, and that I have a letter of recommendation from Mark Douglas, who I believe is not only CEO of Wow-Wow Clothing and my college mentor, but a personal friend of yours, which is how I learned about the job. Not that I'd expect favoritism, but you know the man; he doesn't lie, and his standards are ridiculously high. So when he says I'm a good person and extremely capable, he fucking means it."

"You. Are not. Qualified," Maxwell Cole growled, his beautiful horrible face a blistering shade of red.

"The job only requires a bachelor's and one year of sales experience. So please explain where I'm lacking." I folded my arms across my chest.

Mr. Cole stood from his desk, scowling, and forcing me to look up, up, up. Even in my three-inch heels, I suddenly felt tiny, like he was a huge dragon preparing to unleash his fiery breath and smoke my ass until I was nothing but a pile of ashes.

"What you lack, Miss Snow, can't be captured on a piece of paper."

Just then Keri, his assistant, entered with an armful of files.

Guess she forgot about my water.

"Oh. Mr. Cole. Uhh…" Her eyes darted between her prick of a boss and me. "Is everything okay?"

"Get the hell out of my office and shut the door behind you," he said.

I thought he'd directed the comment toward me, but when I glanced back at him to say that I wouldn't leave until I got an answer—the real answer—I realized he'd spoken to Keri.

She tiptoed backwards out of the room and shut the door.

"You want an answer, Miss Snow?" Mr. Cole snarled with those beautiful sexy lips he didn't deserve. "I'll give you an answer. My salespeople need to step into a room and deliver an image that makes the customer want to buy our products. Not make them search for the nearest hill."

That had been a polite way of saying I wasn't good-looking enough, but the rage inside me wanted to hear him say the blunt, fugly truth to my face. I deserved to hear it. I wanted him to admit what a disgusting excuse of a human being he really was.

"Just say it," I fumed. "I'm fucking ugly, and

you're a fake superficial asshole."

He stared coldly, and there was this moment where my body felt like it was falling through the air without a parachute, just him and me surrounded by nothing, seeing each other for who we were: Him a complete bastard—only beautiful on the outside—and me, the exact opposite.

"Yes," he replied, snapping me out of a surreally vivid moment.

I took a deep breath and felt this strange knot in my chest. Despite already knowing the truth, hearing the words come from his gorgeous mouth cut me deep. Right down to the bone. And for the first time ever, I felt ugly. Truly ugly and unworthy of anything good in this world.

I pressed my lips together and stared down at my black heels. My heartbeat galloped at a million miles an hour, and my brain spun with a thousand ugly thoughts. I'd walked into a dream that ended up my worst nightmare.

When I looked up at his face, that strikingly handsome fucking face with the strong jaw and perfect goddamned chin, I wanted to rip it from his skull. I hated that this man wasn't who I thought. I hated myself for being so naïve and believing I could get anyone in the world to see past my looks.

And then the thought occurred to me; maybe the world had been politely lying to my face and this asshole was the only person who'd ever been honest. Maybe no one had ever really seen me, the real me, except for my family.

Had I been living a lie? Just like good ol' Mr. Cole here?

Fuck. I hated myself for even entertaining the thought, for allowing him to undermine who I was.

I lifted my chin and stared into his cold, beautiful hazel eyes, only they weren't so cold anymore. They were tormented.

I can't imagine why, you dick. Maybe because you're a mess of a human being, and you've just admitted it. Ironically, he'd admitted it to a stranger he considered unworthy of sharing the glorious air he breathed.

"Well, Mr. Cole, at least my problem can be fixed with scalpels. But you'll always be an asshole. A fake, unlovable, shallow prick. Good luck with that."

I turned to leave.

"So why haven't you?" he asked sharply.

"Excuse me?" Halfway to the door, I turned to face him again. "Why haven't I what?"

The condescending look in his eyes knocked me down a peg. "Fixed your problem. If it's so damned easy, why haven't you done it?"

How fucking dare he. "Because there's nothing wrong with me. But you should know that since you've made billions telling women that 'beauty is soul deep.'" It was a slogan they'd used for years.

He crossed his arms over his broad chest, flashing his shiny silver cufflinks. "Don't tell me you don't know the difference between marketing and reality."

"Yes, I do. And the reality is you're a fake."

He nodded with a chilling gaze. "Takes one to know one, Miss Snow. Now if you'll excuse me, real life is calling and there's no room for self-righteous, delusional little girls. Big boys only."

Motherfucker.

I straightened my spine, pasted on a smile, and gave him a cordial nod. "It was a pleasure meeting you, Mr. Cole." *Because now I won't feel any guilt when I start my own company and take you down.*

Someday.

I turned and left his office, hearing him telling me to wait. Wait for what? More insults? I left without looking back.

chapter two

The entire drive to my apartment was a blur. I don't remember getting in my red Mini and putting the top down. I don't remember hitting the freeway north, and I don't remember driving for an hour in the stifling August heat like a madwoman. I simply opened my eyes and found myself standing over my stainless steel kitchen sink with the cold water running, my face dripping wet and my blouse drenched in water.

I was in shock.

I shut off the faucet and patted my face with a dishtowel, my hand shaking with rage. Thank God my roommate, Daniella, was still at work so she wouldn't see me like this. If I was lucky, she'd head over to her boyfriend's place tonight. This was not how I wanted to be in front of anyone: falling the hell apart.

I grabbed a bottle of white wine from the fridge, poured myself a giant glass, went into the living room, and sat on the couch. My entire body felt numb and on fire at the same time. All I could see was that hateful man's face and the disgust in his eyes when he'd looked at me.

I'd never felt like this.

Ashamed.

Humiliated.

Angry.

I even felt pissed at myself because I'd let him get to me. He'd made me feel like a monster.

Not even growing up in the beautiful beach town of Santa Barbara, California, where some of the kids made fun of me on a daily basis, had I experienced this feeling. And trust me, kids can be cruel little bastards. Pug face, pig face, puke face...you name it, I'd been called it. But my mother and father always made sure I knew I was loved, and they never sugarcoated. They never told me I was pretty on the outside or tried to make me feel better about my looks. Instead, they fed it to me straight: "No one gets to have everything in life. They just don't." All I had to do was look at my older brother, a pretty intelligent guy with a boyishly handsome face—big brown eyes and blond hair, just like me—to understand what they meant. He was in a wheelchair. Born that way due to a rare deformation of the spine.

So that was my perception growing up. I got to have everything I wanted, except good looks. I didn't like it, but at the same time I wouldn't have traded my smarts for beauty.

I threw back my wine and lay down on the

couch, thinking I'd be able to pull myself out of what just happened, but this wasn't the sort of thing a girl simply shook off.

When I opened my eyes again, the haze of sleep shielded me for a few precious moments from the realities of yesterday, but sadly, it didn't last.

Then I started to cry and *almost* called my mother. A big mistake because she'd probably hunt down Mr. Cole and castrate him. That honor should belong to me.

I'm not doing this. Sulking was for suckers.

I threw on my white sports tank, shorts, and running shoes and then headed outside for a morning jog in a nearby park with a nice long running trail and lots of shady trees.

By the time I got back to my apartment building, I didn't know the time because I never wore a watch, but the Illinois summer air was too hot to breathe for outdoor exercise once the sun came up unless you had a death wish or were crazy, which I must've been. My body dripped with sweat and shook from heat exhaustion. But running had always been the one thing that helped clear my head.

Still panting, coming off of my exercise high, I made my way down the sidewalk that ran alongside my small six-unit complex. It was a red brick building with three stories and white shutters. Nothing fancy, but it was driving distance to Chicago, ten minutes to the train, and affordable.

When I turned the corner, heading for the front entrance, I didn't think much about the black car with tinted windows parked out front. In these parts, a lot of people used town cars to get to the airport, especially business people.

Muscles burning, I lethargically climbed the stairwell that wound through the middle of the building, stopping on the second floor to check Mrs. Jackson's door. She always left a Post-it outside when she needed help taking out her trash. Everyone in the building kept an eye on the eighty-year-old since she didn't do stairs well.

No Post-it. Someone else had probably helped her already. I'd stop by later, after my shower, and check on her anyway.

When I got to the third floor, my heavy pants caught in my throat with a gag. Maxwell Cole stood right outside my door, wearing a red tie and sleek black pin-striped power suit tailored to fit that athletic body. His full lips were pursed, and his slightly bloodshot hazel eyes held an emotion in them I couldn't decipher. Nor did I try. I was too angry and shocked to see him.

"What the *hell* are you doing here?" I stopped with my hands on my waist and felt the beads of sweat running like a little river down my spine.

His eyes moved over my body, almost reaching

the top before they made another sweep, lingering an extra moment on my breasts. He still hadn't uttered a word.

"What did you expect? Scales on my legs and a uni-breast?" I couldn't believe I'd said that, but pretending to be civil to this horrible man felt like a lie.

His eyes reluctantly settled on my face, his revulsion immediate. "Not the uni-breast." He cracked a dimpled smile. Totally forced.

I hissed out an unappreciative breath and marched straight to my door, pushing past him. I dug my key from the little pocket of my waistband while he just stood there staring at the view down the front of my panties.

Asshole. I shot him a look and released the elastic waistband with a snap. As I turned the key in the lock, I decided I'd be slamming the door in his face before he had the chance to say a single word. My guess was he feared I'd tell his little secret or sue him or something.

Let the man stew.

But the moment I pushed open the door, he said something that made me think twice. "Invite me in."

Okay, it wasn't so much what he said, but the way he'd said it: a demand. It gave me the urge to do far worse than shut a door and leave him on the other side.

I turned and looked up at him, shooting my own

breed of disgust his way. I hated the gorgeous bastard. I hated every perfect hair on his perfect head, and I wanted him to know it. "Why the fuck would I do that, asshole?"

"You have a dirty mouth." A subtle smile, laced with a hint of sadistic delight, twitched across his lips. That time his smile was real.

"You bring out the ugly bitch in me. Why are you here?"

"I want to talk. Invite me in," he demanded again with that deep authoritative voice.

I laughed at his attempt to boss me around. "If you're worried I'm going to tell anyone the truth about you, don't. I'd actually have to give a crap about you." The only thing I cared about was getting on the road to starting my own company as quickly as possible so I could build a company where women like me were genuinely valued.

"Miss Snow, stop being such a hostile bitch and invite me in."

My knee twitched with the urge to salute his balls.

"I've got a job proposal for you," he added, "the opportunity of a lifetime."

This sonofabitch wanted to offer me a job? After everything he'd said? *Hell yeah, I'll invite him in. Just to tell him to go fuck himself.*

I stepped aside and replied with a noxious sweetness, "Why…won't you come in, Mr. Cole?"

He dipped his head of thick dark-brown hair.

"Why, thank you, Miss Snow."

"Oh, please. Call me Lily. I insist."

I showed him in, past the doorway leading to the all-beige tube kitchen, and into our small living room. We didn't have much beside a secondhand floral sofa, a green armchair, and a small glass coffee table. No television. We were never home enough to watch TV (though I occasionally liked to catch *The Fashion Police* or *Masters of Sex* on my laptop). On the wall hung a painting of a lily I'd found at a yard sale. A white lily. The symbol of chastity and virtue. My mother said she'd named me after the flower because she thought they were elegant, beautiful, and timeless.

Maxwell Cole, whose shiny silver cufflinks, expensive suit, and supreme good looks made him look like a duck out of water in my fugly apartment, paused for a moment to take in the room. He subtly lifted a perfect dark brow, indicating he wasn't impressed.

"Can I offer you some water?" *With spit? Or some sweat wrung from my underwear?* I asked while he took a seat in the green armchair, still surveying our humble abode with disgust.

"No. Thank you," he replied stiffly.

Smart choice.

I traipsed back to the kitchen and found the tallest glass we owned—a Chicago Cubs pint glass—and filled it with tap water. I was sweaty and hot and dehydrated as hell. And now I got to add pissed because this bastard had come to my home.

I walked back into the living room, holding the glass in my hand. "You have until I chug this to tell me what you want, and then I'm kicking your ass out."

He shook his head. "Must you be so garish and hostile?"

"You dismissed me from that interview in three seconds because I didn't make your dick hard."

He blinked with a forced calm, and I smelled blood. He was about to lose his cool, and it made me feel damned good, because I wanted to ruffle this man's pretty feathers. Then I wanted to pluck them out and make a fancy headband.

"Yes. I did. And no, you didn't," he replied.

"Wow." I decided now might be a good time to finish my water. I gulped so fast that half the contents spilled down my white sports tank. Hey, what the heck. I was already wet, and it felt damned good on my hot body.

I wiped my mouth with the back of my hand and then looked down at Mr. Cole, noticing him staring at my breasts again.

Pig! "Okay. Time for you to go." I tipped over my empty glass.

He didn't flinch that exquisite body. Not even a dark brow twitched. "I spoke to Mark yesterday after you left. He says he offered you a job, and you turned him down."

Mark Douglas, a fellow Stanford alumni and Maxwell Cole's old fraternity brother, was CEO of a large clothing chain called Wow-Wow (a name Mark's daughter—who was two at the time—came up with). He became my mentor during my graduate studies after I worked on a project related to price elasticity for his company. We kind of clicked. Or maybe he felt sorry for me? Now, I don't know. But he and his wife, who I'd met later on, were hands down two of the kindest people I'd ever known—devoted parents, philanthropists, and just plain cool. Mark invited me into his life, his home, and even had me babysit his two beautiful spunky little girls—Elle and Sarah, now nine and ten. College wasn't cheap, so I was always grateful for extra money, but I felt eternally indebted for the respect and encouragement he'd given so freely. It was how I hoped to give back when I got a shot at running my own company. I wanted to inspire and mentor young women.

Then, after I graduated, Mark graciously offered me a great full-time, permanent position on his marketing team. That was when I reluctantly confessed I had my sights set on the C.C. sales team. Mark told me the door would always be open, but if my dream was C.C., then he'd call Mr. Cole, a close personal friend, and make it happen. I'd given it some thought, because I wanted a job at C.C. pretty badly, but in the end, I needed to know that anything I had was due to merits and sweat.

Not as a favor to Mark.

I did take that reference letter, though. That seemed like fair game.

"That is correct. I turned the job down," I replied, wondering where he was going with this.

"Why?" Mr. Cole asked with a hint of criticism.

At this point, I didn't want to tell him the truth. He didn't deserve to know what I'd done for the chance to be in his presence. *Dammit.* How stupid had I been?

"I have my reasons—what do you want, Mr. Cole?"

"Mark says you're the sort of person I can trust with things of a more personal nature. That means a lot coming from him, but is it true?"

The answer depended on what sorts of "personal" things he had in mind. If it was playing Lady Gaga dress up for five hours with Mark's sweet and wild little girls while he and his wife had to quietly deal with his drunk father getting arrested, then sure. If it was kicking Maxwell Cole in his ass on the way out of my apartment, I could be trusted with that, too.

"I repeat: what do you want, Mr. Cole?"

He ran his hand over the top of his silky head of hair and leaned forward in my armchair. I couldn't help notice how fucking perfect he looked— masculine, elegant, handsome as hell, and freshly shaved, yet still with a black shadow across his square jaw—and I wanted to punch him in the nose for it. Then punch myself for noticing how damned hot he was.

"I...uh..." The striking expression in his hazel eyes startled me. I suddenly felt like he was looking at me again, past my face. "My proposal is this: you come work for me."

This was my moment to tell him to shove it, but before I got the chance, he held up his hand and added, "But not the job you applied for; as a senior manager—the role you are *actually* qualified for."

My mouth fell open. Senior manager was two levels above the junior sales manager job.

"And you'd be reporting directly to me, instead of to a director," he said.

My mouth fell open a little more. I really didn't know it could open that wide.

I blinked at him, speechless. Just yesterday, he'd said I was too ugly to work for his company, and now he wanted me on his direct staff? He must've been quaking in his designer boxer briefs that I'd tell everyone how he'd treated me.

Whatever. I didn't want the job. I didn't want to work for a man like this. A fake. A heartless asshole. Nevertheless, I had to ask...

"Why?"

He leaned back in the chair, all smooth and cool, like he was delivering a sales pitch and knew he couldn't lose. "To use your own words: I am a superficial asshole. I did not necessarily get a choice in the matter; however, we are all dealt a hand in life and must play with the cards we're given."

I scratched the back of my sweaty head. "That reply didn't come close to answering my question."

"We can help each other."

"Oh, really?" I spat. "Mind telling me how someone like you, who finds it offensive to be in the same room, believes I can help?" *Or that I'd ever want to?*

His large hand glided up to the knot on his red tie, his eyes digging into me. "You are the most unattractive woman I've ever met. And you are exactly what I need."

He did not just say that to my face. I didn't know whether to run to the kitchen and grab a knife to stab him with or drop on the floor laughing.

He continued, "Which is why I will also pay for your plastic surgery—top notch, no expense spared—if you agree to work for me."

He's fucking serious. "You're fucking serious."

He nodded with a calm stare and blinked those big hazel eyes at me. There was a hint of something behind them.

Oh my God. Is it fear? Fear I might turn him down? I knew my brown eyes were probably bulging from my head like two chocolate orbs.

"I am dead serious," he replied. "And you're a smart woman—prickly as hell with a surprisingly crude vocabulary, but smart—so there's no need to point out that the role pays extremely well and will allow you to take your pick of positions at any company when the time comes. With a new face and that very beautiful body of yours, there will be nothing in your way. Nothing. You'll have superficial assholes like me at your mercy, licking your shoes, eating out of your beautiful hand the rest of your beautiful life. All you must do is come work for me."

I was speechless. Literally speechless. Except that it was time to say those magic words. "Go fuck yourself."

He stood, shaking his head. "I fucking love that you fucking speak your fucking mind, but you'll need to tone down that filthy little mouth of yours when we aren't alone." He glided past me as if he hadn't heard a word I said.

"I didn't say I'd work for you."

He flashed an arrogant grin. "Then I'll expect your yes in the morning."

He left, and I remained standing in the living room, wondering if what just happened wasn't some bizarre hallucination after hours of running in the heat. But it wasn't. The delicious scent of his expensive cologne lingering in the room was proof.

Finally, I willed my feet to carry me to the sofa and sank down. *A senior manager role at C.C.*

Setting Maxwell Cole aside, it was a job that could act as a springboard for my entire career. However, what he wanted from me was...was...Well, what did he want from me? He'd said I was "the most unattractive woman he'd ever seen" and exactly what he needed.

So what the hell did that last part mean?

I covered my face and groaned.

Twenty-four hours ago, I'd felt like a stable, well-grounded person with a bright future.

Now I am a bitter, foulmouthed cynic. I don't know who I am anymore.

And I certainly didn't know what I would do next.

chapter three

No doubt about it, I had had a long, turbulent day filled with fruitless inner debate. After Mr. Cole left, I spent an hour—or three—looking at open positions online and postings from a recruiter I knew. I still had the option of going to work for Mark Douglas at Wow-Wow Clothing, but it felt wrong taking a role knowing I wouldn't bring my A-game passion.

Are you saying you would bring it to C.C.?

I didn't know. Yesterday, I would've said yes, but then Maxwell Cole entered the picture, the biggest asshole in the world, and offered me...*the world.* (Insert visual of me knocking head against the wall.) I could either accept the terms, him being the boat anchor, or I couldn't. It was an all-or-nothing situation where I wanted nothing to do with him; meanwhile a part of me felt like this could change my life. And I wasn't talking just about the job.

Surgery. I sighed. It was something I hadn't thought of in years.

To be clear, I learned the importance of loving myself at the ripe old age of eight when Tania Reilly, my best friend at the time, who had a severe overbite, was verbally accosted by the too perfect, too pretty Lisa Walters. Lisa came up to her in the lunchroom for no reason at all and said, "Joel thinks you look like a dog. And so do I, so we voted you our class pet." Joel was the official cute boy and every third-grade girl crushed hard on him. But the look on poor Tania's face when she heard those words wasn't child's play. She would probably carry that moment around with her forever. I know I did. But that could also be because I stood up from the lunch table, took my fruit cup and threw it into Lisa's face. "You're mean, and mean people burn in hell," I'd said. Okay. Don't judge me for that. I was eight, and I'd overheard two other girls talking about something they'd heard at church. The point is that Tania would remember that moment, too. At least, I think she would. The smile on her face told me how good it felt to have someone stick up for her. It made her feel loved. And that's when I realized how love could insulate a person from just about anything. Especially self-love. It could also help them—me, in particular—make friends for life.

Sadly, though, it had never been enough to win me the other kind of love. I'd never had a date, a flirty smile, or a kiss. No, I won't bother walking through the parade of tragic stories filled with painful memories—guys laughing at me, making the standard dog jokes—but trust me, they're there. Ironically, I remember that not even the pretty girls were exempt from this sick breed of torment. And if they couldn't escape it, what about me?

Which is why I always told myself there were more important things, like family, friends, your journey in life, and the mark you leave on this world. But I think deep down inside I always knew that being genuinely ugly (not just "unattractive" as Asshole had called it) would slow me down.

The uglies of the world simply don't have it as easy as the beautiful people.

And there was no denying that having men look at me, and want to look again because they liked what they saw, had an appeal.

But the price of surgery, Lily. The price.

There were no words. I would have to endure the worst emotional pain, suffering, and humiliation on a daily basis. I would have to drink buckets of it. Because—no way—would I have surgery on work day one.

Oh no, Mr. Cole will have strings attached. Probably time and performance; I do well for him, be a good little C.C. employee, and he'd buy me a new face. Until then, every time I'd be in the room with that beautiful, hateful, smug piece of garbage, I'd know what he was thinking: *She's disgusting. I can't stand the sight of her. Please, God, don't let her touch me.*

Who could possibly endure that? From a man they'd once idolized? And why the hell would he want me to? What did Mr. Cole get out of this? He could hire anyone he liked from the top schools, his competition, and any Fortune 500 in the world.

Fuck, the man's probably a sadist and wants to watch me suffer. So then why was I even considering this?

But as I sat there, staring at my laptop displaying page after page of jobs I could probably get my hands on and blow out of the water, none of them were what I really wanted. Call it something to prove to the world, call it ambition. I didn't know. But wanting big and bold was who I was. I also hadn't racked up one hundred and fifty thousand dollars in student loans so I could live like a college student for eternity.

"Lily, you home?" my roommate's voice called out moments after the front door opened. Daniella and I met through a friend after I graduated and moved to Chicago last year. On the outside, she was a prim and proper associate finance manager for an investment bank, while on the inside, hilariously vulgar. She also looked a little like Katy Perry but with brown eyes, like mine.

"In here, Danny," I replied from my bedroom, sitting at my vanity, which was an old whitewashed thing I'd found at a yard sale.

She entered my room, which was decorated in classic "Fashion Junky" with stacks of magazines piled in the corner and a huge collage of my favorite outfits pinned onto my oversized corkboard. She plunked down on my bed with a loud sigh, beginning to shed her standard summer work ensemble: black skirt, heels, and a solid color blouse. Today it was green.

She kicked off her shoes and unzipped the back of her skirt, her eyes freezing on my face the moment she looked up. "Oh shit. They didn't offer you the job."

"Not the job I wanted."

She pulled her brown hair from her ponytail and then began rubbing her feet, "Fucking heels. The only reason I wear them is so the guys don't think they can step on me. So what happened?" She was on the short side, so I got the whole "must wear heels" ridiculousness.

"They offered me..." I debated whether to tell her everything. On the other hand, I could really use an external perspective, and I did consider her among my best of friends.

I decided to go with a partial truth until I knew what I'd do. "They offered me a senior manager role, reporting directly to Maxwell Cole."

Her eyes bugged from her head. "Seriously? Mr. Pleasefuckmenow Cole would be your direct boss?"

Like me, she had Mr. Cole on her top ten list of men to masturbate to. And yes, before you ask, I had already removed him and replaced him with Boris Kodjoe. A girl's gotta have a nice even ten on the roster, especially someone like me who only had her imagination to keep her warm at night.

I nodded.

"And you are debating...why?" she asked snidely.

I shrugged pathetically, lacking a proper answer.

"If you don't want the job, then I'll take it. What's it involve? Bringing him coffee? Morning blowjobs? I'll so do it."

"Gah! Danny," I scolded.

She smiled. "What? Don't judge me for wanting to be his right hand—he is right-handed, yes? Because whatever hand he jerks off with, I want to be it." She sighed contentedly and stared at the ceiling.

"I don't think you understand."

"No? What am I missing? He's a hot-as-fucking-hell CEO—and we know he's hot because he posed naked for us ladies in his quest to sell lip gloss," she shook her head, savoring the memory, "so, so generous. And he's a successful businessman and all-around awesome guy, and he's asked you to work for him. In your dream job. What's the problem?"

How could I put this in a way that would net me the advice I needed, without spilling the extremely uncomfortable and confusing beans?

"He doesn't really like me," I said.

"Oh, sweetie." She leaned forward and placed her hand on my knee. "I know it must be disappointing, but don't take it personally. He'd be your boss, and he can't flirt with you or anyone on his staff. That would be inappropriate. Can't you just be happy knowing he sees value in you and that you could learn from him?"

Okay. My plan for extracting advice from Danny blew. She had drunk the Maxwell Cole stud-spiked party-punch, but I couldn't fault her for that. Less than twenty-four hours ago, I'd been sipping from the same fountain of delusions.

I looked at Danny, thinking aloud. "He and I have different views on the world, so I'm not sure we'll get along."

"Really, Lily. You only need to work for the guy for a year. Maybe two max. Then someone else will steal you away."

What? One to two years. Uh-uh. I wouldn't survive that long.

"Either that," she added, "or Cole Cosmetics will go public, and you'll be a millionaire before you're thirty if you can score some stock options."

I blinked at her.

"Didn't you hear?" she asked.

I shook my head dumbly.

"According to the rumor mill, his company is getting ready for the big IPO."

Wow. Going public. That was big. And no, I didn't know.

She went on, "But I heard from my coworker Terri, whose boyfriend works with G.S.—"

"Goldman Sachs?" I asked.

"No. Gary and Smitty—a day-trader outfit they

run out of Gary's parents' basement."

"Oh." *How terribly reliable.*

"But she said that he said that Cole's competitor, B&H, is trying to do everything it can to derail the stock offering. They know if that capital infusion happens, they'll be wiped out. C.C. will eat up their market share."

I sat back in my vanity chair and let that sink in. I was suddenly in a position to destroy C.C., because if the truth about him got out, it would trigger some serious outrage from his adoring, everyday-woman customer base. He did not respect them or care about anything other than making money.

I gave it some thought, the little vindictive devil on my shoulder rubbing its hands together. *No, stop.* It didn't matter how horrible that man was, I wasn't the vengeful sort. But I could be an opportunist.

Whoa. I suddenly realize I wasn't in some weak "take it or leave it" kind of situation. I had leverage. I had some power of my own here to negotiate a different deal.

So what exactly did I want? It wasn't plastic surgery.

Was it?

"Can I ask you something, Danny? And I want you to be honest with me."

"The answer is yes. You should get a tattoo of Maxwell Cole on your back."

I flipped her off with my eyes.

"Sorry." She held up her hands. "Ask away."

"Do you think I should have my face done?"

Her eyes flickered with shock. She hadn't been expecting that question. "Does this have anything to do with your meeting Maxwell Cole today?"

Yes. But not in the way she probably thought—that I wanted to be his girlfriend or something stupid like that.

"Just answer the question," I said.

"Umm...that's a hard one."

"Danny, I want an honest answer. No BS."

She nodded and looked down at the floor. "I think that if it's something you want because it'll make you happy, then great. But if you're considering it for any other reason, then no. You shouldn't change who you are just to make other people like you. You're also the happiest, most genuine person I've ever met. So I'm not sure messing with your face would make you any happier."

I sighed. Danny was right.

"What's brought this on, Lily?"

"Nothing." I cracked a smile to lighten the mood. "But you're right. All of the pretty girls I know are miserable dirty whores. And, yes, that comment was directed at you."

She laughed. "Bitch."

"Crazy bitch," I countered.

"It's a dirty job." She stood from the bed and grabbed her heels from the floor. "But not as dirty as the rim job you'll be giving Max Cole, you sick little slut."

"Ewww!" I laughed. I was anything but a slut, and we both knew it. But even if I were, I doubt I'd ever go around licking butt holes. *Yikes.*

"Did you at least offer him your customary 'thank you' blowjob?" she asked, trying not to crack herself up.

"Yes. I offered. He accepted. And next I have my sights set on getting pregnant with his love child just to make you jealous. My years of hard work and graduate school are finally about to pay off."

"Excellent. And be a good friend, would ya? Ask him to throw in a quickie for me as part of your signing bonus?" She made a dreamy little sigh. "Okay. I gotta mix up some vitamin water and take a shower now."

"Meeting up with Calvin?" Calvin was her new boyfriend, and for whatever reason, she always drank a bunch of vitamin water before seeing him. It was kind of strange.

"Yep, I'm meeting up with my real man for some real dinner and real, very mediocre but vigorous sex. Let me know what happens with my dream lover, 'kay?" She left the room, leaving me there with my thoughts. My very indecent sex-fantasy-filled thoughts.

No, I decided. That was ridiculous. I would never ask for *that*. I didn't even want Maxwell Cole. Especially after learning what a disgusting pig of a human being he was.

I groaned and pushed my hands through my hair.

So I didn't want surgery. Or sex. (Ridiculous.) What did I want out of this deal? A line on my résumé and a paycheck didn't cut it, considering what I'd have to endure seeing that man on a regular basis. Maybe I should be asking for stock options to fund my own company.

God. What am I thinking? I can't take this job. It's degrading. Besides, he only wanted me for some hidden agenda and not because he believed in me, which meant accepting the role would go against everything I believed in.

But then why had I already made up my mind to see him in the morning? Was it to turn him down to his face? Or was it because I had a burning desire to see him again and find out the truth?

What did he really want with me?

chapter four

The next morning I put on my favorite navy blue skirt, tan heels, and a tight cream silk tee with a low-cut neckline. Simple. Sexy. Elegant. I wore my blonde hair loose and wavy—my natural look—and applied a little bronzer to my cheeks and mascara to my very light lashes. Yes, I enjoyed feeling feminine. Even my underwear was known to be a little racy, and it didn't matter that no one would see them. I had never deprived myself of the pretty things in life most women enjoyed, and I never would. I had just as much right as any to want soft skin, nice clothes, and a great job. I was no different from any other woman with needs either. And right now, I needed answers. As painful as the truth might be.

He's probably some fucked-up creep with a fetish for ugly women. It would explain his dating track record. Though, I now suspected all those "girlfriends" were really PR stunts.

Time to find out.

I got in my red Mini and drove back to C.C.'s headquarters, located not too far from the Chicago Board of Trade building downtown. When I entered the spacious, bright-white, heaven-like lobby (minus the pearly gates), I told the receptionist—different from the day before—I was there to see Mr. Cole but didn't have an appointment. That won me the "oh, another female stalker" look.

"He really does want to see me. Would you mind calling his assistant, Keri?" I told the woman.

Skeptically, she dialed. "There's a Miss Snow to see Mr. Cole." She listened. "Okay. I'll send her up."

She handed me a visitor's badge and gave me a strange look. She was gorgeous, by the way, and now I knew why: Mr. Cole didn't want to be greeted each morning by someone who wasn't up to snuff.

As I got inside the elevator, a man in a suit—slender build, light brown hair, and pretty brown eyes—got in with me. He held a laptop and some files in his hands.

"Can you push the top floor, please?" he asked, looking down his nose at me.

"Already pushed," I replied.

"Oh. You going up to the big guy's office, too?"

"Yep."

His expression leaned toward judgmental, like he didn't understand why I was there.

"Are you new?" he asked, sounding overtly snobbish.

"Not exactly."

The elevator chimed and the doors opened. We

both stepped out, and Keri was already waiting for me.

"Miss Snow, nice to see you again." She shook my hand and then dropped her smile, looking at the guy who rode up with me. "Hey, Craig. Mr. Cole says you'll have to wait a few minutes to start the meeting." She dipped her head at me. "Right this way, Miss Snow. Mr. Cole will see you in his office."

Wow. If looks could kill, Craig was in the process of dismembering me. Hannibal style. I guessed he wasn't too pleased about getting bumped.

"Nice meeting you," I said anyway. No one wanted to be on an AMY's (Angry Middle-Aged Yuppy) shit-list.

"Good luck," he said, but really meant "fuck you" by his tone.

Changed my mind. "Thanks, Amy." *Fuck you back.*

I entered Mr. Cole's office and found him once again on his phone, sitting with his large feet propped up on the desk, looking like the picture-perfect sex god, his broad shoulders pushed all the way back into the chair. His thick brown hair was a mess, a few loose strands falling over his forehead like he'd forgotten the hair product this morning or had just gotten laid and passed on the comb.

Keri closed the door behind me, and the sound snagged his attention.

His eyes did that weird wash and scrub over my body while he continued his conversation. "Yeah,

Jer. I get it. But this is not the time to cut orders, so do whatever it takes to make sure it doesn't happen." He listened for a moment, his eyes still on me. Well, on my tits, anyway. It was an odd sensation, almost like he was forcing himself not to look away and my breasts were his home plate—*safe!* It made me feel kind of naked. "All right. Send an update at close of business." He hung up and pasted on a smile. "Well, this is a surprise."

"I figured I owed you since you showed up at my apartment unannounced."

He stood from his desk, giving me a glimpse of his outfit. No suit today. Instead, he wore jeans—loose around his hips, faded and sexy—and a dark gray button-down that perfectly hugged the contours of his very fucking sexy and hate-worthy body.

"Well, I'm pleased you caught me. I only came into the office to take care of a few things; then I'm off to the airport." He gestured toward the light gray table and chairs near the window. "Would you like to sit?"

All right. This was strange. He was being extremely cordial and pleasant—completely phony.

I sat, and he took the chair across from me, this time not pushing away. I could see a sheen of sweat collecting on his brow. Was it physically paining him to be this close to me?

"So, Miss Snow. Are you here to accept my offer?" he asked, sounding like he'd won some giant victory.

"No."

"I'm sorry to hear that. Then do tell. What brings you and your dirty little mouth back to C.C.?" He grinned, seeming amused.

No. He looks...he looks...nervous. But he's trying to hide it. Or was that just my imagination?

"My dirty little mouth and I have some questions." I noticed again that he wasn't looking at my face, but at the base of my neck. And the sweat on his brow had grown to a visible dew.

"Then, by all means, ask away," he replied.

How was it possible he looked cool and calm and falling to pieces all at once? I didn't know. But it had to be the same skill he used to look hot and masculine while simultaneously revolting me.

I cleared my throat, forcing myself to look past his perfect face and body. I needed to see him for who he was, just like I needed him to see me. "This is only going to work if you and I are honest with each other."

"We seem to do rather well with that, you and I."

"True." I had to acknowledge that for two complete strangers, neither one of us seemed to have a filter with each other. Not that I wasn't normally a direct person, but something about this man brought it to a whole new level.

"Go on," he said.

"I want to know what you meant when you said

that I am what you need. What do you really hope to get out of hiring me?"

"I think I made myself clear yesterday." His gaze only hit my eyes for a moment, but the hardness shook me. My question had displeased him.

Well, too bad.

"You only told me you wanted my help, but not why," I pointed out.

He scratched the back of his thick head of hair, and I noticed his rolled-up sleeves, or more accurately, the hard ropes of muscles popping up on his forearm. "I'm afraid that's none of your business."

"It is if I'm going to come here every day, knowing you're disgusted when you look at me."

"And you will be disgusted when you look at me. I'd say we're on an even playfield. Except, I'll be paying you. Quite well."

As I looked at his face, I saw a bead of sweat trickle down his temple.

"Seriously?" I sighed. This was too much. "I can't do this, Mr. Cole."

"Why the hell not?"

"Look at you. We haven't been in the same room for more than a minute and you look like I've got a gun pointed at your balls." I laughed bitterly.

He frowned. "Does this seem funny to you, Miss Snow?"

"Yes," I spat.

"Not to me. Not one bit."

"Then how *do* you find this? Entertaining? Are you getting some kick out of degrading me? Is that what this is about—some weird fetish you have for making the ugly girl your slave or—"

"I'm not that sort of man," he said bluntly.

I stared at him, waiting. He'd have to give me more, and he knew it.

A long moment passed before he finally spoke. "Some people have a fear of heights or small spaces. I have a fear of..." He looked straight at me, and my mind filled in the blank.

"Ugly people? Oh, come the hell on."

"It is called cacophobia, Miss Snow. It is a disorder."

I blinked at him, trying my best not to laugh hysterically and roll on the floor. "Oh, boy. I get that you have a huge ego and probably don't want to admit you're a disgusting, shallow bastard, but don't hide behind a doctor's note. That's pathetic."

His fist came down on the table, jarring me in my seat. "That's enough, Miss Snow. I see you enjoy being a coldhearted bitch, but my issue isn't here for your goddamned amusement."

My smiled vaporized as his angry hazel eyes burned.

"You're serious," I said. "You really have a disease."

"A disorder. And yes, I'm dead fucking serious."

I wanted to ask how he'd gotten it, but did that really matter?

"Wow. So hating me has a scientific name. How wonderful." I folded my arms across my chest and looked out the window. Being disliked because a person was a complete superficial asshat was one thing, but to know that Mother Nature created people who were predisposed to see you as a plague or threat or something to steer clear of really stung. Later, I would look up "cacophobia" and learn it also drove a person to pursue their own perfection. It would explain his body.

"I do not hate you, Miss Snow," he said, his voice low and sincere. "But I am the way I am. Don't take it personally."

I shook my head at him. "God, you're such an insensitive prick. If anything is personal, this situation qualifies."

"What's personal is you're being quite the bitch."

I narrowed my eyes. "Can you blame me?"

"No."

At least he was fair. "But I'm not getting it," I said, trying hard to let it all sink in and not succeeding, "you've dated some pretty unattractive women."

"Not exactly."

"So they were all just for show?" I asked, referring to the multitude of photographs I'd seen in the tabloids.

"The press likes to make assumptions. I simply allow them to."

I had guessed that might be the case. "And the models you use? Or your company's slogans?"

His expression showed no sign of shame. "My affliction provides me with some very unique and valuable insights regarding what women face. I've used it to my advantage."

So that meant he was fully aware of how hurtful his behavior toward unattractive women felt to them. Then he used those insights to sell them the antidote. Was that a good thing or a bad thing? On one hand, it was like a wolf becoming a politician, telling all the rabbits of the world not to feel bad when his kind chewed off their legs and maimed them. On the other hand, it was also like telling the women of the world not to fall victim to the fucked-up, degrading, judgmental ways of men. *Don't listen to us Maxwell Coles of the world—we're idiots.*

Yeah, I liked that second analogy better. Still, I found this all very confusing.

"So why not see someone for your little problem. Why hire me?"

"I am seeing someone, and she advises the only way to eliminate the problem is to accept it into my life, to confront it—similar to any phobia."

"I see." I bobbed my head and then stared at his large hands. They were laced together on top of the light gray table. He had beautiful hands. He had beautiful everything. And now I knew he wasn't just an asshole. Okay, yes. He was still an asshole, but part of his behavior was attributed to a disorder he was trying to get help with.

I whooshed out a breath and lowered my forehead to the table, rolling it from side to side. "I can't take your offer. It's wrong."

"Wrong? Please explain what's so *wrong*."

Half speaking to myself and half speaking to him, I muttered, "I can't work for you. Not like this." I needed to know I was there because I'd earned it and deserved it.

"Like what?"

My head shot up. "You *know* like what."

He leaned back and folded his fit arms over his chest. The way his biceps stretched the fabric of his sleeves caught my female eye like a fish to a worm.

"We are two people who can help each other," he said piously. "You can help me overcome my obstacle. I can give you a better life. Why is this wrong?"

Because seeing you every day and knowing I cause you pain, just because I'm not pretty, makes me feel ugly.

"You want to give me a job I haven't earned," I replied. "You want to buy me a face I wasn't born with. You want to rob me of my self-esteem so you can have an easier life." I stood from the table. "I can't feel good about any of it."

He stared up at me with an unreadable expression. "Then tell me what you really want. What will make you feel good about it?"

"There isn't anything."

"Why did you want to work here in the first place?" he asked.

"Because I wanted to learn from you. I want to run my own company someday."

He laughed. "You? You don't have the backbone and you certainly don't have the killer instinct."

"Are you saying I have to be an asshole like you to be successful?" I asked.

"Absolutely. A leader has to fight for what they want and be willing to step on a few toes. But you? You're running for the door, like the fake that you are."

Yesterday, he'd called me a fake, too. I wondered why. "How can you call me that? *You* of all people?" It was really insulting.

"Because you only pretend to be tough and confident. But you will never be me, never run a successful company, and never amount to shit in this world if you don't truly believe in yourself. You won't even make it to the next goddamned block because you don't have the balls to ask for what you want."

"I have balls. Look at me; I'm here, talking to you and turning you down."

He grinned. "For all the wrong reasons."

"For *my* reasons." I scowled.

"Stop playing games, Miss Snow. Tell me what you really want. Demand it. Let me see your claws."

I glared at him. This man was such an epic bastard.

"As I thought," he said arrogantly, "no real backbone."

His words pinned me under a rock, infuriating me, challenging me. I wasn't weak or afraid. I just found his reasons for wanting to hire me to be outrageously insulting. Degrading. I mean, where did he get off? Asking me to work for him like this was insane.

It's like if I were to tell him...

"Fine. I'll come work for you, Mr. Cole. If you sleep with me. You can be my first fuck. Because I won't have surgery. I won't ever be beautiful. And I will never have a hot piece of dick like you in my bed. So if your terms require me to do something I find morally repugnant, then it will be quid pro quo. All the fucking way, buddy." My chest heaved with heavy breaths as I stood there with my angry fist parked on my hip.

See my damned point, asshole?

Maxwell Cole stared at me for several awkward moments, not a twitch on his lips, not a flicker of fear in his hazel eyes. "Deal."

"What?"

"I said deal." He got up, walked toward his desk, and began gathering his things.

Me, on the other hand, stood there feeling like a giant invisible truck, filled with regret, had run me over and was backing up.

What did I just do?

You just threw your own ass under the bus. I didn't want to fuck him. I certainly didn't want to work for him.

"Be here tomorrow morning. Keri will show you your office," he said flatly.

"You—you're serious?"

He turned and frowned at me. "Don't go backpedaling on me now, Miss Snow. Not after you've just shown me your pretty little teeth and sharp claws. We might make a CEO out of you yet."

I shook my head no. "Not. Back. Pedaling." Just wondering where the nearest exit was. Now I really felt like an idiot. I'd just proposed to my future boss that he have sex with me in exchange for my acceptance of his offer.

Wasn't it usually the other way around?

And what was that other feeling? It was...shock or excitement or something connected to that little spot in my brain that controlled my sexual fantasies.

"Good," he said. "Have your ass to my house Friday at eight p.m. sharp. And bring your running clothes."

Today was Wednesday, so that meant I had two days to get psychiatric help. *Wait. You're not doing this. You can't.*

"You okay?" were the words he asked, but his tone and expression accused me of being a spineless coward.

I stared at him, trying to comprehend what was going through this man's mind. Honestly, I was confused as hell. Possibly frightened, too. He, on the other hand, looked like he'd been given an injection of piss and vinegar. He also looked sort of…happy? Okay, maybe not happy, but excited or determined, like challenging me turned him the hell on. But that couldn't be right.

"Why aren't you sweating anymore?" I asked.

He blinked as if startled by himself. "It seems you're already having a positive effect. Too bad it's your ability to piss me the fuck off that's doing the trick."

Speechless, I turned for the door again and grabbed the handle. I needed to retreat. I was way over my head with this situation.

"Oh, and Miss Snow?"

"Yes?"

"Do me a favor, would you? Fire Craig on your way out. He's the one waiting for me out there."

I blinked. "Sorry?"

"It's your first lesson in running a company: You'll have to come down off that pedestal of yours and get your hands dirty."

"What did he do?"

"He's an asshole."

"Yeah, but so are you," I pointed out.

"I have an excuse. He does not."

"You can't be serious," I said.

He looked at his watch. "I'm afraid I am, and I'm

afraid it's time for my departure."

Right on cue, there was a light knock on the door.

"Yes," he replied in a deep, full voice.

Keri's head of silky red hair popped through the doorway only a foot or so away from where I stood shaking in my heels, probably pale as hell.

"Sir, your helicopter is waiting," Keri said meekly.

He nodded. "Thank you, Keri." He then looked at me, but only briefly, before turning to his desk to grab his leather bag. "And thank you, Miss Snow. I'm eagerly awaiting the chance to become acquainted with your many talents."

Oh shit. That was a sexual pun. No one had ever made one with me before. And the fact it was this guy did something to me. It made me feel a little naughty and sexy and...

No. No way. Absolutely not.

Okay, I hadn't decided what I'd do about this possible employment situation. But I sure as hell wouldn't agree to firing that guy sitting outside in the private lobby.

Mr. Cole sailed past us without another glance, leaving behind a trail of his delicious cologne mixed with a spoonful of "don't fuck with me. I'm the boss." Did alpha males have their own distinct scent that subconsciously told others to watch their step? Because this man shouldn't be fucked with. Not ever. He had no fear.

Except of ugly people. Yet, he'd clearly said he would...

Oh my God. I can't even think it.

Keri and I watched him disappear into the stairwell, to the roof, I supposed.

Once out of sight, I released the breath I'd been holding in. "Holy shit. That man's...that man's..." I didn't have a word. Domineering? Fearless? A huge coldhearted prick? Sexy as fucking hell in the most aggravating way? "...different."

Keri grinned and nodded. "Oh, you don't know the half of it, but I prefer the word eccentric. You'd never know from looking at him, would you?"

I shook my head slowly from side to side, feeling like I'd just been trampled by the world's biggest pair of balls masquerading as a human man. A gorgeous insane man who had the world at his feet, yet had serious issues. "Um...no. I can't say I would've guessed it."

She smiled warmly and patted me on the shoulder. "Well, if it's any consolation, he's a damned marketing genius. Even if only a tenth of what he knows rubs off, you'll be a god. If you can survive working for him."

I lifted a brow.

"Just look up 'perfectionist' in the dictionary. His picture will be right there."

Oddly, it was the only thing about the man I'd guessed correctly. A perfectionist. But now as I stood there, my heart pounding inside my chest, my nerves sparking erratically like black market fireworks, a greedy part of me hungered for what he'd offered: Power. Over my own damned life. I was beginning to see there was so much more waiting for me if I was willing to take it, to fight for it.

I took a deep breath, feeling like I stood high on a hill. Off in the distance was a tall rugged mountain with snow on its cap, surrounded by a forest of green trees, its peak so high, it touched the clouds. That was *my* goddamned mountain. All that stood between us was a whole hell of a lot of rough terrain—quick sand, tar pits, and an enchanted forest with a big, mean sexy ogre toting a huge fucking club.

Suddenly, I felt the surge of determination welling inside me. Perhaps because I now saw how this path clearly lead to my endgame. A beautiful future awaited. All I had to do was push forward and take the job.

I looked at Keri. "See you tomorrow, bright and early."

"Welcome aboard, Miss Snow," she said cheerily.

I marched over toward the elevator banks and the seating area where Craig sat with his laptop open, typing away. He glanced up at me with a flavorless expression. "Mr. Cole ready for me now?" he asked prickishly.

I shook my head no. "No, he had to leave."

Craig let out a huff. "What a fucking dick," he whispered to himself. "I was up all night preparing this bullshit for him."

Now, I get how strange this is going to sound, but good old Craig here calling Mr. Cole a "fucking dick" somehow rubbed me the wrong way. I inexplicably felt like I was the only person in the world who'd earned that privilege. Also, I was at least brave enough to say it to Mr. Cole's face, and not to some stranger I didn't even know, behind Mr. Cole's back. It was completely unprofessional to speak about your boss like that to someone who wasn't a trusted friend or family member you leaned on for the requisite boss-venting.

"Craig, I'm going to give you some advice: don't be such a whiny asshole. It makes you look weak." I walked over and pushed the call button for the elevator.

"Excuse me? Who the hell are you?"

I shrugged, completely blown away by my need to stick up for Mr. Cole. "Lily Snow. And by the way, Mr. Cole says you're fired."

His jaw dropped. "He can't fire me."

The elevator doors chimed and then slid open. "Apparently he just did. Have a great day."

As the doors closed, I distinctly heard Craig call me a "fucking ugly bitch." It was the first time in my life I recalled being unpleasant to someone, who probably deserved it, and it felt kind of...*ugly*. Maybe because Mr. Cole had just gotten me to do his dirty work.

On the other hand, I did need to toughen up, because working for the boss probably meant doing things outside my comfort zone all the time.

I laughed at myself. *Ya think?*

I really needed to sit down and figure out how I'd deal with seeing Mr. Cole every day and not allowing it to get to me.

He's expecting you at his house Friday night. How are you going to deal with that?

chapter five

Later that afternoon, I went for an insanely long run in the heat, trying to digest my meeting with Mr. Cole.

My conclusion?

Temporary insanity.

Mine, of course.

It was the only explanation for why I'd asked that man—now my boss—to fuck me. I'd wanted to push him and make a point by asking for something as equally appalling as his request to help him with his phobia. It had been a knee-jerk reaction, and I never really expected him to say yes.

Only, he had.

Obviously, I couldn't go through with it, but now I really wanted the job for my own damned reasons. And I wanted Mr. Cole to respect me. No, not because I needed the man's approval, but because I needed him to teach me everything he knew and he was not the sort of person who'd waste his precious time mentoring someone he saw as weak and hopeless.

Well, having sex with him is not the way to get his respect. I'd have to think up some way out of it that didn't paint me as spineless. Hell, he couldn't stand the sight of me, so it wasn't like he would mourn the lost opportunity. If anything, it would be the opposite.

I kicked off my running shoes and stripped off my socks, getting ready to take a shower, when my cell rang on my desk.

Oh crap. It was my brother, and I knew exactly why he was calling. "Hey, John. Tell Mom and Dad to stop using you as their spy."

His deep laughter poured through the phone and immediately put me in a better mood. John, who was three years older, had that effect on everyone. He was warm, genuine, and feisty like me, but there was a sprinkle of shameless comedic smartass in everything he did.

"Sorry, Lily, but they promised to stop coming over to my place unannounced if I give away all your secrets." John had moved out on his own about six months ago, and my parents had been freaking out ever since, despite the fact John was twenty-eight, very capable of getting around in a wheelchair, and had been basically taking care of himself since he left home for college. Of course, after he graduated, he'd made the huge mistake of moving back home. I think he tolerated the lack of privacy until he started to get serious with his girlfriend. They eventually broke up, and I was pretty sure it was due to my mom's constant intrusions and mothering—making sure he was up on time for work, cleaning his room while they were still in bed, and washing his clothes, despite his very polite and sincere objections. My father would've been just as bad, only he worked during the day—a math teacher at the local high school—and he taught night classes at the J.C. All of which kept him busy most of the time.

Anyway, John's new job—he was a math teacher, too—didn't pay much, so I knew his place was small, but I could tell he savored his space.

"Ha!" I laughed. "I wish I had juicy secrets." Oh, wait. I actually sort of did. It was something I wasn't used to.

"So do I," he said. "That's why I've reverted to making up flagrant, inflammatory lies about you—oh, by the way, if Mom asks you about that itch, just tell her you saw the doctor. All clear."

"John, you didn't."

"And that the police dropped the shoplifting charges. Everyone knows you wouldn't steal lipstick on purpose."

Oh God. "You're an ass. They're probably on the plane to Chicago right now, getting ready to do an intervention."

"That was the point; getting them in another state."

"I hate you." I laughed.

"Be nice, or I'll tell them you got another DUI."

"*Another* one?" I didn't even drink. I mean, the occasional glass of wine, yes. But that was it. "I'm going to text Mom and tell her you've been crying every night because she's not there to tuck you in."

"Don't you dare, Lily," he warned.

Oh. I dare. "So what do you want?" I asked, but I already knew.

"The job? Did you get it? Mom's been texting me every ten minutes, asking if I've heard anything."

I had forbidden my overly protective and nosy parents from prying anymore. No more nagging texts, phone calls, or emails. If I had something to share, I would share it when I was damned good and ready. And if you think I'm being mean, let me set the scene. My first week away at college, my mother and father insisted I video chat with them once in the morning and once in the evening to confirm that I was still alive and adjusting to campus life. After a few weeks of that, I began to feel a little stupid. I was in college, and my parents were making me check in with them twice a day. It kind of screamed "loser!" After a few weeks of arguing with them about it, I just stopped doing the chats.

Mistake.

Then they came in person. It took months before I finally weened them off their worried-parental crutches, but I still had to email or call at least once a week or I'd find one of my parents on my dorm-room doorstep.

And I'll be honest, part of me really felt bad for them. They literally worried themselves sick about me and my brother, which was probably why we never felt unloved. If anything, it was the opposite: "Could you please not love me quite so much? I'm twenty-five now. And I live in another state for a reason."

Those were the words I'd barked so rudely to my mother during her last "surprise" visit. It was the first and only time I'd ever yelled at her. But during my one year in Chicago, I'd seen my parents five times, excluding my trip home for Christmas. They were out of their frigging minds and definitely couldn't afford it on my dad's salary.

"So?" John asked. "Did you get the job or not? And if you say 'not,' please tell me it's because the guy demanded sex and got fresh with you. That would guarantee Mom and Dad getting on the red-eye to console you."

I felt my blood pressure do a little dip. His comment hit too close to home.

I sat down on my bed, thinking about how to respond in a way that would prevent any parental concern.

"I start tomorrow, but I'm not sure it's going to work out with my new boss," I said. In my heart, that was the truth.

"Well...congratulations! But why aren't you sure?"

"I really don't want to talk about it." I wasn't in the mood to spin a big fat lie, and the truth wasn't an option.

"Lily, you'll have to do better than that or get ready for the avalanche of text messages and phone calls from Mom. What happened?"

Okay, so this was the part about my family that I loved, but also drove me crazy. They were protective to the nth degree. They wouldn't stand for anyone treating me badly for any reason. My brother had been known to show up a few times unannounced, along with my father, to my high school after learning a guy had said something mean to me. My mother had the principal on speed dial. For as long as I could remember, they acted like a vicious pack of wolves when it came to protecting me, and I couldn't exactly claim to be much better. I'd kicked the crap out of a girl who'd once decided to use my brother as her personal trash can for her unwanted lunch tray. Then there were my friends—the Lisa "fruit cup" incident was only one of many.

Regardless, we were grown now and didn't need protecting. We could stick up for ourselves just fine.

"I can't deal with this right now, John. I gotta go."

"Lil, tell me what the asshole did."

Jesus. "He didn't do anything. I just need to decide if C.C. is really what I want. Mr. Cole is very...tough to work for," I said.

"Liar. You've been talking about this job for months. I think you're afraid you can't cut it. But you will, Lily. You're our little flower who fears nothing."

"Thank you, John. But I really have a lot to do." Mainly some serious thinking.

There was a notable pause. "Good luck, Lily. I'm proud of you no matter what."

John could be such a shithead, but he was also a good big brother.

"Thanks. I'll call you next week and tell you what happens."

"Okay. But don't forget, or I'll tell Mom you're in jail."

I laughed and ended the call. I knew my family meant well and just wanted to know what was going on with my life, but I wished they weren't so neurotic about it.

Staring at my phone, feeling a little pang of guilt, I picked the damned thing up again.

Me: *Hi, Mom. Interview went well. But not sure the job is what I really want. Will keep you posted. BTW, I spoke to John. Sounds like he's not eating or sleeping. Think he's lonely. Maybe you should check up on him?*

I grinned, imagining John's face when my mother showed up tonight with groceries and her slumber-party gear. She'd probably stay on his couch for the next week.

My mom: *Oh, honey. Thanks for the update. Break a leg! And yes, I will check on John. You know how we worry.*

Now, for the first time ever, maybe they had a reason to. My head was about to unravel and so was my life.

The next morning, I began drinking through the C.C. firehose—laptop, account setup, work cell, company card, employee badge, HR and benefits, expense reporting, company policies, and all of the other busywork a new employee went through.

Oh, and my new office.

Seriously, it was…amazing. New, modern, bright-white office furniture and the red lips C.C. logo on the wall instantly made me feel like I'd been transported to a shiny new glamorous planet. Then there was the view. Only a floor below Mr. Cole, though much, much smaller, my office overlooked downtown Chicago. Later, I would find out he'd actually moved someone to another floor so I could have it, which made me wonder if he put me there as a reminder of his position above me. My mouth didn't seem to acknowledge the concept of hierarchy when it came to him. Or politeness. Regardless, I had to pinch myself every ten minutes. I kept feeling like I'd somehow faked my way in and, at any moment, the security guards would show up looking to throw me out. But I hadn't faked my way in; I'd just come in through a very, very strange hidden door.

That was just Thursday morning.

The rest of the afternoon was spent digging out from underneath an avalanche of client files Keri had brought over upon Mr. Cole's request. I was going to be one busy bee.

Thursday night, after spending an hour with Mrs. Jackson downstairs, helping her clean her fridge, panic set in. I would have to see Mr. Cole tomorrow, unless I decided not to show, which I knew was not the way to go. I had to be fearless with the man, so that meant confronting my error head-on.

I'm going to tell him I never meant it—heat of the moment sort of thing—and I want stock options instead. All true.

Then I received two entertaining texts from John damning me to hell because my mother *had* shown up the night before and wouldn't leave. She'd cleaned his apartment, tidied his underwear drawer, and started organizing his porn. *"My fucking porn, Lily! Mom put her hands on my porn. Spoiled forever! P.S. Hope first day of new job went well."*

I really had to wonder why he even owned porn. Who did that these days?

Me: *Sorry. But that's what you get for making crap up about me. Do it again, and I'll tell Mom you've started hiring hookers to fill your lonely nights.*

She'd never leave him alone again if I said that.

My brother: *evil cow*

The ritualistic taunting gave me a few moments of blessed distraction from my nerves until I got a text from Mr. Cole on my new phone, which sent me into a frenzied tailspin.

His first message said he'd introduce me to the troops on Monday at his monthly staff meeting, but in the meantime, I should get to work familiarizing myself with the accounts I'd been given—some of them blew my mind. Saks, for example, would be my baby. Pinch me. Slap my bare ass. Call me giddy.

Me: *Yes, sir. Hope trip is productive?*

Mr. Cole: *Boring as fuck. Looking forward to some quality time with your dirty mouth tomorrow.*

Now *that* text pushed me over the edge—it sounded like he actually looked forward to screwing me. Impossible.

But the next message he sent traumatized the ever-living hell out of me...

Mr. Cole: *And change of plans. Pack for weekend. Bring something nice for Saturday evening.*

Oh, Christ. I covered my mouth, reading the message five times. *He wants to make a weekend out of it. But why?*

Then it hit me. Perhaps he saw sex with me as

some sort of intense therapeutic device. *Oh crap. That's it.* That was why he'd said yes so easily. He had mentioned his therapist advised him to "accept it" into his life and to "confront it."

This was one hell of a way to confront his fears, but "it" wasn't going to happen. And I knew he'd understand why—he was my boss and I hadn't really meant this to be part of our deal. I had way more respect for myself than that. Then there was the fact that I didn't want to be some vaccination for his ugly illness. I wanted my first time to be a good memory. Preferably with someone I didn't hate.

Needing something to ward off the butterflies in my stomach and clear my head, I put on my running shoes. I was about to head out when another text came in.

Mr. Cole: *And don't forget your exercise clothes.*

Okay. So this was good. He might be enticed with going for a run or hike instead of his "therapy" session.

Me: *Got my running shoes all warmed up for you*

Mr. Cole: *It's not your shoes I'm interested in.*

I stared at the message for a moment and threw my phone down on the bed, treating it like a poisonous snake.

Oh God. He's probably testing me. The man knows I'm going to back out.

Leaving my phone behind, I headed out for that run to avoid texting him back. No, it was best to let his last message go and confront him tomorrow.

Of course, that's not what happened. About a half hour into my run, I turned around and headed home, intent on calling him and setting things straight tonight. But by the time I got there, I'd lost my nerve and hopped into the shower, where I decided a better course of action was to blow off some steam and rub one out.

Nope. Wasn't happening.

I found my mind unsatisfied with anything in my mental library—Brad, Jason M., Thor, Mr. Thornton—none seemed to hit the spot.

After my shower, and against my better judgement, I finally broke down and texted him back.

Me: *What are you interested in?*

Wrapped in a white towel, my blonde hair obscenely over-conditioned so it would be silky and wavy tomorrow despite the humidity, I nibbled my thumbnail, waiting for a reply. When I heard the chime on my phone, I could hardly look.

Mr. Cole: *Watching you run.*

I spouted out a laugh. *Sonofabitch.* He *was* testing me. Or taunting me, knowing I'd get cold feet. He'd flat out said that he thought I was spineless. *Think you can play with me?* Because I could give as good as I could get.

Me: *Yes. I forgot. Men like you aren't equipped to keep up. However, watching is very admirable. Will bring binoculars so you can see everything from a distance*

I let out a few self-congratulatory snickers.

Mr. Cole: *Thank you. Binoculars would be helpful so I can observe you from the finish line while I wait.*

I laughed. Okay, I'd successfully turned the sex talk into a pissing match. Time to turn it back.

Me: *Wow. Being so fast must be a huge disappointment for all those women who run with you. (Sad face)*

I chuckled. "Take that, Mr. Pompous Egomaniac."

Mr. Cole: *Let's not fool ourselves. We both know I'll be running alone tomorrow.*

So he basically had just called me a coward and implied he'd be jerking off tomorrow because I'd be a no-show? Of course, my thoughts had to come accompanied with a mental image of him lying on his back naked, stroking his long, thick cock, his cum erupting all over his hands.

I shook my head, trying to ignore how turned on I suddenly felt. Something about a beautiful man taking care of himself really did it for me. Not that I'd ever seen it happen in real life, but I occasionally satisfied my curiosity and needs with a little Internet exploration.

I was about to type a response, indicating that I would not disappoint him, but I knew that wasn't true. He was right. I didn't have the backbone to go through with it, and it certainly wasn't the right thing to do.

But then why was the idea beginning to grow on me? A girl like me would never have the chance to be with a man like that ever again.

chapter six

After another long day of reading through client files, sales projections, and product offerings, my brain felt like a tater tot, but I'd welcomed the distraction from the crazy thoughts spinning in my head. I'd also welcomed the fact that Mr. Cole's staff wasn't in the office this week because they were all traveling, either visiting clients or at a big trade show in New York. Sounded pretty dang exciting to me, but I knew there'd be plenty of time for that stuff later. Right now, I needed to get up to speed quickly because come Monday morning, I'd be meeting the team, likely assigned a few projects, and have to start getting out on the road to meet customers. Oh, and I'd be recovering from sex. Okay, maybe not.

Yes, this morning I'd packed and went to work with the full intention of going through with the weekend. Crazy. I know. But after a night of the most erotic sexy dreams of Mr. Cole fucking me, licking me, and touching every part of my body until all signs of my virginity were obliterated, I'd woken up in a state that failed words. Horny, aroused, turned on—none of those cut it.

By lunch, my sanity had overcome my body's needs, and I'd made up my mind not to be a coward, per my own definition. I would tell Mr. Cole the truth: I hadn't been serious when I'd put fucking on the table.

I'd just have to use that backbone of mine to come clean. He would have to respect that, right?

There was a knock on my office door as I started packing up my things.

"Come in," I said, still unable to believe I got to say that. I had an office. At Cole Cosmetics. It was a dream come true. *Mostly.*

Keri's head popped through the door. "Oh, good. Glad I caught you before you left. Thought I'd have to drive out after you. Mr. Cole just called and asked you to bring these to his house tonight." She held out a large white envelope.

Oh, shit. I felt my face turn tomato red. She knew I was going to his house? What else did she know?

"Um. Yeah," I said. "He wanted to go over some things before Monday."

"Go over a few things?" She smirked and gave me a look. "Oh, that man just loves fooling around."

Dear Lord. She knew? I thought I'd die of embarrassment.

She went on, "Mr. Cole has to attend the big fashion show in Milan tomorrow night. The designer is revealing our new fall colors line."

Oh God. I hung my head and let out a sigh of relief, wanting to laugh. He'd been fucking with me about this weekend.

Head-game point goes to you, Cole.

Even I knew that C.C. did these product-release fashion shows four times a year. It was always a big hush-hush until the event when they revealed the models were wearing the new look. They used a different clothing designer every time. I'd read that Mr. Cole did it that way to keep C.C.'s image fresh and it gave C.C. some "runway" before the competition knocked off their products. That was the name of the game: be first to market and set the trend. Just when everyone else caught up, they changed the trend again. *It's how number one stays number one.*

Keri shook her head and grinned. "Mr. Cole can be such a little boy sometimes. He loves to mess with people. Says it's good to always keep 'em guessing."

I gave Keri a smile, trying to hide my discomfort. "He got me. I had no idea."

She shook her finger at me. "Gotta stay on your toes with that man—be ready for anything. But usually when he has you meet him at home it's because he's taking the company jet out of Wheeling."

Wheeling was north of Chicago and not too far from where I lived. There was an executive airport there.

I laughed. She had no idea how relieved I felt. We'd be on a plane all night, and with the time difference, we'd probably be landing in Milan sometime in the afternoon. This was a business trip.

Then part of me realized I was going to Milan on C.C.'s company plane to attend the big fall reveal. The little girl inside squealed with delight. There may have been some pom-pom shaking, too. *Go awesome me!*

"I'll be ready for his little surprises next time," I replied.

"I doubt it. He always finds new ways to shock the hell out of me, and I've been working for him for two years." Her eyes flashed on the envelope she'd laid on my desk. "That's your passport and VIP tickets to the event—Mr. Cole forgot them on his desk."

Keri had asked me to bring in my passport this morning for HR reasons—citizenship verification and for their travel department records.

"Have fun," she said.

She left, and I finished packing up my things, thinking that this weekend would be the perfect opportunity to set the record straight with Cole.

I picked up my phone and decided to send Danny a little "rub it in" text.

Me: *Guess who's going to Milan tonight? Me. That's right. And guess who I'm going with?*

She didn't know that being with Mr. Cole wasn't

the fantasy it was cracked up to be, but why not make her a little green anyway?

Danny: *What? No! You whore! Stay away from my man or I'll cut you! (Smiley face)*

Me: *I'll send him your regards, you crazy bitch. C U Sunday. Pls. check on Mrs. Jcksn. XOXO*

Danny: *Bite me. Yes on Jcksn.*

I laughed. She was so awesome. I'd definitely have to bring her back something nice like some Italian condoms.

༄

Later that evening, I pulled up to Mr. Cole's gated house on the lake, about forty minutes north of Chicago and about a half hour east of my apartment.

The home was every bit as impressive and intimidating as the man himself. To describe it would take about an hour and I still wouldn't do it justice, so I'll just say the thing was a two-story mini castle with a gray brick and stucco exterior. A high-pitched roof made the home appear more daunting and larger than it probably was, which was still pretty dang large.

As I reached to buzz the little pad near the gate, the wrought-iron fence slid open, and I pulled my red Mini up the long driveway lined with green lawn on both sides. The view of the lake to my right, where he had two boat docks and a beautiful yacht, was breathtaking. The entire place was exactly the sort of palace a girl like me dreamed of owning.

I pulled up between the front door and the circular fountain, wondering why I suddenly felt all nervous again. I knew he'd just been toying with me—testing out my backbone—and we'd be getting on a plane to Milan.

I guessed that was a good reason to be nervous, too. For me, this was an exciting trip to a place I'd always wanted to go. For him, it was therapy. He'd be shut up in a plane with me for twelve hours. Then he'd get a break and get to drool over the gorgeous runway models during the show. He'd probably snatch one up for the night, and then we'd see each other on the plane again to come home.

Look on the bright side, he'll be a captive audience. Somewhere between now and the end of the trip, I'd tell him I had been joking about the sex but that I wanted to trade up—that's what I'd call it—for shares in the company. If I did a good job, of course. In exchange, I'd put up with his shitty disorder and work my ass off for him. I'd also make it clear that I didn't expect any special treatment just because I knew his ugly little secret. It was a fair deal.

Nervous as hell, I stepped from my car. I'd decided to change at the office and had worn my running clothes—as my own little joke—white tank top, pink and black running shorts, and my favorite black running shoes. My hair was loose around my face, though. Not how I usually wore it when I ran.

After ringing the doorbell twice and knocking a few more times without a response, I tried the door. It was unlocked, so I pushed. Hell, someone had let me through the front gate, and I'd been invited, so perhaps Mr. Cole expected me to show myself in?

Or the butler has gone home for the day? Did he even have a butler? I didn't know.

The door creaked open. "Hello?" I called out.

No one answered as I stepped inside and looked around the opulent foyer that included a winding staircase, raised ceiling with chandelier, and grand arched doorways leading to several dark rooms.

"Mr. Cole?" I called out again.

"In here." I heard his deep, hypnotic voice coming from the room to my right.

I followed the sound and stopped in the doorway.

"You're late," he growled.

No. I wasn't. I'd arrived to his gate at exactly 7:55 p.m., but when my eyes spotted his silhouette seated in an armchair in the corner of what looked like his formal living room, the last thing on my mind was arguing.

The lights were off and with the sun setting outside, a faint shadow crossed over his beautiful face, giving him an especially intimidating and angry look.

He added, "But I'm glad you decided to show up. I'm not in the mood for a solo run tonight."

*Uh...*was he speaking literally or figuratively? My heart started pounding inside my chest.

"Mr. Cole, what's going on?"

He stood, making me realize he wore only black shorts and running shoes. No shirt. His ripped-as-hell chest and abs were on full display, and I couldn't pretend I wouldn't be fantasizing over the image later on. He'd also added to his tattoo collection since he'd modeled almost nude last year. The intricate tribal pattern now covered both of his upper arms instead of just one.

Yum.

"What's going on," he replied, "is your second lesson."

Lesson one had been getting my hands dirty—aka, doing things I didn't feel one hundred percent comfortable with simply because the boss asked me to.

"Please don't tell me you're going to have me hire Craig back," I said sarcastically.

"No. He'd been harassing Keri. Repeatedly. He won't be coming back."

Oh. And Keri, a huge credit to her, never once dropped her professional demeanor around the shmuck. Point for Keri. It was also nice to know Craig really deserved to be canned.

Had that been part of the lesson, too? That I needed to trust that Maxwell Cole had his reasons for the things he did or might ask me to do?

He continued, "Lesson two: from now on, if you want something, you'll have to fight for it."

Okay. "What exactly are you asking me to fight for?" And why the hell was he shirtless and sitting in the dark...

Oh. It dawned on me. He didn't want to see my face. *Fuck. This hurts.*

"I'm sure by now," he said, "Keri's told you about Milan."

"Yes."

"Good. Because if you want to go, you'll have to run."

"Run-run?" I asked.

"Yes."

"You want me to race you?" He couldn't be serious. The idea was almost as crazy as him accepting my proposal to sleep with me.

"Why not?" he asked.

Because you're built like a stallion, have a personal trainer, and could probably outrun me by a few clicks per hour with those long powerful legs of yours.

"I'm not really sure it's a fair fight," I replied, still reeling from the fact the lights were off. The reality of our relationship was beginning to sink in, and I wasn't sure I could deal with it.

He crossed his arms over his bare chest, and I

wished to hell he'd turn the lights on because I'd give anything to see his eyes. Was he fucking with me again?

"That's the point," he said. "You want to run a company, then you better get used to things being unfair. The competition plays dirty every day."

I swallowed. I understood what he was saying, I really did. But racing against him?

"So what's it going to be, Miss Snow? You in, or are you going to run to your little red car and drive back to your shitty little apartment to whine about how unfair the world is?"

What an ass. "Fine. You wanna run? Let's run." I had no clue how I'd win, but what did I have to lose besides a trip to Milan?

※

As the final rays of daylight faded and the fireflies began making their flashy moves in the trees around the edges of his front lawn where we stretched, I did my best not to run to my car—but I wouldn't go back to my shitty little apartment; I would drive into the lake. I also noticed Mr. Cole glancing at me from the corner of his eye, perhaps trying to read me or size me up.

"So where are we running?" I hoped it would be straight to the plane to Milan and that this was a joke.

"I frequently run at night during the summer,

unlike some other people I know with a death wish."

Lily jab. He was referring to the fact he'd caught me running in the day.

He went on, "We'll run along the road for about two miles. Then there's a path that cuts toward the beach and loops back here."

"So about four or five miles?" That was it? I began feeling cocky. I could do five miles with my legs behind my back. Okay, an exaggeration, but you get the point.

"What? Can't handle it?" he said smugly.

What I couldn't handle were the feelings I was beginning to have with him parading around without a shirt. His body was nothing shy of a male miracle—strong, lean, fiercely muscled in all the right spots. It dawned on me that the magazine spread had not been airbrushed. *Nude and natural*.

I pffted. "I can handle it. Lead the way."

"With pleasure, Miss Snow." He headed down the driveway, exited through a small gate, and hooked right, toward the north. I trailed behind him closely, not wanting to burn up all my energy in the first few miles. Pacing was always the key. Yeah, I'd run track in high school and college.

The first mile passed quickly, and Mr. Cole kept his pace steady, making it fairly easy to keep up as we passed house after house along the road, their driveway lights illuminating our way given there were no streetlamps. Just lots of trees and big houses. What little light there was, however, allowed me a nice view of his muscular back and tight waist. Then there were those athletic legs. Not tree trunks, but hard, sleek man-legs. I could clearly imagine all of those ropes of muscles flexing and straining with force as he pumped himself between my—

"How you holding up, Miss Snow?" he called out, panting lightly.

Uhh...a little hot? "Just wondering when you'll start running, Mr. Cole."

"Feel free to pass me anytime."

So damned cocky! "And miss out on the sweet view? No, thanks." I hoped my brazen comment might make him trip or something. Seriously, how else would I win?

He laughed. "Hope you brought those binoculars, Miss Snow, because the view is about to disappear."

"You're all talk, Mr. Cole."

He didn't reply. Instead, he began running hard, fading out in front of me down the dark road.

No, you don't. I pumped my legs and arms, pushing my body as fast as it would go, my lungs burning deliciously. Still, I could barely keep him in sight. *Dammit. That man is in great shape.* My only hope now was that I'd outlast him and pass him up ahead. The thing was, I wasn't really a sprinter, but a long distance kind of gal. Hanging in there was my thing.

Fuck. It suddenly hit me—what he'd said earlier. It wasn't a fair fight. That was the entire point of this run. So if I wanted to win, I had to play dirty. Because aside from finding a shortcut and cheating, I would not be going to Milan.

Then I had an idea. A very crazy one.

I glanced up ahead, barely able to see him as he took a path that cut eastward, through a stand of trees and toward the lakeshore.

Okay. He had to be getting tired because he'd been sprinting. If I pushed hard, I could overtake him right before he got to his house and then...he was going to get a little surprise.

I picked up the pace, my body pouring with sweat, the nocturnal bugs—crickets and whatever the hell else lived out here—clicking away. In the dark, I could barely make out the trail, but I kept charging on until I saw his faint silhouette again.

Okay. Here goes.

⁂

"What took you so long, Mr. Cole?" I said, standing on the edge of the dark dock, with my arms crossed over my chest, watching him approach in a cool-down walk.

"Seems I had a little accident back there. Thank you for stopping, by the way," he said sarcastically.

It was dark, so I couldn't see his expression, but if I had to guess, he was looking shocked as hell that I won.

"Yeah, well. Someone told me that fights aren't always fair."

Now standing a few feet in front of me on the dock, I could smell his delicious scent. Expensive cologne mixed with his fresh sweat.

"Here's your shirt back." He held it out. "Quite the bold move, Miss Snow."

Seriously, I wished I'd had an infrared camera to capture the look on that man's face when I'd whipped off my tank at the exact moment I ran at his side. Now, before you get the wrong idea, I normally didn't wear a bra when I ran because I used those special sports tanks, but tonight I'd worn a regular tank. "What the hell are you..." he'd said, looking over at me several times while running, probably either trying to get a better look at my breasts jiggling in my white lacy push-up bra or wondering if I'd lost my marbles. Then I'd thrown my tank top in his face, causing him to trip and fall. I kept running and didn't look back, just hoping and praying no one would see me running along the beach, cupping my breasts.

Yes. It was a full-on insane thing to do and not at all like me, but I'd done it. A calculated move, knowing it was dark out and would win me what I wanted.

I shrugged. "What can I say? I really wanted to go to Milan."

"I would've taken you anyway."

Ugh. Asshole! "So I just ran without a shirt for a quarter mile and would've gotten to go anyway?"

"Not really. But I wanted to make you feel bad. By the way, has anyone ever told you you're completely mad?"

I laughed and turned around to unravel my tank top and slip it over my head, a huge smile on my face. "So, what time do we leave for the air—"

I suddenly felt his hot sweaty body pressed up against my back, his one hand on my bare waist, the other sweeping my long hair to one side. "No need to put that back on."

My breath caught in my throat. "Wha-wha-what are you doing?" I whispered, feeling his hands slide up the front of my body and begin touching my breasts over my bra. He was hard. Really, really hard, and straining against my lower back.

"I think that's fairly obvious; keeping our deal," he said, his hot breath tickling my neck.

I was about to say something to explain how I didn't really want him to do what he was doing, but it would've been a lie. The heat of his skin on my back, his hard cock pressing into me while his hands massaged my breasts felt better than anything I'd ever experienced.

His lips trailed down the side of my neck and stopped right on the little spot where my shoulder started.

How was this happening? Because wasn't he…didn't he have that problem with…?

"Oh my God. That feels...that feels..." My words faded as one of his hands left my breast and slid down my stomach, reaching to rub me over my thin shorts. I let out a little moan.

"Mmmm...your body is amazing," he said. "So fucking sexy."

His words shocked and excited me. No one had ever used the word "sexy" to describe me. Not once.

Then reality arrived like a boulder on my head. He didn't like me. Not even a little. This really, truly wasn't what I wanted. A fuck. With some guy who had serious issues just looking at me.

And he's your boss. Doesn't get much more screwed up than that.

I grabbed his hand. "Stop. Please," I said.

"Ah. I wondered when your weak spine would make an appearance."

I stepped away from him and went for my tank, which was a white little wad on the dock, barely visible. I slid it over my head. "I changed my mind. That's all."

"Why?" he said.

This time when I turned to face him, I wasn't wishing I could see his face; I was wishing he could see mine. This was painful for me. "I'm not comfortable discussing it with you."

He chuckled. "The topless runner is timid all of a sudden?"

He had a point, but being a little ballsy wasn't

the same as exposing yourself emotionally. Those were two different animals. And a man who'd posed nude—practically nude—should know the difference.

"No. I just really don't want to have this conversation with you—my boss," I said flatly.

"Don't pull the boss card. I shared my secret with you. You can share yours."

Why the hell did he even care? I was just a therapy tool for his phobia. And to be frank with myself, I wondered how he'd planned to finish what he'd started. Would we be in the dark so he could imagine some other woman's face?

God, how degrading.

"All right," he said, "if you don't want to tell me, then I'll guess. You've never been fucked before. And you're probably stuck on some fantasy of your first time being with some knight in shining armor who will sweep you off your feet and tell you how beautiful you are."

"No. I'm not delusional." *But I'd settle for someone who doesn't find me repulsive.*

"Good. Because we don't get everything we want in life. We just don't."

I made a little half-laugh. It was what my parents always said. "Trust me. I know."

"Then what is the issue?"

"Why do you care?" I asked.

"Answer my question, and I'll answer yours."

"Fine. I never wanted to sleep with you." My

words came out all rushed like a Band-Aid coming off.

"Really?" He laughed. "I hope you don't think me an arrogant prick—oh yes, you already do—so there's no harm in saying I think you're full of shit."

This man was...he was...

Sharp.

I suddenly felt the undeniable and simultaneous need to hide myself and open up. He was just that magnetic. Like a weird madness I felt the need to invite into my life.

I took a breath. "When I asked you to have sex with me, it was just something that came out of my mouth on the spur of the moment because I'd wanted to punish you with a nasty, spiteful price tag after you told me why you really wanted to hire me."

"I wanted," he said slowly with a deep, sincere voice, "to hire you because I like you. I like the fact that you're genuine and say what's on your mind. I admire that. Quite a lot, actually. You're unlike anyone I've ever met."

My heart fluttered. It was a really, really nice compliment. Especially coming from someone who didn't seem to hand them out so freely.

"Thank you," I said.

"And to answer your question, regarding why I'm curious about your sudden lack of interest in fucking me, it's because I think you have potential, but not the backbone to truly pursue what you want, without shame, without asking for forgiveness. You behave like you don't deserve a seat at the table because your face isn't perfect."

Oh my God. This guy wasn't afraid to say anything. He brought the art of bluntness to a whole new level. "Well, if you haven't noticed, I'm not like everyone else. It hasn't been easy, but I've managed to make it this far."

"Being audacious is not enough, Miss Snow. You have to believe you deserve the things you want and expect them to happen. Then you need the determination to see them through despite the obstacles. But you behave like a second-class citizen; it's written all over your body—the way you carry yourself."

I wanted to react to his words with the typical denials and arguments most of us throw up when we're told something unpleasant about ourselves; however, his statement genuinely hobbled me, like being slapped in the face and waking up. I had been seeing the world through my face, always feeling just a little unsure of myself, like I was just one notch below everyone else.

I groaned and pinched the bridge of my nose.

"Well, I'm glad we had this little chat," he said. "But I've got a company to run and problems to deal with, and I'm not paying you to sit around and snivel. So if you're not in the mood for fucking, you can shower in the bathroom just off the foyer. We leave in ten."

Oh, look. The asshole is back. "Ten minutes? Wooow," I yelled as he walked away. "Good thing that fuck is off the table. I'd be finishing the job alone, you big stallion."

He laughed, his deep wholly masculine voice cutting through the darkness. "The fuck is *not* off the table."

What? I tensed for a moment until I realized he was just messing with me. "Yes, it is!" I screamed back. "And I want stock options."

"No!"

"But you're mean! I don't want you and never will!"

"You're lying. And a deal is a deal, Miss Snow! Get your ass in the shower, because I wait for no one."

Crap. What if he wasn't kidding?

Of course he's joking. And if not, it wasn't like he could fire me for backing out. In fact, now that I thought it through, I was probably the least fireable person on his staff—not that getting fired was ever my concern; I'd wanted his respect. Nevertheless, it had only just dawned on me what a huge risk he'd taken with me, which was probably why he'd talked to Mark Douglas about my trustworthiness. I already knew enough to ruin his reputation, and he had to realize that.

So why is he taking such a huge gamble? It didn't make sense. Maxwell Cole had exposed himself to me. Not just now, but from the first moment we'd met. And there had to be a reason.

Lily, hellooo? Maxwell Cole just had his hands on your tits and his dick pressed against your back, and you turned him down. I whooshed out a breath. *That really just happened, didn't it?*

And I suddenly wanted it to happen again.

chapter seven

Awkward. A word that defines something that is difficult to deal with or makes one feel uncomfortable. That would sum up my feelings after my "moment" with Mr. Cole on the dock. It would also describe every moment after that for the next few hours.

First, there was the fact that when I'd packed this morning, my mind had been in an entirely different place: sexscapade weekend with Maxwell Cole. Now, we were going to Milan on a business trip.

Why does this matter?

Because I'd brought all the wrong clothes, with the exception of my little black dress for Saturday night. The rest of my wardrobe consisted of running shorts and sports tanks, or tight jeans and short-shorts. I'd brought zero blouses or grown-up clothes.

"That is a lovely outfit, Miss Snow," Mr. Cole said, seeming very amused as I approached the awaiting limo, where he stood next to the opened door, looking like he was modeling his outfit: jeans, a regular button-down, and a casual-looking, but perfectly tailored blazer.

Pulling my suitcase behind me, I looked down at my low-cut, cream-colored, full-body tank top that showed ample cleavage and had a lacy thong bottom. Of course, I wore my skintight jeans over the truly racy part, but the outfit was pretty sexy in the boob area.

"Next time," I snapped, "tell me where we're going, and I'll bring a suit."

He dipped his head. "Then not a chance."

Oh, he was so enjoying this, wasn't he? Yes, I was sure he got off seeing what a girl like me would've worn had we actually been having a very, very wrong, illicit-sex kind of weekend.

I huffed out a little laugh. "You can stop the childish gloating now, Mr. Cole. It cheapens your alpha-male mystique."

He was about to say something when the driver scrambled from the front seat and ran over to take my luggage.

Carrying my laptop case and purse, I slid inside. Mr. Cole came around the other door, got in, and immediately began typing away on his phone. It was just after nine o'clock at night and we hadn't even made it out of his driveway, but I already found myself wondering how I'd handle forty-eight hours with him.

Oh, stop. You're not afraid of this guy. But that wasn't really the problem. I was beginning to realize that I liked him. Not his body or his good looks, but his prickly personality and unabashed approach to life. I liked...*him*. The person. Just a teensy, weensy bit, and that unsettled me. The man was cold, ruthless, and...okay, he was hot. His unwavering self-confidence, smoldering hazel eyes, and smokin' hot, male-model body were turn-ons, too. I liked that he didn't shy away from showing me who he really was. Not that I knew him well, but it was clear he didn't give a fuck about anyone's opinion. And when I thought about his phobia, well, I wondered how many people out there would admit to having it, let alone tackle it head-on like he had.

Take an arachnophobe, for example. I wasn't a fan of spiders, but I wouldn't invite one into my bed. Yet, in this analogy, seeing a spider gave him panic attacks. Did that trip him up? No. He said, "Hiya, Spider. Come inside. Let's get it on."

Okay. Strange analogy. But when he saw something—or someone, I guess—that he found ugly, it triggered a physiological response that alerted his fear receptors. Yes, I took the time to read up on phobias. How could I not? The point was, his brain produced all of these mixed and erroneous signals that told his body he was in danger.

I sorta loved that because it made me feel bad. Me. Lily Snow.

And his way of handling his "challenge" made me start to seriously question how I'd been dealing with my own. Had I been facing it head-on? Or had I simply been trying to live with it? There was a huge difference between accepting and conquering. Accepting meant one tried to work around an issue, knowing it would never change. Conquering meant one pushed the obstacle out of the way. Total annihilation or domination.

That was when I realized I could learn more from Mr. Cole than the mere basics about running a company. He had his ugly. I had mine. He owned it. I did not.

By the time we arrived to the private airport, Mr. Cole was on his phone, speaking in fluent Italian—impressive—to someone about the show. He stayed on that call as the pilots—two nice older gentlemen with silver crewcuts—introduced themselves and got the plane ready for takeoff. Meanwhile, I occupied myself with trying not to gawk at the awesome corporate jet with full bar, five rows of sleeper seats (three in each row), television, workstation, bathroom with shower, and stocked kitchenette, where I found and attacked a bean-sprout sandwich. It was heaven.

Anyway, the travel accommodations were seriously nice. But of course, if your life was flying back and forth all over God's green Earth, it probably felt less like an episode from *Secret Lives of the Super Rich* and more like *Man* (or woman) *Versus Wild*.

Nah, it's cool no matter what, I thought, settling

in toward the back to give Mr. Cole some space while he finished his call. I got out my laptop and started going over numbers from some of the client files. It seemed that Cole Cosmetics' number one issue was overselling. Ten percent growth, quarter after quarter, and each customer had a double-digit percentage of order cuts. Meaning, C.C. couldn't keep up with demand even with the new factory they were building in New Jersey.

I guessed that was a good problem to have. Except that shorting orders probably pissed off the customers, which opened the door for our competitors to come in and make them happy. Not good. And it wasn't like Mr. Cole was stupid, which meant he had some other plan to boost supply that he hadn't made public yet.

I'd have to ask Mr. Cole about it later. For the moment, however, the long day and effects of the emotional roller coaster were catching up. I shut off the overhead light and tilted back my seat.

I wasn't sure of the hour, but my subconscious alerted me to a person in my space while I slept, awakening me from a very erotic dream comprised of a merry-go-round that had nude male strippers instead of horses. You fill in the rest.

When my eyes creeped open, hoping to hell it wasn't my mother standing over me with a suitcase in hand, I was immediately jarred by a very curious view of Mr. Cole staring at my face, his body inclined in the seat right beside me.

I blinked a few times to moisten my dry eyes and sharpen my vision. "What are you doing?" I whispered.

"I couldn't sleep," he replied, lying on his side, his face less than a few feet from mine.

"So you're staring at me?"

"Yes." He kept staring. And then I noticed he wasn't sweating or cringing, but really looking at me.

"Therapy," I said, understanding the situation.

"You were asleep. Seemed like a good time."

I smiled. Somehow, it didn't bother me despite the absolute weirdness. Something about him just made me feel open to accepting things. "How's it going?"

"Good, but it's easy with you."

"Easy how?"

"There are many things about you to like," he replied in a low voice.

It was very sweet.

"And many things not to like." He grinned.

"Ha-ha."

He smiled, and it was a warm, genuine, heartwarming smile that made me wonder why he wasn't like this all the time. And I don't know what it was—maybe the dimmed lights and the isolating hum of the engines—but I felt like we were inside a safe cocoon, just him and I.

"What happened to you?" I whispered, wondering what could've caused this man to be perfect in almost every way, except for this.

"I'll tell you, but then you'll have to answer one of my questions."

"What question?"

"A simple yes or no is called for."

"Control freak." I smiled. "Fine. Deal."

He gazed into my eyes, and I wondered if that too was a safe zone for him.

"My mother happened," he replied.

Oh no. Maybe I didn't want to hear this. On the other hand, I'd asked. I couldn't slam the door on this.

"What did she do to you?" I asked.

"She used to beat me and my older sister with wire hangers until our rooms were cleaned."

I gasped, and then I noticed a spark of amusement in his eyes.

"Oh, you're such an ass," I said. "Mommy Dearest, huh?"

His smile melted away, his expression shockingly serious. "My mother was too good for wire-hanger punishments, but her obsession with perfection was always taken to the extreme. She couldn't help herself—a behavior she passed down to me. My sister, on the other hand, just ended up being a very distrusting person."

I remembered reading in his online bio—

interview research, of course—that he had a sister who was a year older. I wondered if they were close like I was with my brother. I was about to ask when my mind suddenly made sense of what he'd just said.

"Wait. You inherited your phobia from your mother, didn't you?" I asked.

He didn't reply, but he didn't have to. And his confession hit me right in the heart. Probably because it made me sad to imagine what it might've been like for him. The irony was that my mother was the exact opposite. My imperfections gave her purpose.

"Why are you smiling?" he asked.

It wasn't really a smile, it was more like a smile-frown. "Because I don't know what my mom would do with herself if I'd been born as perfect as you."

"Perfection is an illusion," he said. "So now it's your turn. Tell me why you turned down my offer for surgery."

I suddenly didn't want to have this conversation any more. I inhaled a deep breath and looked away from him before setting my chair upright. I was about to say something, but my thoughts and words got all jumbled up inside my head.

"I have to use the restroom," I announced like a moron, standing up from my seat.

Mr. Cole righted his seatback and then looked at me with a frown.

I knew what he was thinking: he'd told me his

truth and now I was denying him mine.

"I'll be right back. I promise."

He nodded, and his eyes jerked to the side, indicating he wasn't getting up for me.

"Fine." I rolled my eyes and stepped over him. As I passed, he took the time to grip my hips and assist.

His touch sparked a moment of sexual flutters in my stomach. I liked his hands on me. I shouldn't, but I did. "Stop that."

He dropped his hands and shrugged. "Just making sure you don't fall."

I flashed a quick little glare and made my way back to the bathroom. I really did need to go, but I also needed to gather my thoughts. Call me weak or anything you like, but his opinion suddenly mattered. No, I wasn't trying to come up with a lie or some BS about the answer to his question; I was trying to rally the bravery to be honest with him. In the exact same way he'd been honest with me. No apologies. No shame. Just the truth. There was power in the way he didn't allow his challenges to pull him down, and I wanted to feel the same.

I splashed a bit of cool water on my face and patted myself dry with a paper towel. *You can be more than brave, Lily. You can be you and feel good about it.*

I opened the door and returned to my seat, where Mr. Cole sat with two tumblers in his hands.

"What's this?" I asked, taking the glass.

"A very fine scotch," he replied.

I scooted past him and sat down, sniffing the very, very tall glass of strong honey-brown liquid. "Smells like gas."

He chuckled. "If gas were this expensive, we'd be flying in a weather balloon to Milan. Try it."

I took a sip, trying not to let the unpleasant sting of the alcohol show on my face. It was sweet and had a cinnamon-like burn, but I didn't like it. "Mmmm..." I tried to smile.

"You don't drink very often, do you, Miss Snow?"

"No, but it's good to try new things." I threw back the entire drink and handed him the glass.

He laughed. "Remind me to stock the cheap stuff for the flight home."

Oops. I guessed I wasn't supposed to chug it.

Following my lead, he finished his drink and set our glasses down on the seat across the aisle.

His gaze returned to me with an expectant look in his eyes.

"What?" I said.

"You know what."

Dammit. I wasn't going to get out of this, was I?

I bobbed my head and looked down at my hands. The scotch had an immediate effect—a warmth in my chest and little rush in my heart. I suddenly didn't feel so awkward sharing any more. Was that why he'd given me the drink?

"The reason I don't want to have surgery," I

finally said, "is because I'm afraid it will make me unhappy."

He lifted both brows. "Unhappy?"

"It sounds absurd, but everyone I know has their issues, too, and they aren't happy. At least, not most of the time. Me, on the other hand," I shrugged, "I've always felt so grateful for everything."

"Maybe because you never expected anything. The higher one strives in life, the more pressure and disappointments you'll come across."

"So you're saying I've been happy because I haven't set the bar high enough?" I asked. *Ridiculous.*

"I don't believe for a moment that you're pushing yourself to reach your full potential. Case in point, you applied for a position you were overqualified for."

I stared at the seatback in front of me for a moment, trying to digest his words, the scotch now running freely through my system. Maybe he was right.

"But tell me," I asked, "if you were free from your *problem*, what would be different about your life? Would you be happier?"

"Good question. I don't know. But I will never find out until I conquer it."

"And you really, really think I can help you do that?" I asked.

He looked ahead for a moment, his stubble-covered jaw flexing. "My therapist believes if I successfully associate positive feelings with the things that trigger my disorder, then I will overcome it."

I snickered. "And there it is. The truth." I hit my knee. "You wanted to bang me so you could see if it cures you." The moment those words left my mouth, I realized how crazy it sounded.

But then why is he looking at me with a cocky grin?

"I'm a man. Sex is a powerful thing. And then there's you."

His words hung in the air. I'd been right?

And me how?

I didn't have to ask because his hand extended and cupped my cheek. The gesture took me completely off guard. He was touching me, his chest rising and falling quickly, while he studied me like some dangerous, exotic creature he found fascinating. No one had ever looked at me like that before.

"Nothing scares you, does it?" he asked. "Which makes you perfect in a way most of us will never experience, especially me. Take pride in that, Miss Snow."

"I'm fairly sure you outrank me on the perfect scale."

"It's the other way around, Lily."

How could he say that? He didn't really believe that he was the more flawed person in this comparison. That would be insane.

But the subtly troubled look in his eyes as they toggled between mine and the window told me he was struggling. He wanted to look at me, but couldn't. And it pained him. I wondered if anyone else but me would ever pick up on it.

I realized they probably wouldn't, and I understood the sadness and frustration of feeling like this thing had been thrust upon you and, as best you tried, you couldn't escape it. It controlled you when it shouldn't. It got in your way and held you back. It was that horrible, self-deprecating voice in your head that undermined everything you did. Some days, it was louder than others, but it was always there.

Fuck. I looked up and drew in some air. I don't know what came over me in that moment. Call it scotch. Call it the strange and brutally honest conversation we were having, but somewhere inside my mind, what we were doing felt far more intimate than sex. We were showing our insides to one another and the feeling of closeness—something I'd never experienced with a man—left me wanting more. The feeling was powerful and consuming and I think that only someone who'd been deprived of it for as long as I had could understand why I wanted to do what came next.

I stared down at my hands for a moment, my core tingling with the explicit thoughts.

"Close your eyes," I said, knowing this was

insane and, once I let it happen, there would be no turning back. But for once in my life, I wanted to feel like a real woman. Unashamed to feel sexual. Unafraid to take what she wanted. Powerful.

"Why? Are you going to punch me in the face?" he asked.

I slid my hand over his lap and rested it on his groin. "Not exactly."

I half expected him to push it away in disgust, but he didn't. Instead, he closed his eyes and tipped his seat back.

Well, twist the man's arm. I couldn't believe what I was about to do, but I wanted it more than I wanted to think or rationalize. And he seemed to be offering himself up freely for my personal exploration.

I slid from my seat, pushed up the armrest between us, and got down on my knees. I could already see him straining against his jeans.

God, he's so perfect. I didn't deserve this fantasy, but I wanted it anyway.

I maneuvered my way between his legs into the tight space at his feet and then began unbuttoning his jeans. When I glanced up at him, I noticed his sharp breathing and rigid posture. Both excited me. I liked having this effect on him.

Slowly, I finished unbuttoning his fly and found hard pink flesh awaiting me. No underwear. Did most men go commando? I didn't know, but it was sexy as hell.

I placed my hand on him, and he gasped as I pried his hard cock free. I'd never seen a penis up close and personal, but it was more erotic and sensual than I could've imagined—the soft velvety head glistening with a drop of moisture, the veins pushing against the soft skin, and the thickness and length so substantial. I wondered how something like that would ever fit inside. Then there was the patch of male hair surrounding the thick base like a wreath of sin.

I must've been staring at it, holding it in my hand for way too long, because he grumbled, "Are we getting on with this or not?"

I glanced up at him and smiled. His eyes were still closed, and he looked tenser than hell. But something about conquering this man's fears made me wet. I just hoped the videos I'd seen during my Internet explorations were accurate.

I lowered my mouth over the tip of his head, and he jerked his body. I assumed from his groan, he liked it. I, on the other hand, didn't know what to make of the flavor. Salt and male musk. It was different from anything my lips could've imagined.

I slid him further in and enjoyed the instant power I felt from having his cock inside my mouth. I slid my head down, his hips pushed up, and his breath whooshed out. I drew back, and his hips pulled back. It was strangely delicious and sexy, and with each stroke of my tongue and mouth over his shaft, I felt like I was the one who was going to come.

He slid his hands to the back of my head, urging me to move faster, his hips pumping his thick cock in time with the movement of my mouth.

"Oh yeah. Suck it," he groaned. "Harder."

The gravelly, carnal sound of his voice mixed with his dirty words were like warm gasoline on my fire.

I moved my mouth faster and let the length of him slide back a little further.

"Fuck yes," he whispered, cupping the back of my head more firmly with those two strong hands. "Fuck yes."

This was the moment that I usually saw women do one of two things in the videos; take it on the face or suck it up. Both options did not seem too pleasing to me, but I'd started this little therapy session, and I had to end it. Him coming on my face was...well, embarrassing for me and probably counterproductive for him.

Then the thinking part of this first encounter was over.

He came. Hard.

He groaned with a deep thrust that hit the back of my throat, pouring himself into my mouth. I swallowed the salty heat of him down and looked up, meeting his eyes as he watched me take him.

That moment of connection—crude, primal, sensual, and erotic all at the same time—was oddly satisfying. Or maybe triumphant was the right word. I felt powerful knowing I could turn this man on and get him off. Especially given the obstacle.

He finished with one final little thrust and then threw back his head, panting hard. "Fuck. That was amazing, Lily."

He'd called me Lily, and I couldn't remember if he'd used my first name before, but it made the moment feel even more intimate.

I stared up at his face. He was so beautiful sitting there with his afterglow, totally free from his thoughts about his phobia or anything else. He was just a guy who'd had his dick sucked and felt fabulous.

I suddenly felt jealous. *Oh, to be on that cloud where nothing else matters*. I sighed and wiggled my way from between his legs, leaving his pink cock out for me to look at one last time. It was so damned beautiful. Just like the rest of him.

I slid into my seat and reclined, turning away from him. I didn't know how to feel about what I'd just done to him. I think I liked it a little too much, which was a huge mistake. A man like that was way out of my league.

"Something the matter?" he asked.

"Just tired, Mr. Cole. Goodnight." I should've called him Max, but I didn't want to—I felt the need to keep a little distance between us.

I heard him get up and leave. Probably to his own seat or something. Frankly, I didn't care. I had no business wanting the things I suddenly wanted. And it scared the hell out of me.

You can't let this go any further, Lily. You'll just get hurt. I could feel it in my gut.

chapter eight

Around three p.m. Milan time, I woke up to a gentle prod from one of the pilots alerting me that the flight was over. When I sat up, Mr. Cole was heading out the door, screaming at someone on his phone in Italian.

I hoped everything with the show was okay. From his tone, it didn't sound like it.

"Thank you." I nodded to the pilot, stretching my arms.

"Miss Snow!" Mr. Cole screamed from outside. "Hurry your ass, please."

I looked up at the pilot and shrugged. But then I realized I didn't have to take the rude talk lying down. And I was capable of reciprocating.

"Hold your pants, Mr. Cole. I have to pee!" I supposed I should've used the word "piss" to mirror his rudeness, but pee sounded nicer.

I stood from my seat and gathered my things. As I passed the pilot, he gave me a wink, and I smirked like we were in some secret club belonging to the serfs.

In the bathroom, I took my time brushing my teeth for obvious reasons—*yeesh, don't think about it*—fixed my hair into a ponytail, and washed my face. The entire twelve-hour flight felt like a dream. An erotic one. And now that the afternoon Milan sun shined bright, I needed a moment to gather myself. Mr. Cole and I were no longer inside our intimate, scotch-infused bubble. I hoped it wouldn't be weird between us now.

You're two grown adults. Of course it won't be, I lied to myself. Still, I would make it absolutely clear that it had been a onetime thing—not that he'd want more from me—and as far as I was concerned the "deal" was fulfilled, not to mention he'd voided his right to accuse me of spinelessness.

I heard a knock on the bathroom door. "Lily? Are you all right" It was Cole. And he'd used my first name again, but I still felt uncomfortable using his. Distance was good. It would protect me.

Still, his concern made my heart do this little weird skip thing. "Yes, Mr. Cole." I shoved my toothbrush into my accessory bag and then unlatched the door.

Mr. Cole stood there, arms crossed, his impatient frown greeting me. "There's a shower at the hotel."

"Good news. Because I'm feeling a little dirty," I said, sliding past with a grin. I'd meant it in a good way, but the look on his face was filled with confusion. Or maybe curiosity? Then his cell rang, and the yelling in Italian commenced.

We made our way through immigration and

customs, then on to the hotel. The area, at least from the limo, going down the *Autostrada dei Laghi,* looked so different than I imagined: normal with a lot of flat countryside, some trees, and I think I even saw...two McDonald's?

How very Italian!

Once we got closer to the hotel, however, the Milan I'd seen in pictures started working its way into the scenery—the classic Italian-style architecture with that light brown and gray stone, wrought-iron balconies, and cute little shutters around the windows. The cobblestone one-way streets, barely wide enough for cars let alone the pedestrians or people on bicycles, were lined with art galleries, museums, and every pricy shop known to woman—Dolce, Pierre Cardin, Gucci. And then there were the crazy drivers in teeny-tiny cars or riding mopeds. The city buzzed with life, including tons of tourists and shoppers. Sadly, I wouldn't be there long enough to do any of that, but I'd happily take whatever I got, which wasn't bad at all.

From the limo, I snapped off a few shots of the Milan Cathedral and its elaborate Gothic-style turrets that stood off in the distance. However, when the driver turned down an adorable little street—filled with immaculately maintained, three- and four-story buildings tightly packed together—and then stopped in front of the Four Seasons, I put my phone down and stopped breathing. The beautiful arched doorways, the stone façade, the...everything. Later, I would do a little exploring and learn it had a full spa, indoor pool, cloistered garden, and had been built in the '90s, to look like something from the fifteenth century. I would also make a mental note to have my ashes spread there.

"We're staying here?" I asked, but Mr. Cole was busy yapping away on his phone. Pissed as hell.

The valet opened my door and let me out.

While Mr. Cole stayed absorbed in business, I absorbed the surroundings. The lobby—soaring arches, elaborate crown moldings, and antique chandeliers—was an eye-gasm. Italy on steroids with old-world style and modern drool qualities.

I resisted the urge to squeal. When the receptionist asked me about our reservations, I looked over at Mr. Cole, who gave me the scoot-scoot hand gesture.

"The reservation should be under the name Maxwell Cole," I said.

"*Sì, signorina*. Here it is," said the young brunette with an immaculate bun and red lips. "Two rooms, one night."

"Yes. Thank you," I replied.

She typed in a few things and then handed me the room cards. "If you need anything, *Signorina* Snow, please let us know." The bellhop had already zoomed past us after gathering our luggage from the limo, so I assumed my things would be waiting.

I grabbed the keys, but when my eyes registered the room information printed on the envelopes, I coughed.

Holy shit. We were on the same floor in the executive suites with terraces. I had been sure he would put himself in the presidential suite and I'd be in one of their still fancy, but regular rooms. Had he downgraded just to be near me? And didn't he realize the room he'd gotten me was way nicer than I needed? I was not Pretty Woman. *I'm sorta the opposite, actually.* Nevertheless, Roy Orbison's voice still made an appearance in my head.

Holding up the keys, I looked over at Mr. Cole so he'd see we were all set.

Once again, he made the scoot-scoot gesture. I shook my head, trying not to appear ungrateful or nervous as we hit the elevator and he continued his call on his supersonic cell phone that stayed connected as we rode up. All the while, I kept wondering if he might ever decide to say anything about last night.

He had to say something, right? Or maybe I should? Then again, I didn't want it to be weird between us.

The doors slid open, and I exited with him on my heels, subconsciously feeling a heat that wasn't really there.

"*Molto bene*, Mauricio. *Molto bene*. But if you fuck this up, they won't find the body," he said.

I laughed as he disconnected the call.

"Something funny?" he snapped.

I handed him his envelope and then slid my key card into the reader at the door. "No, sir, Mr. Cole." I held back a laugh.

"Good. Be ready at five o'clock." He kept on going down the hall, and I watched him disappear around the corner. I felt relieved to see he wasn't in the room next door. I don't know why that would matter, but I suppose I didn't want him hearing me sing in the shower.

I stepped inside my suite and instantly felt some of the tension drain from my body. I hadn't realized how being around him really wound me up. He hadn't said a word about last night, and while I would never resort to behaving like a needy woman, his lack of engagement had left my emotions stirring. Good or bad, I needed to know where we stood after last night.

Are you kidding me, Lil? Where we stood seemed rather clear to the negative fugly bitch inside my head. He was an extremely attractive, high-powered man who got anything he wanted from any woman he desired. Probably to him, my first coveted encounter with a penis was like a drive-thru chocolate milkshake. Sweet and tasty, but cheap and nothing special. I needed to act like a mature woman and put it all into perspective.

You gave your boss a blowjob on the corporate jet. Which perspective might that be, Lily? That you're a dirty, dirty woman?

No. I'm an opportunist with extenuating circumstances. Yeah, that sounded better.

I turned, and my eyes swept through the fancy room. "Holy crap." Then I spotted the huge panoramic windows and glass doors leading outside. All of Milan was right there in front of me. The entire thing. I walked out onto the terrace and made a giant shame-free squeal. Just beyond the wrought-iron, waist-high railing, an ocean of little red tile roofs, the Milan Cathedral, and pristine gardens were laid out. I could seriously die happy on this terrace.

I snapped off a bunch of photos and posted them everywhere I could—FB, Instagram, Pinterest. *A view like this should be shared.*

I set my phone down on the cute little café table outside and went to explore. The place was about twice the size of my apartment. Why had Mr. Cole put me in this suite? I felt like a princess, with its crystal chandelier, elegant black and tan furniture, expensive art, and marble-everything bathroom with a two person tub that screamed "pamper me!"

I spent the next couple hours taking a long hot bubble bath, shaving my legs, straightening my hair, and doing my makeup. I hadn't been on a vacation in years—there was never any time, and every dime I made went toward paying for school—but these few precious hours more than made up for it.

By the time the door buzzed, I didn't look beautiful, but I felt it anyway. I'll admit, part of me wondered how much better this experience might've been if my face matched everything around me.

I opened the door, expecting to find Mr. Cole and expecting him to pay me a compliment for the effort I'd made to be presentable.

I only got one of those right.

Dark hair immaculately disheveled and wearing a dark gray dress shirt and a very, crazy-nice, black suit that didn't hang, but hugged his manly, fit body and accentuated his broad shoulders, Mr. Cole's eyes scaled up and down my torso as I held open the door.

"You're wearing *that*?" he said.

I looked down at my plain black heels and little sleeveless black dress that tastefully showed off my C-cup cleavage. "What's wrong with this?"

"Everything."

I wanted to punch him in the dick. No, seriously. I did. "Who says that to a woman?"

"An asshole like me. Get your purse."

"I think you can go and—"

"Before you tell me to fuck myself, Miss Snow, I'll offer that you're in Milan."

I was "Miss Snow" again. *Okay. This is good.* We were back to the way things were before last night, including his rudeness.

"Really?" I pointed toward the terrace. "I was

wondering what all that Italian-looking stuff was outside. Thanks for clearing that up." I gave him a bitchy smile.

He snarled at me with his hazel eyes. "And you're going to be sitting front row at Babs's fashion show, so you'll be in every photo of the runway, including *Vogue*."

My bitchy-smile evaporated. I suddenly felt mortified. Was it because of my fab-less dress or because the world would see my face? *Don't think like that, Lily. There's nothing wrong with you.*

I was about to tell him I didn't care. I wore the best dress I owned and that was that. Nothing to be ashamed of. But before I could speak, the man was on his phone again, doing the circle-the-wagons gesture with his index finger, indicating we needed to go.

I glared at him, and he turned away, heading toward the elevator. I grabbed my black evening bag from the little side table and followed, closing the door behind me.

Right as the elevator doors slid open, I got inside behind Mr. Cole. He said a few more words and then ended the call, slipping his cell into his pants pocket. "You might want to start making punctuality a priority, Miss Snow."

I'd gotten in the elevator three seconds after him. What was his problem?

"Yes, sir, Mr. Cole. Absolutely. And might I just say that I'm glad there's no awkwardness between us after I sucked your cock last night. You're still the same insolent bastard."

He smiled proudly, but didn't look at me.

I shook my head and decided staring at the doors was a far better option than looking at the man. Seeing him standing there in his perfectly tailored suit with his perfectly messy hair, full sensual lips, and unshaven jaw was too unsettling. I didn't want to feel any attraction for him. But I did.

Asshole.

When we got into the limo, I noticed that Mr. Cole was still smiling. Or was it more of a smirk?

"Okay, what the hell is so damned funny?" I seethed.

"Nothing." Grinning ear to ear, he shrugged innocently.

"Don't tell me 'nothing,' because there's obviously something that's amusing you."

Looking ahead at the road, his grin grew into the shit-eating sort, and he toggled his head from side to side. "Nope. Nothing. Just feeling happy."

"Well, stop it. It's freaking me the hell out," I said. But, honestly, it was kind of cute. For a few minutes. But then we pulled into traffic, and I could swear the bastard looked downright giddy—a total distraction from allowing me to soak in Milan. "Okay. I can't take it anymore. Are you laughing at my dress? Is that it? Because it's not nice to make fun of someone just because they have nothing nicer to—"

His gaze flashed my way just for a moment, and that smile of his melted right off. "I may be a heartless prick, Miss Snow," he said sternly, "but I have better manners than to laugh at a woman's dress."

I looked away toward the window. "Such a difference from telling me 'everything' is wrong with my outfit," I mumbled. And for the record, he had laughed at me before—the time I told him I wanted to run my own company.

He touched my leg, and I looked at him. "Lily, I am happy because…" His words faded away.

Ignoring how good his hand felt on my bare thigh, I crossed my arms over my chest. Big mistake because his eyes immediately gravitated to my pushed-up breasts. I dropped my arms. "Why are you happy?"

He shook his head. "Never mind."

"Fine with me." Now that his grin had evaporated, I kind of missed it. It was a breathtaking smile that made his handsome face light up and produced little divots in his cheeks that weren't really dimples, but more like deep smile grooves. Not smile lines either, because they disappeared when his smile left. I wished he'd smile more often.

Fifteen minutes later, we pulled up to a six-story brick building with beautiful carved gray stone details around the doorway and windows. A golden plaque next to the exterior door read "Babs

Lavine." It was one of her boutiques.

My heart jumped and started doing cartwheels. "What are we doing here?" I asked.

"Getting you a proper dress," he replied, gesturing toward the door where the limo driver appeared and pulled it open.

"You're joking," I said, already realizing he wasn't.

"No. Now if you'll please step out of the car? We're already running late."

I was too stunned to get out. Babs's dresses ran anywhere from five thousand to fifty thousand for the hand-beaded stuff. "Mr. Cole, I...I really appreciate the gesture, but I can't take a gift like that. The suite is already too much."

He shot me an irritated look with those stunning hazel eyes. "Miss Snow, you're a representative of my company who's about to be photographed and in every major global magazine, sitting by my side. So while I applaud your moral standards, you're missing the fact if you look bad, it makes my company look bad."

Oh. So this was about him. I felt silly for thinking that he was...well, trying to do something nice for me. Like a man might do for a woman who interested him romantically.

I mentally slapped my palm on my forehead. *I'm so out of my league here.*

"Sure. Fine. I'll wear the dress," I said with a polite smile and slid from the limo, feeling a bit deflated. But the truth was I needed to focus on the positive. When all was said and done, this was like living in a dream...working for C.C., going to a fashion show in Milan, wearing a Babs Levine dress. Minus the indiscretion with my boss—who some might argue should be part of my dream because he was part of theirs—this experience was about as great as it got when it came to work. This was my job. This!

Don't get too carried away with yourself. You're also Mr. Cole's therapy tool. Yes, I needed to remind myself of that and stay grounded.

"I'll wait here. You have five minutes, Miss Snow," Mr. Cole said.

"Is Babs going to fit me herself?" Her company was based in New York—at least I think it was—but Babs was in town, so I could only hope!

"She's at the show, but Margharita, her assistant, is waiting inside."

Wow. Good enough for me! "I'll be as fast as I can."

I trotted up the cement steps that led to an arched doorway in the center of the building and rang the buzzer to enter the shop. I supposed they were an appointment-only sort of place given the cost.

The door popped open, and I stepped inside, immediately blinded by the bright lights, white marble floors, and sparkly dresses worth thousands displayed on elegant manikins. A few champagne-sipping shoppers stood on low platforms while seamstresses made adjustments to their hems with pins.

At the far end of the shop, a set of French doors with smoky glass popped open, and a petite brunette waved at me. "Lily! Come in. Come in," she said hurriedly, with a thick Italian accent. I headed inside to what looked like a small private showing room, the walls lined with two tiers of racks and packed with shiny, colorful dresses.

"Wow. I think I just died."

"And I will be di next to go if I do not get you into a dress queeckly." She yanked down on the straps of my dress and peeled the thing off my shoulders. "Hurry up. Get out of dat thing."

Whoa. Okay. She hadn't even bought me a drink.

Now with me in my heels, black lace thong and matching lace, strapless bra, she whipped out a measuring tape.

She quickly sized me up. "*Bene,*" she said in that thick accent, "you are a beet fawt, but I think we have a few dresses for you."

A bit fat? I was a size six. I shot her a sour look, but she didn't care.

"But your teets are nice, *si*?" she added.

"Jeez. Thanks. Did you and Mr. Cole go to the same school of compliments?"

"No," she said sharply, looking at me with a peculiar frown. "I went to di fashion school."

"Never mind."

She turned away and rushed to the rack at the far end of the room. "Yes. I think deez will work nicely." She grabbed a black sequined thing, a red silky dress, and a pink satin gown with a beaded cream cinch around the waist.

She handed me the pink one first. I kicked off my heels and stepped into it. She tried the zipper, but it wouldn't go up.

"You are too fawt. Next dress." If she called me fat one more time, I was going to bite her.

"What are you? Like a size ten?" I asked, wanting to point out the obvious. Of course, there was nothing wrong with a size ten, but still.

She shrugged. "I am not di one asking for a dress one hour before di big show." She opened up the back of the black one, which was strapless and looked to be formfitting with eyelets in the back instead of a zipper.

The door swung open, and I heard that deep, familiar, masculine voice. "Miss Snow, are you rea—"

Oh crap. I turned my head, and Mr. Cole just stood there staring at my nearly naked body. I could've sworn I saw his Adam's apple do a little bob. I liked it. I liked his eyes on my body. Which was why I let him look.

Margharita prompted me to step into the dress, which I did. She then went to work on the hooks and eyelets in the back. Mr. Cole's eyes slowly moved to my face.

My breath hitched. A morbid part of me, the one that couldn't help looking at car accidents as I drove by, waited anxiously. What would happen when he looked at my face? Would he be able to handle it without any discomfort?

God, this situation kind of sucked. Okay. No. It flat out sucked.

His eyes met mine, and then he quickly turned away from me. "Wear that one. I'll wait outside."

My heart did a little dive. Being around this guy was like riding an emotional roller coaster. Up, down, fast, slow, spin in a loop. I couldn't quite seem to stop myself from feeling one way and then another.

I straightened my spine and lifted my chin. *Don't let it get to you, Lily. You knew this was the deal.* I had to keep reminding myself that he couldn't help it. And as horrible as he behaved sometimes, he was trying to fix his problem.

"Suck it in, girl. Suck it in," Margharita barked, trying to fasten the last hook, which hit me mid-back.

I did as she asked, feeling the fabric squeeze my rib cage. "*Eccellente!*" she chirped. "Di fawt is in!"

Ohmygod. I was about to give her an earful, but then I caught a glimpse of myself in the mirror and forgot what I was going to say. My breasts pushed up into voluptuous pillows at the top, almost like a corset effect, the waist darted in to give me a classic hourglass figure, and the hem hit me just above the knees, making my legs look long and graceful. I felt...so damned sexy. Me. Lily Snow felt really sexy.

"Wow. Thank you, Margharita."

"It is nothing!" She handed me a pair of shimmery black satin heels with a strap that went around the ankle. She quickly helped me get them on since I couldn't bend over so easily. The dress was really frigging tight.

Once the last buckle was on, I thanked her and scurried off, trying to keep my composure in the three-inch heels.

When I exited the door, Mr. Cole was standing there, talking on his phone. Then he stopped talking and just stared, blinking at my breasts and hips and legs and everything.

"Now *that* is a dress worthy of your body, Miss Snow."

The moment that passed between us was difficult to articulate. There was this strange hollowness in my chest when he looked at me. I guess you could call it a sadness or an emptiness. And the look in his cold, hard eyes made me all too aware that he felt the same. But not about me. About himself—his inability to get past this boat anchor around his neck. At least, that's what I guessed. But the two of us just looking at each other, seeing each other once again, profoundly affected me.

"How is it possible that the only person in the world who really sees me, can't stand to look at me?" I asked.

The expression in his eyes softened. "I did look. And you are stunning."

"Thanks." I didn't know if he meant it, but I wanted to believe he did. I looked down at my feet, my heart pounding away inside my chest.

"Now if you don't mind. We have a fashion show to get to." He marched out of the building, leaving me to my own devices to navigate the door and stairs.

He's still an ass. But he was seriously starting to grow on me. "Uh...thank you for the dress!" I called out.

chapter nine

Going to the fashion show reminded me of eating a bowl of chocolate ice cream: so, so good, and over way too fast. And like my favorite dessert, it was addictive—the buzz in the room, the excitement and glamour. *Over. Whelming.* But in an "I must be dreaming" kind of way.

There were so many famous—at least I think they were—beautiful people at the show, many of them rushing to greet, kiss, hug, or snap off a photo with the infamous bachelor and sex symbol Maxwell Cole. It was a feeding frenzy of photographers and fashion reporters, who knew the moment he walked in the room that this show was the secret reveal for the new fall makeup line. Of course, given the amount of press, I suspected the news had been leaked.

And as I hung back, away from the lenses and crowds that gathered around him until we took our seats, I noticed an ease about him. The way he smiled and carried himself with confidence was utterly magnetic. This was his element, surrounded by all the beautiful people who didn't make him sweat or panic or feel helpless.

It was the first time in my life I remember feeling jealous. Truly and utterly jealous. Not of him, but of everyone in the room he looked at and touched as if it were nothing.

I didn't want to acknowledge these shallow feelings, but I was only human, imperfect in more ways than I'd ever understood. And I'd been burying my emotions, lying to myself for so long that it felt normal. Only now, being there in that room made me realize how tainted I was on the inside.

So what are you going to do about it?

It was a question I put out of my head for another day, because when the lights dimmed and the loud, pounding techno music started, my mind transported to another world. Gorgeous, tall women with long slender bodies floated past me in twenty-thousand-dollar, hand-beaded dresses worthy of the Oscars, Cannes, or any other glamourous event. Before I blinked, it was over.

Like I said, ice cream. Sweet. Delicious. Never enough.

After the models concluded their sassy struts, Maxwell Cole joined Babs on the stage. The crowd roared, cheered, and clapped. A million bulbs flashed, lighting up the room in a constant stream of lightning bolts.

Maxwell Cole put his arm around Babs, a middle-aged woman with a kind face, but no glamor queen herself, especially standing next to the enigmatic Mr. Cole. He then looked down at me and winked.

I had a fan-girl moment, remembering the first time I'd seen a picture of him in a magazine. It had made my heart race with gnawing need, like how a girl feels the first time she goes to a rock concert and sees her idol on stage. It's a sort of all-consuming, magical attraction at a very primal level.

The show ended, and while I waited for Mr. Cole by the limo, I got to chat with Keri's boyfriend—a very handsome black guy with a super cute smile who'd actually gotten the job through Mr. Cole. I wondered how he and Keri made it work since he was based out of New York. *I guess when people are in love, they just make it work.* I wondered what that felt like: "making it work no matter what." Would I ever get to love someone that much?

Finally, Mr. Cole said his goodbyes to a few more people standing around outside, and I got into the backseat ahead of him.

"Wow," I said. "That was fun. Thank you for taking me to this."

He glanced at me. "You're welcome," he said, sounding shocked by my gratitude. Had I really been acting like such an ungrateful turd that a thank you was a rare thing? I'd need to try harder.

"Well, now I know why you were smiling earlier. You looked like you really enjoyed it."

"I do. I especially enjoy knowing that we'll be getting great publicity from this event, which costs me almost nothing, but will help us sell a billion dollars of makeup next quarter." He glanced at me. "But that wasn't why I was smiling earlier."

Hmmm... "Okay. Don't keep me in suspense, Mr. Cole."

"I think it's best that I do. I wouldn't want to sour your evening."

Of course, that only got my wheels turning faster. "You're evil."

"I prefer shrewd and calculating." His voice hinted at humor, but I wasn't sure. "Speaking of, you'll be meeting two very important customers tonight. One is Franco Morrano, the other is Krissy Walters, the head of purchasing for Libby Loo."

Wow. Okay, so Libby Loo was this really fantastic retail chain for older teens and twenty-somethings, sort of like an H&M, but less messy. Franco Morrano was the CEO of makeitless.com the biggest online makeup website in the world. I knew because I bought stuff there all the time for their discounts.

"Oh no," I said. "I didn't have time to prepare anything."

"There's nothing to prepare. You smile, shake hands, pay a few compliments, and then tell them you'll call next week to book time on their calendars in one month."

Okay. That sounded easy. "Sure. No problem."

And it would give me something to do at this party, where I'd surely feel a little awkward.

"And word of warning, Miss Snow?" The limo pulled up to some hotel I didn't know. The red carpet swarmed with photographers.

"Yes?" I asked as the door opened and he got out, bending down to quietly warn me.

"Franco gets a little free with his hands when he drinks. Steer clear of him later on."

"Is he cute?" I said, completely joking. Mr. Cole's eyes told me he did not find that funny.

Okay... I exited the limo as gracefully as I could, hanging back a little as the press had their fill of Maxwell Cole from behind the ropes.

Our limo pulled away and another pulled up. Out of the corner of my eye, I saw a blonde in a bright red dress step out.

Holy sacred fashion cow. It was Adeline Taylor. Supermodel turned actress. The moment she hit the carpet, the photographers started splitting up, going after her. Then she walked right toward me. I was a little starstruck and didn't know what to do.

"Excuse me?" she said with a snotty tone.

Oh. I was standing in her way? No. I wasn't. But the woman could move one foot and go around me.

I gave her a look but didn't move. She rolled her eyes and then glared as she went around, pasting on a fake-as-hell smile the moment she laid eyes on Mr. Cole.

"Max, baby!" she squealed, which got his attention. He turned and seemed extremely happy to see her, taking her hand immediately and placing a kiss on the top. Meanwhile, the photographers moved their attention to the next celebrity, an Italian actor, I think. Honestly, I couldn't take my eyes off of Mr. Cole as he leaned in, saying something to the woman that made her burst out laughing. They then walked on ahead, leaving me trailing behind like an invisible pet.

Wow. Well, at least I knew where I stood with him, right?

I put on my work hat and lifted my chin. I wasn't pretty, but I had self-esteem. And healthy eating habits. *So there.*

Once inside the packed, dimly lit ballroom buzzing with lights and loud music, I searched for Mr. Cole, but couldn't see him.

Great. Thanks for leaving me all alone at the most intimidating party in the world. I made my way to the bar and grabbed a glass of champagne. Sipping slowly, standing on the edge of the crowded room and feeling like a duck out of water, I watched the people flowing in. Some were dressed a bit more casual than others, but everyone looked fabulous. *And so uptight.* Weren't they here to have fun? Or was this really all just an excuse to get some publicity? There were photographers everywhere, like ants at a picnic.

"Lily?" I heard a strange man's voice.

I turned and found a short older gentleman, handsome with black hair and a lopsided smile, staring at me.

"Yes?"

He extended his hand. "I'm Franco Morrano. Max said I'd find you over here. He said, 'She's the blonde in the sexy black dress with the tight body.'"

My eyes flared, and I nearly spit out my bubbly. "Sorry?" No way would my boss say something like that. Would he? I looked over my shoulder and then the other. I still didn't see Mr. Cole anywhere.

Franco snorted. "He wasn't lying. You look…pretty nice. Let's go dance."

"Um…" *Shit.* From the subtle happiness and slur in his voice, I could tell he'd already been drinking. I wondered how much time I had before his magic hands would make an appearance and I'd have to go hide in the bathroom.

"Well, I think I need another drink first. I'm not much of a dancer."

"I gotcha!" He snagged two glasses as a waiter just happened to float by with a tray. For the next forty minutes, I watched Franco pound down the champagne while he talked to me about online consumer trends and shopping habits. He mentioned that he'd been fighting with Mr. Cole about the fact that they never had enough product to sell at a discount. I tried to keep the convo light and casual since I wasn't up to speed on any of the issues. I only knew that Franco's company moved a few million dollars of product for C.C. each year.

"Well, how about that dance?" he asked, now thoroughly trashed. I really wondered why with a room full of gorgeous models he'd want to dance with me.

"I really need to use the ladies' room," I said politely.

He shook his finger in my face, slightly swaying. "But you come right back, young lady."

Dear God, no. I was going to take my sweet time. Maybe take up knitting while I was in the loo. I'd always wanted to learn.

I turned to find the powder room, and Franco gave me a swat on the ass. I yelped and then immediately bit my tongue. *That sonofabitch.* If he did that again, I might not be keeping my job. Breaking your customer's arm would definitely be a career-limiting move.

On the other hand, if I was going to do this job, and do it well, I needed to learn how to start dealing with people from the good and the bad to the creepy and vulgar, like Franco.

Or I let the boss handle this guy. But where the hell was Mr. Cole?

I kept an eye out for him as I weaved through the glamorous partygoers toward the ladies' room.

Nada.

The man had ditched me?

After listening to several women vomiting in the

stalls, and trying my best not to get anything on my dress as I went up to bat, I practically ran from that bathroom. Those poor women. What would possess them to do that to their bodies on a regular basis?

Maybe the same thing that possesses you?

No, I didn't scarf and barf—I liked my food going one way only—but I had been known to punish myself with extra running when I felt bad.

I exited the bathroom and heard a familiar chuckle to my right. Mr. Cole had that Adeline Taylor woman against the wall in a dark corner behind some large potted plants. They were intimately close, his lower torso pressed against her body as she laughed and sipped her drink.

I knew I had no right to be jealous. But for the second time that night I was.

He must've noticed someone staring because he glanced in my direction at the precise moment that I saw her slide her hand over his groin.

My jaw dropped, and then I snapped it shut, turned, and walked away.

It was too much. Not that I couldn't handle everything that was happening, but I couldn't handle it all at once. I needed to get back to the hotel and gather myself before I said or did something I'd regret. Sometimes the heart—an inherently reactive creature and immature at times—needs to burn off its steam so the mind can step in with a grounding kick in the pants.

We are not in a relationship. He's my boss. We have a strange and disturbing relationship. This is all.

I headed for the door and heard Mr. Cole calling my name. I looked over my shoulder and waited for him.

"Miss Snow, where do you think you're going?"

"I'm suddenly not feeling so well. Thought I'd go back to the hotel."

He tilted his head to the side. "You're running away."

"No."

"Really?" He crossed his arms over his chest.

"Yes. Really," I lied, feeling irritated that he could see through me so easily.

"I'm sorry, but you can't leave until you shake hands with Krissy Walters."

"Well, where is she?" I asked. I would've introduced myself, but I had no idea what she looked like and Mr. Cole had been too busy with Adeline.

"She generally comes late to any function where there's press."

"Oh." I shrugged. "Well, I guess I'll wait, then." I turned toward an empty table and Mr. Cole grabbed my hand to stop me.

"Miss Snow, about last night—"

I tugged back my appendage and held it out. "Please. I don't want to talk about it. I'm fine. Just go back to your gorgeous actress girlfriend and enjoy yourself."

He shook his head. "I'm beginning to think I was wrong about you."

I frowned. "Why?"

"I thought you were the sort of person who always speaks her mind. Fearlessly."

"Some things are better left unsaid." *Fucker.*

No. You did not think that. He's done nothing wrong.

"Not between us," he argued.

I drew a deep breath. "I really am fine. I've had the best time of my life tonight. The best. And I'm grateful for it. And the job. And the opportunity you've given me." I meant every word. I really did.

"But? There's a but coming."

"But nothing," I said. "I'm here to help you. You're giving me the opportunity to pursue my dreams. What else is there?"

"All right, then. If you're having so much fun, then act like it. The pouting version of you is unflattering."

Sometimes I wondered if this man had a soul.

"Lily! There you aaare." Franco stumbled into Mr. Cole. "It's time for that dance nooow."

"Franco," Mr. Cole said in an overtly charming voice, "I'm sure Miss Snow would like to—"

"I'd love to dance, Franco." I stood and took the man's hand and pulled him to the crowded and chaotic dance floor. At first, I felt like a one-legged grasshopper—clumsy and awkward—but then

Franco grabbed my hands and started making me do all kinds of crazy moves—a tango thing, a very bad waltz, and some other polka-esque bullcrap. I danced along. Horrible step for horrible step. I decided if I was going to be there, I might as well enjoy myself. Franco and I made another trip to the bar, and I pounded down my fourth glass of champagne—a lot for someone like me who rarely drank.

Roughly thirty minutes later, Franco disappeared to the men's room while I stood by myself at the edge of the dance floor.

"You looked like a woman who knows how to have fun. Mind sharing a little of that with me?" said a man with a slight Italian accent. He was lean, nicely built and had brown hair and bright green eyes.

"I saw you earlier getting out of your limo. You're an actor, right?" I asked.

"Yes, Patricio Ferrari."

Oh. Like the car.

I extended my hand. "Lily Snow. I work for Cole Cosmetics."

"Oh, do you now?" he said.

"I started this week, actually."

"Well, Maxwell is a pompous asshole, but I won't blame you for that."

I like him already. "Thank you. So how do you know him?"

"Who doesn't know the man? He's almost as

famous as me." He leaned in. "But not nearly as good looking. Or fun."

I laughed, and we took to the floor. Patricio was a little wild, his arms waving in the air, his ass wiggling all over the place, but he made me laugh and it was fun. I knew I'd landed in his "friend zone," which was totally fine with me, but every time I glanced over across the crowded room, Mr. Cole's eyes met mine. The irritating part was that he held Adeline Taylor's hand.

I turned my back to him, deciding I needed a little dose of "grow the hell up." When the fourth song came on and the music turned into some sexy tango-styled techno, Patricio wrapped his arms around my waist and pulled me snugly to his body. Frankly, I wasn't uncomfortable, but confused. Call me crazy, but this guy acted like he was hitting on me.

"You have the most stunning body I've ever seen, Lily." He swayed from side to side while I stood still.

All right. He's definitely hitting on me. "Uh...thanks?"

His hands slid down to cup my ass, pulling me into his crotch. There was something very hard there. "I think I'd like to see more of it." He smiled with a charming grin.

Okay. Now this is awkward. But was it really? I didn't have a frame of reference, considering no one ever hit on me. Not ever.

What would Danny do?
She'd crack a joke.

"I'm a decent and proper woman. So I only show my body to men who ask me to marry them first. You should see my collection of diamond rings."

He laughed. "In that case...marry me."

"Got a ring?"

"I'm sure I can get you one."

"Make it outrageously big. Okay?"

He laughed. "I find you very refreshing, Lily. So unlike these other women here, obsessed with their looks."

"Oh now, I bet you say that to all the girls." *The fugly ones.*

"I don't."

I stopped moving and stared at him. "You're serious, aren't you?"

"Yes."

I had to admit, I felt extremely damned flattered. Like...amazingly flattered. I wouldn't go to bed with him, but I'd certainly ask for his number. That was what I was supposed to do right? *Damn, I'm like in dating kindergarten.*

"Thank you, Patricio. And I mean that from the very fiber of my being."

He looked at me with a peculiar expression. "Why are you thanking me?"

I bit my lip and looked away, unable to feel the same candid comfort I felt with Maxwell Cole.

"Lily?" Patricio pushed.

"No one has ever—"

"Lily, it's time to go." Maxwell Cole stood next to us, straightening his tie in a manner that could threaten a matador.

I looked at him, then at Patricio, and again at Cole. "Sorry?"

"Krissy texted. She has the flu and isn't coming."

"And?" I asked expectedly.

His hard gaze didn't waver. "And we have an early flight."

I didn't know what to say, so I dropped my hand from Patricio's steamy grip.

"Thank you for the unforgettable night," I said.

Patricio bobbed his head. "Likewise, Lily."

"Miss Snow?" Mr. Cole's voice was stern and angry. No, I didn't understand why.

I flashed him a look. "Be right there, sir."

Mr. Cole walked toward the door, and I took the opportunity to dig into my evening bag for one of my cards. "If you're ever in Chicago?"

He took the card and shoved it into his pocket. "You will be the first person I call."

I had to admit, the thought made me all bubbly. "Great. Don't forget the ring." I smiled and walked toward the doorway. The toxic vibe left behind by Mr. Cole stuck in the air all around me. When I arrived to the limo awaiting curbside, I found the world's most irate man simmering in the backseat.

"What the hell is with you?" I fumed the moment the door closed.

It took only a second for the volcano to erupt, but it came, spewing its ugliness all over me. "What's with me, Miss Snow, is your lack of discretion."

"Are you referring to the fact that I danced with Patricio?"

"And Franco," he added accusatorially, poking his index finger into the leather seat between us.

My mouth launched into the customary offended position. "Are you criticizing me for dancing?"

"Your behavior represents mine, Miss Snow." He straightened his tie. "The public display of pelvic grinding isn't an image I'd like my company to portray."

Was that the real reason, because…"Your fondling that woman in the dark corner is all right, though?" Okay, she'd been fondling him, but still.

"You're here for me. Not the other way around."

"What the hell is the matter with you?" He was acting like some strange possessive dictator.

"Did I not just make that clear? I brought you to Milan to establish business connections, not to throw yourself at our clients or make a drunk ass out of yourself with men."

Wow. Just…fucking wow. "So you think because you find me disgusting to look at, that it's impossible for anyone to want me."

He shook his head and glanced out the window, his jaw pulsing.

"I'm sure you'll find this shocking," I said, "but I wasn't doing the hitting tonight; they were. Not everyone is hung up on my face or is trying to push me down for something I can't help. It *is* possible for men to actually like me." Although, that had not been my experience prior to tonight, and I still hardly believed any of it myself.

He turned his head to shoot me a furious look. "Is that really your aspiration—to be wanted for a quick fuck by a man like Patricio who screws anything that walks? I thought you had higher goals in life, Miss Snow."

What. The. Hell? I couldn't believe the words coming from his mouth. It was as if he'd abandoned all sense of rational thought. And where did he get off judging me like that? Or Patricio, for that matter?

"And now you're angry because that guy *wants* to fuck me," I fumed. "Seriously, Max? Seriously? How many women have you been with?"

He didn't have to reply because his face said it all.

"That's what I thought," I said. "But you were my first. My first kiss, my first suck, my first anything, and I'll point out that I'm still a virgin—which is pretty damned stupid given my age. So you'll have to excuse me if I ignore everything that just came out of your pompous, self-righteous mouth. You have no clue what it's like to be me or what it feels like to want things you'll never have or to get a thrill from a little attention because I know in my heart that's all I'll ever get. So yeah, I wouldn't mind a good-looking guy like Patricio taking me back to his place for a night of cheap sex." I threw up my hands. "Sounds fucking awesome to me!"

He stared with a livid expression, his chest rising and falling rapidly.

"Don't!" I pointed my finger in his face. "Don't you dare get angry with me for wanting to be wanted."

"I'm not," he growled bitterly.

"Fuck you. Yes, you are."

"I'm angry because *I* want you," he barked.

I stopped breathing.

"How's it possible, Lily?" he seethed, his hazel eyes filling with an unfathomable hardness. "How is it possible for me to want someone like you as much as I do?"

The mixed emotions poured in. He said he'd wanted me for more than "therapy," and the thought struck me hard—pulse spinning out of control, skin tingling with excitement, my core producing an overwhelming sensation of throbs and aches begging for one thing and one thing only. Him inside me. On the other hand, the way he'd delivered the message—shock and disbelief that someone so great as him could genuinely want me—was a fucking insult. On the other hand—*yes, I've got three hands*—he was right; a man like him, with a stranger-than-hell phobia, feeling an attraction for me was pretty damned crazy. Or amazingly twisted and masochistic.

I swallowed the shock and excitement. "Someone really smart once told me that if I wanted something, I had to get my hands dirty."

"You think it's that easy?" he growled in a way that made his words sound more like "I already know that; don't be an idiot," which really made me mad.

"Yeah. I do," I snarled back. "You big pussy."

I don't think I'd ever called a person that name for real—maybe just my brother in jest—but I'd definitely have to use it more often. Because I'd never seen a human being more pissed off as Mr. Cole was right then and there. Like he wanted to grab me and tear me a new one.

Finally! Something that gets under your skin. The "p" word!

"Don't ever speak to me like that, Lily," he said, his eyes narrowed on my face, his pulse ticking away on his neck.

But that only made me want to push his buttons harder. I wanted him to snap, explode, lose his cool polished exterior and show me a little of those uncivilized claws he'd tried to bring out in me.

I leaned in, staring into his sexy, fury-filled eyes. "I call it like I see it, Mr. Cole. And right now, I see a fucking coward. I bet the only reason you're holding back is because you're afraid I'll laugh when your dick goes limp."

"My dick is the least of my fears. But fine, you want a cheap, meaningless fuck. Then I'm going to take you back to your room and fuck you."

"Fine," I replied and looked away, folding my arms over my chest. "Can't wait. I need a good laugh tonight."

"I promise you won't be laughing."

chapter ten

The short, ten-minute ride back to the hotel felt like five seconds. Five. My mind kept replaying his words about me throwing myself at men and then him telling me I was wrong to want to be desired sexually, followed by his confession that he wanted me but was unable to believe it.

Asshole. I really hope he doesn't get it up so I can shove it in his face. Of course, that wasn't true. My angry body was on fire for him. Hot, wet, carnal tension aching away between my legs. Did I hate myself for wanting him inside my body so badly?

No. Not even a little. The chemistry was too powerful.

The elevator doors slid open on our floor, and I marched to my room with a furious looking, but silent, Mr. Cole on my heels. When I pushed the door open, he shoved me inside and slammed it shut. His mouth was on my neck, his hands were on my tits, his body pressed against me, grinding and thrusting rhythmically.

Yes, he was hard. Really hard.

It took a moment to realize he was going through with this because he wanted to fuck me as much as I wanted to reciprocate.

Panting, I reached for his shirt and ripped it open, letting my hands grab a feel of those pecs.

"God, you fucking drive me crazy, Lily," he panted against my neck and then yanked my dress down, popping the hooks from their stitches, and shoved the garment to the floor.

We both froze for a moment while he pulled back and stared at my chest. "Dammit. I could fuck those tits."

He dipped his head, bathing the tops of my breasts in kisses while he expertly unhooked my strapless bra. Soon to follow were his expert licks and adoring sucks while I ran my hands through his thick short hair, pushing his mouth into my chest. I'd never had my nipples sucked, but I guessed that if a hundred guys had been put to the task, none of them would've compared to his swirling tongue and hot mouth.

He removed his lips and replaced them with his hands, massaging and pinching, while his hips ground and his mouth sucked the skin from my neck like a juicy buffalo wing.

"I want you, Lily. I fucking want you," he panted, pinning my body against the wall like his personal dry-hump station.

I didn't know the words to express my lust, but my body did. I shoved my hands down to his pants and ripped him free. He felt so hot and hard in my hands that I had to fight the urge to buckle at the knees and take him in my mouth again.

Before I could have my way, he yanked down my panties and bodychecked me to the wall, panting and kissing me like a hungry animal.

"I'm going to fuck you so hard that your dirty mouth won't know what to say."

"Do it," I demanded. I was ready. So damned ready I was losing my mind.

With my thong now gone and his pants down, his arms reached down to my thighs and lifted me. I wrapped my arms and legs around him, feeling the tip of his shaft rubbing against my bud. Good God, he felt so good. He then reached under, gripped his cock in his hand, and found my ready entrance.

There were no words for what came next.

He thrust, but much too slowly, as if testing my readiness. But I didn't want that. I'd always been a "rip the Band-Aid off" sort of person. Because nothing was worse than anticipating pain.

"I said 'do it,'" I demanded, my tone egging him on before I lost my nerve. Or started thinking.

He hesitated for a moment, but then he gave me what I wanted. He slid all the way in with one smooth, firm stroke.

I screamed toward the ceiling, my body protesting from the painful, delicious intrusion. "Don't fucking stop," I said through my gritted teeth.

He withdrew and thrust again.

I moaned loudly, trying to process how the pain and pleasure felt like one giant sensation all scrambled together. He felt so good. So hard. So unrelenting.

"More," I panted. "More."

Still pinning me against the wall, I realized he'd been going easy on me.

His lips kissing my neck, his hips pounded into me, his balls slamming, his chest slapping, his arms flexing and holding me in place. I hung on tight, accepting the fact that the sexual pleasure of having Maxwell Cole unleash his lust on my body trumped any virginal pain I might be experiencing.

"Fucking hell, you feel so good." He fucked his words into me.

I was so close I couldn't speak.

"Come on, Lily, scream for me." He pumped hard, and I realized he was waiting like a gentleman for me to come.

This was where my rational mind began to return and mingle with my sinful soul. Maxwell Cole's hard, thick cock was inside my body, sliding and thrusting. He was likely ambivalent to the emotional impact of having just taken my virginity. Yet, he wanted this moment to be for me. That's also when I realized he hadn't put on a condom. It hadn't even occurred to either of us. Lucky for him I was on the pill for nonsexual reasons, but it really was luck. Because this man had completely overridden my rational mind, and I'd overridden his. All I wanted was to fulfill this unyielding carnal need to feel him come inside me. I couldn't explain it, and there was no excuse in this day and age, but it was what I wanted. Him. Me. Raw. And knowing his lust for me had made him just as reckless made me feel ten times more desired.

As these strange thoughts passed through me, I felt the sinful need building. I rocked my hips into him, and he pumped away at a ravenous pace, our naked bodies simultaneously giving and taking.

Then a big build started.

"Yes. Don't stop, Max. Don't stop," I screamed his name as my body bucked and ground.

"Never. Fucking hell, never." He hit hard, those biceps flexing, those abs contracting, those pecs protruding. Every inch of his sensual body was on display for my pleasure.

He rocked himself faster. "I'm going to come. Tell me you're ready."

Aspirational thoughts of prolonging the moment entered my head, but it wasn't meant to be.

I came, my nails digging into his shoulders, my head pushed back while he hammered me like a nail into the wall.

It was a glorious, carnal moment of two people fornicating like animals. And when he'd pumped his last jet of cum inside me, groaning my name in a low, gravelly voice, my last orgasmic contraction subsided, and I knew I'd made a mistake.

No. Not just because he was my boss, but

because he'd felt so good, so right.

And I'm not the girl for him.

He might be able to look at me with some effort, and fuck me, but that didn't mean anything.

I would never be beautiful in his eyes. He would always be beautiful in mine.

Slowly, Max withdrew and lowered me. His hands then cupped my face, his eyes closed and his tongue sliding over my lips. "That was amazing," he said with a deep, masculine breathy voice. "Better than amazing."

I pulled away. "Please leave."

A long moment of silence passed. "What's the matter?" he whispered.

"Get out of my room."

"What did I do?" he asked, and it was the first time he didn't sound like the tyrant, but just a guy.

I sucked in a deep breath and let it out, still looking away. "You didn't do anything, Mr. Cole. I just need to be alone." I felt emotionally exposed, and I had no clue how to deal with it. I wanted him so badly that it hurt.

"Was I too rough on you?" He squeezed my shoulder, and I jerked away, shooting him a look.

"Don't."

"Lily?" He was pissed.

Well, fuck him and his perfect everything. Then my pride kicked in, and I realized I didn't want him to know how much I wanted him.

I smiled. "Sorry. I'm a bit overwhelmed. It wasn't

what I expected."

He looked down at me, frowning with pity. "You really think you don't deserve anything. Not even this."

He hit the nail on the head, but I wasn't strong enough to face the truth, so I acted like a bitchy punk.

Not my best moment. Not even close.

"I deserve better," I said.

He shook his head, his hands on hips. "I can't argue with that. See you at five a.m."

He slid on his pants and shirt and left my room, slamming the door behind him. I sank to the floor, covered my face, and bawled.

I am in over my head. It was impossible to be around a man like that and not feel something for him.

chapter eleven

The next morning I felt sore all over. Even my ass cheeks felt bruised. But by far, my dented-up emotions trumped everything else.

Every human being had different sides. The rational side. The irrational side. Lust and logic. Love and hate. Pleasure and pain. There was often a difference between doing what was right and doing what we want. You shouldn't eat that gallon of ice cream right before bed, yet you do it anyway. You're happily married with two kids so you probably shouldn't be looking at that hot waiter's ass and imagining how it might feel in your hands; yet you imagine anyway. My rational side had not been in control last night and neither had his. This made me feel all sorts of really, really hopeful things about what that passion meant when I knew I shouldn't.

Was what we felt last night normal? Was it special? Did it even matter?

Maxwell Cole was not the sort of man to grow attached to women, and he certainly wouldn't grow attached to me. I simply needed to remind myself that while our relationship was extremely unorthodox and felt intimate in some ways, it was an arrangement of mutual benefit.

Did I secretly wish things to be different? Maybe. But they weren't. And his distant and formal disposition when I saw him in the morning—oh God, yes, I had on ridiculous white short-shorts and a pink tee—confirmed everything I believed.

Still, I'd behaved like a petulant child running him out like that. The "ugly" episode landed squarely on my shoulders. But when I apologized, he'd barely looked at me. "Don't give it another thought," had been his response.

He then made no effort to make eye contact or acknowledge my presence while he stayed on the phone the entire ride to the airport, so I retreated and busied myself, reading all of the reviews and press releases about the new fall colors lineup. *"Bold." "Daring." "Cole Cosmetics raises the bar again."* Mr. Cole had to be happy about that.

When I toggled my phone to the celebrity gossip section, however, I knew he was probably anything but pleased. There was a photo collage of me sitting next to him at the show and then dancing wildly with Franco, my arms raised over my head. Another pic showed Patricio holding me in a suggestive pose. The fourth set of photos was of me getting into Cole's limo with his hand on the small of my back, staring at my ass. I didn't even remember that moment, but the caption read,

"Cole Cosmetics Manager Goes Wild and Gets Around."

"Oh. God," I whispered. "Who would write this?" I wasn't anyone even remotely interesting.

I suddenly had the urge to hang my head out the car window and vomit.

Mr. Cole glanced over, still talking on his cell. His eyes flickered with annoyance at me.

So he'd likely seen it already. I could only assume he was upset because "it reflected poorly" on his company. But I was the one who'd been called a whore. The only saving grace being the fact that no one would believe I'd slept with those men let alone Maxwell Cole.

I shut off my phone as we pulled up to the private terminal. Mr. Cole ended the call and got out on his side. As we marched through the little checkpoint, I could feel his eyes burning into the back of my head.

Finally, I couldn't take it anymore. "Please stop," I said.

"Didn't say a word, Miss Snow."

"I told you I was sorry."

"And I told you not to mention it. Ever again," he added coldly.

Wow. Point taken. Last night...mistake. Never happened.

We got on the plane in awkward silence, flew twelve hours in awkward silence, and rode back to his house in pissy-awkward silence. The longer he went without saying a word, the more irate I felt. I'd done nothing wrong—except fuck him. Which wasn't technically wrong, as we were both consenting adults, but the other circumstances were not the sort of thing generally accepted by the public. Or my parents. Or anyone I knew. Okay, yes. I was a scandalous woman. And I'd behaved a little rude with him after sex, but I apologized. And I'd really, really meant it, but he hadn't cared.

Now in his driveway, the limo driver unloaded my small suitcase and then Mr. Cole's bags.

I dug through my purse, looking for my keys, eager to get home, crawl into my bed, and sob this one out.

"Miss Snow?"

"Yep?" I said softly, trying not to provoke an argument I didn't have the stomach for.

"Now that this portion of our arrangement has concluded, I'll expect you to behave accordingly."

I blinked at him, my eyeballs feeling like sandpaper after the long trip and sleepless night. "Meaning?"

"Meaning you'll act professionally."

"Aha. So you don't want me running around blowing kisses at you in the office? Darn. That had been my plan."

"Do not make light. I allowed last night to happen because I believed you were the sort of woman who doesn't drown herself in delusions."

He'd "allowed" it to happen? Allowed? Like he

hadn't really wanted it so badly that he'd been out of his mind. *Oh, but he* alloooowed *it. Like he gave me some precious permission slip to ride his cock.*

I frowned. "If by delusions you mean last night wasn't anything more than a fuck, then we're on the same page."

"Yes," he replied.

"No problem there. It was simply a transaction—part of our deal."

"Good," he replied coldly. "And I realize we were less than careful last night. I take very good care of myself, but you will inform me if there are any...other repercussions," he said distastefully.

So he'd basically just said he was STD free, but if I ended up pregnant, shoot him a memo? Or something like that. And the way he'd said it made me feel so dirty.

"I'm on the pill, but I'll let you know if I get any weird rashes." I found my keys and pressed the unlock button on the remote. "See you at the office, Mr. Cole. And thank you for the weekend, especially for the part where you put your dick inside me. It was interesting."

Asshole.

I got in my car, started the engine, and drove away, the entire time feeling his angry gaze pinned to the back of my head like a laser beam.

"You did what?" Sitting on my bed with her legs stretched across my white comforter, Danny spit out a mouthful of white wine, shooting it all over her gray sweat pants. I'd already showered and put on my yellow ducky pajamas, which was what grown women did in the middle of the day when they were preparing to binge on cupcakes and tragic movies to make themselves feel better about their life choices.

"I know you heard me," I said, picking up my suitcase and laying it near her feet on the bed.

She blotted her face with the tip of her long brown ponytail. "No. I didn't. Because what you said sounded like 'I lost my virginity to Maxwell Cole at the Four Seasons in Milan,' and I'm pretty sure that was *my* fantasy. Or something from a movie." She shook her head. "And if it's not, it should be."

I reached into my suitcase and chucked my dirty clothes into the basket in the corner. The torn-up dress I'd worn got left behind in the closet at the hotel. I couldn't bear to look at it, and it was ruined anyway.

"I was really thinking tell-all book instead of a movie," I said sarcastically.

"How the hell did it happen, Lily? I mean...Wow." She blew out a breath.

"It just did." That was only part of the truth, of course.

"I'm shocked."

"Why? You were the one who gave me the idea."

"Me?" She pointed to herself. "Lily, I was joking. I would never advise you to sleep with your boss—even Maxwell Cole."

I gave her a cynical look.

"Okay." She held up her hands. "I'd at least tell you to wait until you had a new job lined up and it was your last day."

"I'm sure it will be fine. This kind of stuff happens all the time." As if I knew what the hell I was talking about.

"Are you going to do it again?" she asked.

"No. Absolutely not. It was a onetime thing, and we both agreed we'd move on. Business as usual." *We-hate-each-other business.*

"All right. If you say so."

I closed my empty suitcase and pushed it into my closet beneath my dresses. "I think he's an asshole. And he's not into me—it was a pity fuck for him. That's all." Or had it been an ego-fuck because I'd called him a pussy?

She looked at me in horror. "Lily, how the hell can you say that?"

"I'm not stupid, Danny. And I own a mirror."

"Are you sure about the stupid part? Because you're a very wonderful person, and you somehow don't see it. Has it ever occurred to you that maybe guys don't hit on you because they're intimidated? Unlike your name, you're not a timid little flower. A guy's gotta have a lotta balls to even talk to you. Then they have to be comfortable with not feeling needed and being disposable."

Huh? I looked at her and blinked. Actually, it had never occurred to me. Not once. "You think I'm mean?"

She set her empty wineglass down on my whitewashed nightstand. "God, no. You're like the most caring, most genuine person I've ever met—but you also don't let anything stand in your way. And you're extremely independent and driven. Oh—and there's that whole competitive thing about you."

"What? I'm not competitive."

"Maybe not on a one-on-one basis, but with the world? Oh yeah."

Wow. She'd basically just said I had a huge chip on my shoulder. I'd never realized that about myself, but maybe she was right. I did feel a little like I was on a one-woman mission to kick ass.

"How come no one's ever said anything?" I asked, going to sit beside her on the bed.

"Honestly, I figured you knew. You're not like one of these assholes I work with who run around saying how great they are, but their heads are shoved so far up their asses that they can't even smell their own bullshit." She placed her hand on my thigh. "With the exception of your small insecurity, you come across as the kind of person who knows themselves—bullshit and all."

I ran my hand over the top of my head and down the back of my long hair, thinking hard about what she'd said. I was beginning to see I didn't know myself.

She went on, "So now that we've established your boss—aka my fantasy boyfriend—may have screwed you for non-pity related reasons, can you go over that part again where he threw you up against the wall and tore off your ten-thousand-dollar dress?"

"Nope. Scandalous porn story hour is over. I have to get ready for a long day tomorrow." And honestly, now that I was beginning to see myself in this different light, I had to start questioning more than just my relationship with Mr. Cole. My entire perception seemed to be contaminated by this one small aspect of my life: my looks. A shocker because I'd never thought of myself as the type of person who could be influenced by something so shallow.

Nevertheless, I suddenly felt like my face had created a cancer that had been quietly undermining me my entire life, possibly robbing me of seeing good things that were right in front of me the entire time.

Crap. Mr. Cole had been so, so right when he'd said I didn't believe I deserved "even this," meaning casual sex. I didn't believe the things I wanted were there for me, so I pushed and fought my way through everything.

I'm so damned confused. Who the hell am I?

"Come on, Lily!" said Danny. "You barely told me anything. How big was he? Do his abs ripple in real life, or were they painted on in that photo shoot?"

I glanced at her, almost forgetting she still sat there. "No more details tonight, but I promise you a good bedtime story tomorrow that will include how I did pelvic thrusts with Patricio Ferrari."

"That cute Italian actor?"

I nodded. "Holy crap, Lily. You're my idol. I mean, my other idol. Max Cole is my first."

The notion of someone as messed up as me being anyone's idol was pure ridiculousness.

My phone buzzed on my nightstand, and I picked it up. "It's my mother." I sighed.

"Oh. Good luck with that." Danny smacked me on the back. "Gotta run."

"Coward," I sneered at her as I fled my room.

"Hi, Mom," I sighed my words, expecting the worst.

"Honey, I understand that you are a grown woman now, but I think we raised you better than this."

Oh, boy. "So you heard about the tabloid."

"Yes. From Beverly." Beverly was her best friend and neighbor. "And I'm extremely worried. Three men in one night? Please tell me this isn't true."

"It's not true." *It was only one: my boss.*

She let out a sigh of relief. "I knew it wasn't. I'm

going to call those people and demand they print an apology."

"Mom, just let it go—okay? It was a fluke. I just happened to be in the wrong place at the wrong time."

"That's the other thing, young lady, why didn't you tell us you were running off to Milan? What if something had happened to you? Where would we know to look if you'd gotten into trouble?"

Oh, God. I really couldn't deal with this right now. "Mom, I love you. But this is my job now, and I can't check in with you every time I take a business trip. And I have a phone if I need help and the company knows where we are—"

"Just remember, Lily, we are here for you. Even if you're halfway around the world, we'll be there to help you."

I sucked in a slow breath and released it. My asking her to not worry was like asking her to stop being my mother. "Thanks, Mom. I appreciate that. Tell Dad I said hi, and I'll send you guys some pictures from wherever I am this month."

"Anywhere fun?" she asked, but I'd better not tell her; she might show up with her suitcase.

"Not sure yet, but—oh, by the way, I spoke to John. How's he doing?" I grinned, so needing a moment of comfort, which meant messing with my brother's life. In the most loving way possible, of course.

"I think he's feeling better after I spent a little

time with him. Did you know he has a porn collection?"

I held in a laugh. "Ummm. No. I didn't know that."

"I mean, really. Who owns porn these days? It's all over the Internet for free."

What?

She continued, "You just click and there it is."

Ohmygod, I chuckled internally, trying not to imagine her at the helm of a mouse, sailing through the superhighway of porn.

"Maybe you should show him," I offered. "I bet he'd save a lot of money, and you know how little he makes." I was completely joking, however...

"I'll do that. Great idea. You have a nice evening, baby."

What? I pinched the bridge of my nose, laughing hysterically with the phone on mute. John was going to kill me!

We ended the call, and I texted my brother immediately, still cracking up: *I am so, so sorry. Please forgive me.*

He'd never see this one coming.

chapter twelve

Monday morning at C.C. wasn't what I imagined. People, in conservative business casual wear, ran around like members of a NASCAR pit crew, dashing to early calls with customers overseas, preparing materials for Mr. Cole's monthly staff meeting, and frantically sharing torn-out pages from newspapers and magazines of the fashion show—I assumed to be up to speed on all of the latest buzz and reactions from the public. The frantic and energetic vibe was completely different compared to my first mellow week when I was practically the only person on my floor.

I couldn't wait for introductions and to get to work.

I made my way down the aisle that led past several cubes and offices toward my door. A few folks, who were congregating in the middle of the floor, turned to glance in my direction. I smiled and waved but was greeted with frowns and cold stares.

What the...? I dropped my hand and entered my office, feeling an icy wave of nausea hit. *Okay.*

Don't panic. They don't know you yet. That's all.

I got out my laptop and turned it on, deciding to go for a cup of coffee in the break room while it did its warm-up exercises. No one even noticed me leave my office, which is why I heard their words: "Can you believe?" "Newby fired Craig." "Not even a director."

I listened carefully, filling my cup. *This is horrifying.* I'd already gained a toxic reputation and hadn't even met a single person besides Keri, really.

"Miss Snow?" said that deep familiar voice behind me. I turned to find Mr. Cole in a well-fitting blue dress shirt, shiny silver cuff links, black satin tie with red Xs, and black slacks. As usual, he looked as handsome and cocky as hell.

I pasted on a polite smile, trying desperately to push away any thoughts of his mouth on my breasts or his body inside mine. "Good morning, sir. How are you?"

"Great. I just came down to tell you that—"

A loud male voice just outside the break-room doorway broke his train of thought. "At least we know she's not banging the boss. Did you get a look at that fucking face?"

The hot coffee in my hand almost slid away as my blood pressure dropped. Then I had to prevent myself from crushing the cup.

Mr. Cole's expression went from neutral to Arctic glacier. "As I was saying, I came down to tell you that you'll be working with Mike Masters on a new project. He's a director who's been with us for three years, and he'll be showing you the ropes."

I swallowed and forced myself to focus on Mr. Cole's words while my anger and humiliation worked on getting the best of me.

"Thank you for the heads-up, Mr. Cole."

He nodded, turned, and walked off.

Me? I stood there feeling a mishmash of pissed and hurt. How could grown professionals be so blatantly cruel? And I don't know what I'd expected Mr. Cole to do about it, but the way he'd ignored the comment got under my skin more than the comment had. He had to know it stung. Did he give a shit?

Nope.

I walked to my office, shut the door, and started poring through emails, my hand shaking with indignation. I couldn't afford to unravel on my first real day. This was my dream. My future. And no one had the right to take it from me.

There was a light knock on the door.

Great. Someone coming to tell me how unwelcome I am?

"Come in."

The door opened and a tall, nice-looking man with an athletic build, black hair, and bright blue eyes popped in. "Lily, I'm Mike Masters. Just wanted to introduce myself before the meeting." He held out his hand, and I stood, leaning over my desk to shake it.

"Nice to meet you." I tried to sound positive but wasn't sure it worked.

"I think the pleasure is all mine. You've been here less than a week and you've already got everyone shaking in their Pradas."

"Sorry?"

He glanced over his shoulder. "You know, the show," he said quietly.

I shook my head no.

"Mr. Cole just hired you and took you with him to Milan."

Yes, but what was I missing? "So?"

"So, he only takes one person, and it's usually his favorite."

What? Were we in grade school? "I'm sure Mr. Cole has no favorites. Just people he dislikes less than others."

Mike laughed. "You catch on quickly."

"Yes. But not quickly enough, apparently, because I had no clue I'd end up with my name attached to a scandal for having a little innocent fun at the party." All true. Because my dirty fun happened after the party.

"Don't worry. You're officially the envy of everyone here," he said with a warm friendly smile.

"Envy. Is that what it's called? I could've sworn the mob smelled of hostility. Or were those welcome torches?"

"They only have the best of destructive

intentions, I promise." He shrugged playfully.

I instantly liked this guy. His humor reminded me a little of Danny.

He glanced down at his watch. "Time for the meeting. Get ready."

"For what?" I asked.

"We like to think of these monthly gatherings as a monster truck show—lots of things getting crushed."

"I thought we were going to talk business strategies," I said.

"We will. But Mr. Cole likes to keep us on our toes with plenty of action."

I cringed. "Sounds fun." Almost as fun as sitting in a room with Mr. Cole and trying to keep a poker face while I also pretended some dickhead stranger outside the break room hadn't just degraded me. *I'm living the dream.*

The meeting with forty-two of Mr. Cole's direct staff members, including Keri, was held in the executive conference suite—a sterile but chic-looking room with bright white walls and the infamous red C.C. lips and logo painted behind the head of a long dark-gray table that stretched from one end of the room to the other.

Mike and I hustled in, only beating Mr. Cole by a minute, and found a place to sit in the corner along the edge of the room. The table had already been filled up.

I had to admit, I was curious to get a look at everyone, knowing what I did about our boss.

Would they all be supermodels? I'd wondered.

But no. Most looked like your average, well-dressed professionals with a fairly equal mix of women, men, younger and older.

When Mr. Cole walked in, the entire vibe of the room shifted from antsy to terrified. Lots of sitting still, no chitchat, very focused eyes. The lion had entered the jungle and the tiny creatures quaked in their fur.

Then I noticed why: Mr. Cole's handsome face had a "don't fuck with me" look on it. It was a scowl I'd seen quite a few times already, but even I felt uneasy.

He shut the door behind him, threw down a tabloid on the table and then looked around the room, his hazel eyes boring into everyone there.

He skipped me.

"I'd like to ask everyone here a question," he said. "Who in this room thinks I should fire Steve?"

A bunch of people looked at a middle-aged blond guy at the opposite end of the table— younger than the rest. That had to be Steve because he looked like he wanted to die. Or wet himself. I wasn't sure.

"And who here thinks I should beat the crap out of him?" Mr. Cole popped off his cufflinks and began to roll up his right sleeve.

Everyone in the room exchanged nervous glances and probably, like me, wondered what the hell was happening.

He finished rolling up his right sleeve and went to work on the left. "Because I just can't decide. On one hand, Steve will probably sue me, but on the other, I'll get the satisfaction of driving my fist into his face." He looked around the room. "Everyone gets how tempting that is, yes?"

"Sir?" Steve croaked. "What's going on?"

Cole flashed a sadistic smile that oozed rage. "You know, Steve. When I stood downstairs in the break room, speaking to our new team member—" he gestured toward me and the entire room turned for a look—"Lily Snow there, who by the way has an MBA from Stanford, graduated top of her class, has worked with two of our competitors, and possesses more balls in her pinky than all the men in this room combined, with the exception of myself, of course—just imagine my surprise when you said..." He paused for dramatic effect, and I felt my head coming unhinged. He was not about to make me relive that moment in front of all these people, was he? "All right, never mind what you said," I mentally blew out a breath of relief as he went on, "but it was offensive. Even to someone like me, which says a lot. But you know what changed my mind from having a talk with you, Steve, to beating you unconscious in front of a room full of people?" Mr. Cole pointed to the tabloid. "That."

Steve's frantic eyes glanced down at the paper showing a picture of me on the front page, but he didn't speak.

"Did you really think I wouldn't find out it was your roommate who wrote that?" Mr. Cole seethed.

Steve didn't respond, but now that I knew he wasn't just the guy who made the comment outside the break room, but who'd also somehow arranged this crap to be printed about me, I no longer felt sorry for him.

Monster truck.

I raised my hand. "Mr. Cole? I vote you fire him and then kick his ass so your liability is reduced to only your personal assets versus the company's." *But whatever you do, get those big hands dirty, sir. Show me how it's done.*

Mr. Cole flashed a glance at me and smiled. "There. You see. She's already paid for herself." He looked at Steve. "Steve, you're fired. Don't bother collecting your things; Keri will see to clearing out your office."

Steve rose from the table and kept Mr. Cole in his peripheral vision as he scurried from the room.

"Steve," Cole yelled, "watch your back, because I'll be coming for you."

If I were Steve, I'd be leaving the state.

"Okay." Mr. Cole blew out a breath and planted

his hands on the table. "In the future, if anyone here feels the need to publically shame me or a member of my staff because they didn't get to go to Milan, please save us all some trouble, pack up your shit, and go home."

Wow.

"Now," he took his seat, "where were we?"

We are feeling very hot for you right now. That's where we are. I forced myself to turn away a thousand different thoughts pertaining to how that man had just triggered a dire need to show some gratitude. With my body.

The rest of the meeting was run like I'd originally imagined—professional, efficient, and drama free—with the heads of each department giving overviews or status updates on major projects. Marketing got a huge pat on the back for yet another flawless launch of a new product line. Operations got a kick in the pants because the new factory in Jersey was two months behind in construction due to weather delays, and C.C.'s contract manufacturers were still struggling to keep up meeting basic orders. So the company was bleeding money. Sales got a stick and carrot because the numbers were up, but margins were down. Of course, most of that had to do with lack of product to sell, but Mr. Cole pointed out that they'd not been pushing the higher-margin, more readily available product like lip gloss.

Raising my hand at the same time my mouth

went to work, I offered up this nugget, "How about another Maxwell Cole spread? My friends still talk about that Nude and Natural campaign." The moment I said those words, I instantly regretted them. Why? Because the entire room gasped, rumbled, and snickered, indicating I'd stepped on a landmine.

Mr. Cole shot a look at me. "Are you suggesting, Miss Snow, that taking off my clothes is the only way for this company to sell product?"

Oh damn. He was angry. Again. But why?

Well, I'd dug my hole, and backpedaling would only make me look weak. I knew that about my boss now. If I was wrong for my suggestion, then so be it, but being wrong and spineless was not a wise choice.

I drew a breath, uncrossed my legs, and stared him in the eyes. "It's not the only way. But let's face it, you could sell ice to an Eskimo."

He tilted his head, looking at me with a peculiar expression as if to say, "Are you mad or crazy?"

The room waited with bated breath. "Anyone else here agree with Miss Snow?"

Mike leaned over and whispered, "Mr. Cole banned anyone from suggesting that again. It's been proposed a million times. The last person that did it was fired."

Oh God. Now I got it.

Surprisingly, almost everyone in the room still raised their hands, and Maxwell Cole shook his head. "I hire the best people in the industry and they can't come up with anything more creative than seeing me naked." He looked at me. "Thank you for your suggestion, Miss Snow. I'll think about it." He nodded and moved on.

Wait. Why hadn't he chewed me up and spit me out? I knew he wanted to, but he hadn't.

No. This won't work at all. He was not allowed to show me any favoritism or special treatment just because...of everything else.

I'd have to speak to him later because I really wanted this to work out. Though, I'd later learn that was impossible.

chapter thirteen

At the end of the meeting, a few people came over to introduce themselves—Susan, head of Marketing; Jer, the head of Operations; Gloria, head of R and D; and a few others in Sales. It wasn't the warmest welcome, but it seemed my willingness to speak up to the boss won me a little respect despite my bumpy start.

Right after we adjourned, I went to see Keri and ask if Cole was available, but she was already off to lunch. Hearing that familiar deep voice on the other side of his door, I figured Mr. Cole was busy on a call or something, so I turned around and headed back toward the stairwell. Just then my phone buzzed in my pocket. A text from the big man himself.

Mr. Cole: *Come see me.*

I didn't want to seem like a stalker standing outside his door, so I replied, *Be there in five.*

I heard a thump emanate from his office. Had he hit his desk because I told him to wait?

Me: *Sorry. Make that ten. I need to wrap up this call.*

Thump!

Dear God. This man had a temper. I quietly stepped out into the stairwell to wait in my office for a few minutes. I had plenty to do now that I had several accounts, introduction meetings to schedule with clients, accounting issues to resolve, and a project with Mike to work on a new tween line, an exclusive for our top ten customers.

The moment I got to my office and sat, Mr. Cole appeared in my doorway, fuming.

"Do you ever *not* look angry?" I hissed.

He closed the door and then sat in one of the two guest seats that faced my desk.

He leaned back, staring at me for a moment. "Are you purposefully trying to get fired on your first real day of work, Miss Snow?"

I held my cool. "No, sir."

"Then why the hell are you behaving like this?"

"Like what?"

He leaned closer. "What are people going to think if you're looking at me like that in meetings?" he asked in a low voice.

"What are you talking about?" I hadn't been looking at him any special way, had I?

"Ogling. And you can't behave like you're not…you're not afraid of me."

My eyes nearly popped out of my head. "I'm *not* afraid of you, but that has nothing to do with…" I flipped my hand through the air, "that…event last weekend. And you're the one giving me special treatment."

"You mean calling that sonofabitch out for what he said or having his buddy print those articles to punish you because you took his place on the trip?"

"God no. I thought that was surprisingly fantastic. And I'd love to get a front-row seat to the ass kicking, whenever that's going to be." In all seriousness, with all the excitement, I hadn't truly had time to process all that. Mr. Cole really had put himself out there to stand up for me. It was really...nice. Really, really nice. "I meant that you should've yelled at me for suggesting the nude photo campaign, but you didn't."

"Why would I? You had no idea I'd banned it."

"Yeah, but I think someone like you would expect me to do my homework before I pop off a suggestion. I didn't."

He stared. "Fine. Point taken. Next time, I'll be an unreasonable hard-ass."

"I'd expect nothing less, Mr. Cole."

He stood up. "And the next time I tell you to come to my office, you drop whatever the hell you're doing and come. Understand?"

I nodded, trying desperately not to check him out. I just couldn't help but want to look at him. *Eyes on his face, Lily.*

"Yes, sir." I wouldn't do what he'd asked, but why fight about it now when we could save that enjoyable little argument for another day?

"Good." He reached for the door.

"By the way, I bought six tubes of lip gloss after

seeing you naked." *Oh, wait.* "In the photo, I mean." Because that would be weird to bang your boss and then run out and buy lip gloss. "I really hope you'll do it again because I'd like a fat bonus this year." Which I'd only get if we all hit our sales numbers.

He shook his head—"Women"—and left.

Once he cleared the room, and I cleared my hot mess of a head—okay, maybe I had been ogling him in the meeting and needed to keep that in check—I realized Mr. Cole hadn't once looked at my tits. Not at my ear or neck or the floor either. He'd looked me right in the face. And while I understood from experience that his symptoms tended to subside when emotions were high, he really had been pretty calm.

I wondered if his "therapy" hadn't worked on some level. However, it was a question I wouldn't get to test out for a very long time.

☙❧

The next three weeks, I saw almost nothing of Mr. Cole. He went to his side of the world, and I went to mine, visiting with clients in L.A., Toronto, Atlanta, and New York.

My mother and father hounded me for photos via my brother at every stop. I'd been so tired after spending long days with customers, hearing complaints about supply, talking about upcoming forecasts, and going through my lists of questions about their facilities, that most of the pics I'd sent to my parents were of me standing next to the window in my hotel room, wearing my pajamas.

Hitting airport after airport, customer after customer, for three solid weeks promised to take my mind off of Mr. Cole—those soft lips, those hot kisses, the feel of his naked body slamming into mine while he groaned my name—but the truth was, the separation had given me time to process my feelings. I wanted more of him.

It was something I desperately needed to get over, which was why, after my return, I avoided Mr. Cole most of the week, spending my time in meetings with Marketing and Mike, hammering out a project plan for our new tween line. It was fun, crazy work, and I really liked Mike's humor, which was also why I decided to accept his offer to go for drinks on Friday.

No. I absolutely did not think that having an office romance—a real one—was a good idea. Bad in every way. But how would I ever start getting over my own issues if I didn't begin opening myself up to men? And drinks with a male coworker did not mean sex. It meant spending a little downtime getting to know someone. Innocent and perfectly acceptable. Right?

Friday, around four o'clock, I sat in a small conference room with Mike, poring over color concepts from Marketing when a text from Mr.

Cole caught me completely off guard.

Mr. Cole: *Come see me.*

"Everything okay?" Mike asked, noticing that I probably looked like a ghost.

"Oh. Um. Yeah." I stared at my phone, deciding not to reply and placing it face down on the table. I was in the middle of something, so Cole would just have to wait.

Several minutes went by and my phone began to vibrate. I could have sworn it sounded angry, too.

"Sorry," I said apologetically to Mike and took a look.

Mr. Cole: *I know you're with Mike in the corner conference room downstairs. Get your ass up here, or I'm coming down and you won't like it.*

Shit. It sounded like I was in trouble.

Me: *be right there*

I looked up at Mike. "It's the boss. And he sounds angry."

"Doesn't he always?"

"More than usual," I clarified. "I'll be right back."

I marched upstairs, past Keri, who wore a bright orange dress and was on the phone—probably with her boyfriend because she had a naughty little smile.

I knocked lightly on his door.

"Come in," Mr. Cole said.

I cracked open the door and found him talking on his headset, staring out the window, wearing a dark T-shirt with the C.C. lips logo on the back and a pair of extremely sexy jeans. His tall, lean, but muscular frame accentuated by those broad shoulders was just as breathtakingly delicious as the first time I'd laid eyes on him. I'd honestly forgotten how damned good he looked and what he did to my pulse. Okay. No, I hadn't. But I'd been working hard on it.

He looked me over, making a pit stop on my breasts, which were highlighted by my fitted, button-down khaki dress.

I cleared my throat, and his gaze snapped up to my face.

He pointed to the table and chairs.

"Yep. Sounds right," he said to whomever was on the phone. "Look. I've got an important meeting, but I'll have Keri follow up with you on Monday."

I'm important, am I? I sat, and he turned to look at me, removing the band over his "don't give a fuck" messy dark hair that left it looking even sexier.

"So. Miss Snow, how are things going?" He folded his arms over his chest, but didn't join me at the table.

"Fine. I've gotten out to see all of my clients, have forecasts started for next quarter, and have begun working through all of the promotional plans." Honestly, it was hard work, but I liked it—especially the customers, who were more like members of the Maxwell Cole cult. One lady, a senior buyer for Lacy's department store, had a Ken doll on her desk with a tiny photo of Maxwell Cole taped to the face. It was pretty mind-blowing how much they worshiped him and wanted to come to our offices for our quarterly meetings just so, on the off chance he was around, they could catch a glimpse. It was almost comical, except that I could relate.

Anyway, there wasn't anything I'd come across in the role I didn't feel I could handle. And being back in the office this week also gave me a chance to meet two more ladies on the sales team who reported to directors but were at my level. We all seemed to click. So I guess...things were moving ahead.

"Good to hear," he said. "I want you at my place tonight at nine."

My stomach fell through the floor in a rush of nerves and shock and...confusion, frankly. "For?"

"Why do you think?" he asked.

Honestly, I had no idea, but my heart sped up and did a little flip. "I don't know."

"I haven't seen you for weeks."

For a moment, it sounded like he missed me. But obviously, that was ridiculous. "You mean...for therapy."

"What else would I mean?" he said stiffly.

Just when I'd begun to feel like life was getting into a normal, manageable groove, he threw this at me. Well, I didn't want this anymore, whatever "this" was.

"I can't. I have plans," I said. "And I have to get back to work; Mike's waiting."

"I don't give a shit about Mike having to wait. And whatever plans you have, you'll cancel them."

"No. I won't. I'm not your dog who comes when it's called. I have a life. And a date tonight."

His eyes narrowed. "With who?"

"None of your business." I stood and fully intended to leave, but then he said something that reopened a few too many fresh wounds.

"Why did you kick me out of your hotel room that night?"

I froze, and my mouth sort of moved, but no words came out. There was way too much emotional content contained in the answer. "I...I...don't want to talk about this right now." *Or ever.*

"Is it because you have a boyfriend and you cheated on him?"

"What? No. I'd never do that." And Mr. Cole knew he was my first everything—I'd told him that. There were clearly no other men.

"Then why?" he demanded.

"I told you; I don't want to talk about this."

"I do," he replied firmly, in that deep authoritative tone.

I gave him a pleading look. "You promised me we'd be professional."

"No. You promised me. And I'm not asking for anything other than an answer. There's nothing inappropriate about that."

I stared at this beautiful man, wondering why the hell he even cared. Was it some ego trip he just couldn't deal with?

I shook my head. "If you want 'therapy,' it'll need to be through our normal interactions, during office hours. And discussing anything having to do with that night is off the table."

He laughed.

"What? You think playing with me like this is funny?" I asked.

"What's funny is your goddamned sense of humor."

"I'm pretty sure I don't have one anymore." I noticed he'd gone back to looking away again. No real eye contact except for a few brief flits here and there. Otherwise, the eyes were back on my chest, hands, or feet.

"Of course you do," he said snidely, "because you believe you're in charge."

Damn him. "Even if you're my boss," I hissed quietly, paranoid someone would overhear us somehow, "I *am* in charge—of me, my life, and my body. And right now, I'm telling you that having this conversation here in your office is crossing the line, Mr. Cole, and making me feel uncomfortable." I turned to head out before I blew my top.

"Be at my house at nine o'clock, Miss Snow. And

bring your running clothes."

I huffed and slammed the door behind me, returning downstairs to the conference room where Mike waited.

Sonofabitch.

"How'd it go?" Mike smirked, blinking those big blues at me, noticing my flustered face when I entered the room.

I let out a frustrated breath and took my seat across from him. "Fine. He just...never mind. Let's get back to work. I don't want to end today feeling like we fell short." We still had a few more hours of work do to in order to be ready for the monthly staff meeting on Monday where we'd be giving an update. And I really, really needed not to do any work this weekend.

"Don't worry. We can stay late and still go for that drink after."

I immediately thought about how late that would be—would it be later than the time Mr. Cole wanted to see me?—but then I pushed the undermining thoughts from my mind. I was not going to see Mr. Cole tonight. "That sounds great."

"I'm sure the others won't mind if we show up late," he added.

Others? "Oh, who else is coming?"

He shrugged. "There's a big group of us in Sales. We try to meet up once a month."

"That's...cool." I sucked at reading men. Seriously sucked at it. I swear I'd gotten the "date" vibe from Mike.

"Actually, it's one of the things most of us like about C.C. We work our asses off and compete like hell, but when office hours are over, we all check our crap at the door and have a little fun. Blowing off steam keeps us sane."

"Yeah. That's pretty great." *Maybe they offer classes on this stuff—Speaking Man 101.*

Mike looked at me. "Oh. Wait. You didn't think that I...?" He toggled his index finger between us.

"What? No. God no. A lot of people prefer to do creative work offsite." I shrugged. "That's what I figured you wanted."

"Oh good. Because I know how uncomfortable women get sometimes with all that."

If you only knew. "Nope. I'm good." Which was a complete lie. I wanted to go to Mr. Cole's house now more than anything. Maybe I still felt I owed him a little gratitude.

You're not going, Lily. You deserve better.

I took any thoughts about seeing Mr. Cole, mentally tossed them to the floor, and stomped them to a pulp.

chapter fourteen

The awkward moment passed, and Mike and I wrapped up the work faster than I'd expected. We were on schedule, prepared to present our recommendation Monday—we were going with recommending the shimmery pinks and light orange pallets so in style at the moment—and I had nothing but a relaxing weekend ahead. The more I thought about it, the better I liked the idea of a little Sales department after-hours fun. It was a great opportunity to get to know a few more people.

Around eight o'clock, I pulled up to the Rusty Bucket, a beer and wings sports bar, in downtown Chicago about ten minutes from the office. The people in Sales were eighty percent male, so I wasn't surprised by the venue.

When I walked in, probably lagging Mike by about ten minutes because I'd stayed behind to freshen up, I immediately spotted our group amassed around the corner of the bar, most of them standing and talking, a few seated along the wall at several small tables.

Even though his back was to me, I recognized Mike's black hair, but one of the guys—I couldn't remember his name—waved to me. Mike turned to see who'd come in and that's when I caught a glimpse of another face his body had been blocking.

Fuck. Mr. Cole. Mr. Cole. Mr. fucking Cole. I hid—pretty poorly—my shock and approached with a smile.

"Hi, everyone. And Mr. Cole, I wasn't expecting to see you here."

"I never miss beer and wings night with my sales team—besides, who do you think pays for it?" he said.

I swallowed. "It's ummm...great that you make the time, Mr. Cole."

"Call me Max." He held his eyes to my face, and I noticed a slight strained look in his eyes.

Mike elbowed me. "But only when we're off the clock. Unless you want your ass chewed out."

I'd had sex with this man. I'd had his cock in my mouth. But had he ever asked me to call him "Max"? No. But apparently beer and wings night was an appropriate occasion for that.

Of course, even if he'd asked, I still didn't feel comfortable using his first name. Barriers were good.

"Okay...Max," I croaked out his name.

"So, Miss Snow, I'm surprised to see you here. What happened to that date?" he asked.

Kill me right now. Someone please. Because while "Max" thought the date thing had been an excuse to blow him off, right about now Mike was figuring out that I *had* thought we were going to go out on a date.

"Date?" I said innocently. "Oh. You mean this? Didn't I say I had plans?"

"No. You said you had a date."

I tried not to look at Mike, but I couldn't help it. Thankfully, he'd put on a poker face.

"I misspoke, then. I'd meant to say 'plans.' Which I did. Being here with you guys."

Max bobbed his head and then continued on with his conversation with Mike and the two other guys. I spotted one of the gals I'd met earlier in the week—Maureen, a middle-aged brunette with a degree from Northwestern and ten years of sales experience—so I decided to go say hi and pretend like I wasn't hiding.

Soon, the waiter came around and I ordered a beer, which I only pretended to drink because I needed to drive home and one beer was enough to put me to sleep. The entire time Maureen and the other lady sitting with her—Nelly or Nadine or some name starting with an N—talked about kids and the latest episodes with their husbands, Mike kept looking over at me and smiling.

Yay. Just what I need. Another awkward relationship at work. Finally, after about an hour, I made my pleasant goodbyes to everyone, who probably assumed I was retreating early like an antisocial coward.

I passed by Mike and "Max," who stood in a circle, talking football with four others.

"Hey, guys," I said. "Nice seeing everyone, but I'm heading home. That beer—woo—made me so sleepy."

"You okay to drive?" Mike asked.

"Yeah. I'm fine. Just one beer." And not even that. I'd taken two sips.

"I'll walk you out to your car," Mike said. "It's not a crime-free zone around here."

"No," I objected. "It's fine. I'm just one block aw—"

"Then I will take you, Miss Snow," Max said, his voice stern and fatherlike.

Damn him. Why did he have to be such a dickhead?

I shot him a fast and furious look and then turned to Mike with a smile. "Mike, thank you for the offer. I'd love it if you'd walked me safely to my car."

He flashed an uncomfortable look between Max and me. "It's no problem." He shrugged.

"Thank you, Mike," Max said. "We wouldn't want Miss Snow here getting into any trouble."

Oh. Because I was such a reckless woman? *Jerk.*

Mike followed me out, and I felt the awkward vibe spike through the air.

"I'm just over here." I pointed to my little red

car sitting at the curb and stopped to unlock it.

"Lily, I'm really sorry about tonight. I should've been clearer," he said, standing a few feet away.

The sun had just gone down, but a warm orange summer glow remained in the sky, casting a light on Mike's black hair.

"What?" I flicked my hand at him. "I told you. I really didn't think anything about it."

He smiled. "Well, now that I know you would've said yes, maybe we should have dinner next week?"

I looked at him. I was about to say that I didn't need a pity date, but then I remembered how bad I was at reading men. Was it a pity date or real date?

"I'm..." I needed to think about it. "I think I'm in Houston part of next week, but why don't I let you know on Monday?"

"Sure." He reached out and gave my hand a little squeeze. "Drive carefully."

I got into my car, wanting to rip out my hair. *Holy hell*. Why did men have to be so confusing? And why was I so bad at dealing with them?

When I got to my apartment, I looked forward to a hot bubble bath and some quality me time with my laptop and a movie. That's not what was waiting for me. It was a shock I couldn't have been prepared for in a million years but should've seen coming. And no, it wasn't Mrs. Jackson's trash. But it was something equally dirty.

She was an older woman with short silver hair and glasses and wore plain beige slacks. Her expression reminded me of the kind of person who'd had a rough life once upon a time, but now devoted her energy to saving orphaned kittens and eating organic vegan cuisine. Yeah, it was strange that she made me think that, but whatever.

"Can I help you?" I asked, thinking maybe she was at the wrong apartment.

"My name is Nancy Little." She extended her hand. "I'm a journalist."

I shook her hand hesitantly. "Okay. And you're here because…?"

"Can we go inside and talk?"

"About?" I asked.

"Maxwell Cole and that arrangement you have with him."

I felt a sharp drop and roll in my stomach. How the hell did she know? Whatever the case, it didn't feel like it was in my best interest to talk to her. *Play dumb.*

"Sorry?" I said.

"You don't have to pretend with me, Lily. You're not the first."

"I have no idea what you're talking about," I partially lied—I honestly didn't know there'd been others. It had to be a mistake.

"Lily, he's had three different women—that I

know of—try to help him with his disorder. One of them was my sister."

This was information that hit me like a barbed baseball bat. "Okay," I said in my bitchiest tone ever. "I'm going to ask you to leave now. Because whatever you're talking about doesn't involve me."

I moved past her, trying to keep my cool. How was it possible he'd had three other women try to help him? How long had this been going on? And why the hell did I feel like the inner sanctum of my relationship with him had been violated?

Just as I was about to slam the door shut, she blurted out, "My sister killed herself, Lily. That's why I'm publishing a book."

Whoa. Already standing inside my apartment, I looked at her, wondering how this tragic event was connected. "What happened?"

"He used her and tossed her aside. That's when I found out there'd been others he'd recruited for what he likes to call his 'therapy.'"

I was shocked. And disgusted. She made it sound like we all belonged to some dirty sex-cult. But before I went into a full-blown rage with Mr. Cole or discarded what she said, I needed to talk to him.

"I'm very, very sorry to hear about your sister." And I meant that. I really did. If anything ever happened to John, I'd be a mess. "But I don't understand; you're publishing a book about my boss and telling the world what exactly?" Whether

I liked it or not, I needed to hear this.

"Don't act stupid, Lily. I know he's hired you to help him. What did he promise you? A new life?"

My blood rushed inside my body, feeling like it was darting all over the place. "I really don't know what you're talking about, but please leave and don't come back."

I stepped inside and locked the door behind me. *Oh God, this is bad. Really bad.* My brain was beginning to see all the ways this could turn ugly for me.

"I'll leave my card," she yelled from the other side of the door, "in case you change your mind."

I picked up the card, threw it in the wastebasket in the living room, and then called Mr. Cole's cell phone. It rang twice then went into voice mail. *Dammit.*

"Mr. Cole, it's Lily—I mean Miss Snow—whatever—I need you to call me back. It's important. A Nancy Little came to see me, and I…fuck. Just call me when you get this."

I went into my room, plugged in my cell, and left it charging on my nightstand. I don't know how long I lay there staring at the ceiling, trying to come up with some explanation that could possibly justify why Maxwell Cole had been recruiting these women and discarding them or why he hadn't told me.

Nothing.

There was no reason under the sun for that. But

what I did know was that I felt betrayed and afraid. This private affair, I naïvely believed existed in an insulated room that only Maxwell Cole and I could enter, wasn't so private. There were others inside with us, and soon the world would get a peek.

Oh God. The things they would say about me and assume.

I began to cry. Yeah, it was time.

⁕

Around three in the morning, I woke to my cell vibrating on my nightstand. I rolled over, my brain foggy with sleep, and looked at the number. It was Mr. Cole.

"Hello?" I mumbled.

"Open your fucking door."

He was here? At my apartment? Sonofabitch had some serious explaining to do. "One sec."

I hopped from my bed and made a quick pass into my bathroom. I looked like shit—even for me—like I'd been crying because clearly I had been. I rinsed with mouthwash and hurried to the door. Yes, I had my yellow ducky PJs, but this wasn't a time for putting on something sexy like a lace teddy.

Mr. Cole stood there, still in his jeans and black T-shirt, his hair looking even messier than ever. *Is that a chicken wing stain on his shirt?*

"Nice pajamas. And what the hell took you so

long?" he asked with a slight slur to his words.

"Are you drunk?" I whispered, poking my head into the hallway.

"Yeah, so what." He pushed past me, and I closed the door.

"Did you drive like this?"

He headed into my kitchen and opened the fridge, immediately looking disappointed. "You now make two hundred thousand a year, but you have no food or beer?"

With the light of the fridge, his hazel eyes looked redder than hell. Had he been crying, too? No. Hell no.

"I've been traveling and haven't had time to shop. Let me make you some tea."

He slammed the door shut. "I don't want tea."

"Okay. Can I give you a ride home, then?" Because clearly he was in no state to talk sanely about Nancy Little, and this wasn't the sort of situation we could resolve by screaming at each other with one of us being shitfaced.

"My driver is downstairs." He stumbled past me and went into the living room. "God, this place makes me sick." He plopped down on the floral sofa.

"Thank you. I'll be sure not to have you over uninvited again." I sat in the green armchair, leaning forward. His troubled stare really made me nervous. Simply put, he wasn't the sort of person to unhinge or let things get to him. "Let me get you back into your car, Mr. Cole."

"You're going to stab me in the back, aren't you, Lily? You're going to turn into one of those backstabbing bitches."

I blinked at him.

He continued, "She thinks I killed her sister, but I tried to help her. She was more fucked up than me—if you can believe that shit."

"So you know about Nancy Little's book?"

He shook his finger at me. "I never promised those women anything, Lily. But I treated them with respect. I was nothing but a gentleman, and when things weren't working, I stopped." He ran his hands through his hair. "I just don't understand why they turned on me. Maybe they wanted more. Maybe they wanted what they couldn't have or they felt used—I don't know, but they never said a word. Then they stabbed me in the back—people I trusted." I tried to pick through his rant and piece together the entire story, but there were too many holes.

"I'm not going to stab you in the back, Mr. Cole. I promise. But I need you sober for this. We can talk in the morning." *Not like this crap is going to crawl into the toilet and flush itself away in one night.* No. This was not that sort of problem. And I was absolutely terrified.

"Where's the bathroom? I'm going to throw up," he said.

Speaking of toilets... "It's right there." I pointed

to the door between my bedroom and Danny's. "Second on the right."

He staggered to his feet, and when I rose to help him, he pushed my hands away. "I got it," he said belligerently.

"Fine." I held up my hands. "Call me if you need any help."

I waited for a few minutes, and when I didn't hear anything, I knocked on the door. "Mr. Cole? Are you okay?"

Nada.

I opened the door and found him sleeping with his head on the toilet seat. Yes, I desperately had the urge to take a photo, but lucky for him, I wasn't a complete bitch.

I gave him a quick shake, but he was out cold. *Fabulous.* What was I going to do with him? He was twice my size or damned near close to it.

I went over to our living room window and looked out at the street. There was no limo parked there. Had his driver dumped him here?

Okay. What am I going to do with you? Danny was with her boyfriend tonight, so I couldn't ask her for help—probably a good thing because she'd be molesting Mr. Cole or posing him in compromising positions with herself and posting pics all over the place.

I decided I'd lay down some towels and slide him off the toilet so he wouldn't crack his head on anything. As gently as I could, I got him onto his side and covered him up. Lying there, passed out on my bathroom floor, I couldn't help but stare at the man and wonder what was truly going on with him. Had he really been using these women, or had it been the other way around?

I guess it's going to have to wait until morning.

I left the night light on, in case he woke up later wondering where the hell he was, and got back into bed.

chapter fifteen

Saturday morning, Danny's voice whispering in my ear woke me from a vividly sexual dream involving Maxwell Cole's hard body grinding against my ass while he fondled my breasts and groaned my name in sweet sexual agony as I denied him.

"Lily? Lily?"

I slowly opened my eyes to a grinning, giddy Danny.

"Ohmygod. Ohmygod. Is that Maxwell Cole?"

Huh? I looked over my shoulder to the man spooning my body, his strong arm wrapped around my midriff.

Crap. He must've gotten up at one point and found me, which meant that hard thing sticking into my tailbone wasn't a dream.

"Get out," I grumbled.

"Just one picture? Please, I'm begging you."

"No," I hissed, "now get out."

She obeyed, mock-pouting the entire way.

I looked at my phone. It was seven in the morning—Danny usually went to the gym at this time and her boyfriend did some sort of bike riding—which was why she was up. Mr. Cole, on the other hand, needed to get the hell out of my apartment. What if that Nancy lady was watching me? It would not help me avoid getting dragged into whatever the hell she was doing if my boss was seen doing a walk of shame from my apartment after a night of drinking.

I shoved him off me, sat up, and gave the lump of dead-to-the-world manliness at my side a little shake. "Max, wake up."

He didn't move.

"Max? Mr. Cole? Maxwell? You have to go."

He rolled over, giving me his back.

"Uh-uh. You can't stay here. You have to go now," I said sternly.

"*You* go. My fucking head hurts."

"Yes. I know, but it will hurt much nicer in the comfort of your own bed."

"Fuck off," he mumbled.

Ugh. Fine. I reached down and pinched his ass. "Wake the hell up, Mr. Cole."

He sat up, his eyes moving around my room and then glancing at my face. "What the fuck am I doing here?"

"Good question. One we can answer later by phone when we talk about Nancy Little's book and the fact that you've fucked me over in a way I never dreamed possible. Time for you to go—I don't want anyone seeing you leave my apartment."

"The book." He stared at the wall for a moment,

obviously trying to sort a few things out.

"Mr. Cole, I'm trying very hard not to blow a fucking fuse here, so please just go."

Instead, he kept on staring at the wall, his jaw pulsing. "You're moving in with me."

"Huh?" Was he still drunk?

He looked over at me. Well, at my neck. "You're moving in with me."

I didn't respond with words, but the "are you nuts?" look on my face was sufficient.

He stood from the bed, rubbing his face and making a little groan as his biceps flexed into half-hard mounds. "I knew about Nancy Little. It was the reason I took a risk on you."

"So this entire time, you were aware that this journalist was writing a book about you, using testimony from two other women to call you out as a fraud."

"Yes."

"Why didn't you tell me?" I fumed.

"I didn't want to discourage you from accepting my offer."

"So you withheld information that could potentially damage my life and drag me through the mud?" How could he fucking do that? "You're such a selfish prick."

"I thought we'd established that already."

Flippant bastard. "No. That's my answer: No. I don't want anything to do with your little scandal, and when I clear my head, I'm going to try my absolute best not to fall apart because you've hurt me worse than every cruel motherfucker I've ever known rolled into one."

He tilted his head, looking offended. "It was never my intention to get you dragged into this, but you're part of it now whether you like it or not. That's Nancy's doing, not mine."

Dammit. I didn't want to argue about this; I wanted it to not happen.

"Can you sue her, or get a judge to stop her?" Defamation of character wasn't legal, was it?

"My lawyers hit a wall despite my hopes I could make it all go away, so that book is being published in four weeks."

Stay calm. Stay calm. Do not murder the billionaire. "So what does she want me for?" I asked.

"She probably feels you'd be of value if you spoke publically after the release of her story," he said.

"This is crazy." And I wasn't referring only to this woman's book, but to his reaction to it. He was so calm, like it was just another business issue he needed to deal with. No prob.

"Yes," he responded.

"So why not just tell the truth?" It was an honest question. He could come out publically and speak about his disorder. People might understand.

He looked at me. "Tell millions of customers that the sight of unattractive people gives me panic attacks? Or that while I do believe women should be more focused on their self-worth, the number one thing I judge them on is their looks. Yes, I can see how that will work."

I stood and stared across the bed at him, feeling exposed. "Why will my moving in with you help anything?"

"Accelerated therapy. When the book comes out, I need to be cured of this. I need to be able to look any woman in the face and prove to the world the stories are lies."

"But they're not."

"It's none of their goddamned business, Lily," he fumed. "And the relationships I had with those women—years ago, by the way—were private, just like my relationship with you."

I could understand his point. I mean, if the guy had erectile dysfunction and was trying to work through it privately with a girlfriend, it would be genuinely wrong for her to write a book about it. On the other hand, Maxwell Cole had built his company on a philosophy he physically couldn't prescribe to. The only way to deal with this was head-on before the book came out and to talk openly about his problem. He could make people understand that he'd been trying to overcome his issues any way he could.

"What happened with the others?" I asked.

He looked down at his black shiny shoes—yes, he'd worn his shoes to bed—my bed. "I guess they lied to me and couldn't truly handle it."

"That's it?" There had to be more.

"Yes, that's it."

"So you...what? Tried to work on desensitizing yourself and—"

"I paid them money to spend time with me. I had no progress with one woman and moved on. The next eventually wanted more from me and we quit when I couldn't reciprocate—she seemed to understand. I broke it off with the last one, Sarah, because she was unstable. She killed herself six months after we ended our sessions, but not because of me. She was depressed. That was four years ago. I gave up trying despite my therapist's insistence I continue confronting my issue."

I believed him. I really did. But still. Knowing he'd had other women in his life like this made me feel disposable or cheap somehow.

"Did you fuck them, too?" I asked.

He gave me a sharp look. "No. I just told you, it wasn't like that. At least not for me."

"Oh." I nodded, trying to think that through.

"You're the only one I've been able to make progress with, Lily. The only one in seven years since I started therapy. Which is why I want to move things faster."

Seven years? He'd been trying to overcome this for seven damned years? "I think you should find a new therapist."

"The problem isn't her, Lily. It's me."

Yeah, no kidding.

"Well, you should've told me before dragging me into all this. And now it's time for you to go." What the hell was I going to do? I'd been at C.C. a little over a month, and I didn't want to leave—I loved working there—but once this book came out, that Nancy lady was going to pull me into all this. I'd never get a job at another company because I'd be known as...whatever...one of Mr. Cole's ugly women. I honestly wanted to beat the crap out of him. How *dare* he do this to me?

"*Lily,* I know you're upset with me, but you can't run from this—"

"Yeah. I get that, *Mr .Cole*, but I need to think."

"Fine. I'll go, but think about what I'm asking. Come live with me. No one will know."

I still just couldn't make sense of how that made any sense to him. He'd spend more time with me, accelerate his "healing," and then face the world and tell them what? Was I missing something? Because this man wasn't stupid or crazy. So for whatever reason he wanted this, I simply wasn't seeing the rationale.

Or he's not telling you everything. I shook my head, biting my tongue.

He turned to leave. "One other thing," he said, stopping in my doorway, "if you think this is really about me or you, then you're wrong. There are thousands of people who will lose their jobs—and homes and cars and won't be able to pay for their children's college—if C.C. goes under because of this."

"Then resign. Hand the company over to someone else."

He blew out a breath. "My leaving now would be just as destructive—especially right before we go public."

I supposed he was right. That man was the face of the company.

"I'll call you later," he said. "Please think about it."

Think about it. Think about it? Think about it! I wanted to run over him with my car.

"Sure," I replied, just wanting him to go. "I'll think about it."

I watched him leave, trying not to get emotional. If I got hung up on getting angry and playing the blame game, it might make me feel damned good, but it wouldn't save me or C.C., the only place I'd be able to work after this was all said and done.

God, Max. How could you do this to me? On the other hand, I had only myself to blame. I agreed to this arrangement, and I should've known something was going to happen.

chapter sixteen

All right. So when most people find themselves in a position where everything hinges on a single decision, they go to the people they trust for advice. But my situation was already set to destruction mode, only there were two degrees. The lesser degree would be that when the book came out, Mr. Cole would refute the women's stories and I would end up a footnote of sorts and the center of a lot of tabloid and office gossip. That was the best case. Worst case was no one believed him, the company tanked, and my name still got dragged through the mud. Either way, I was ruined.

Ruined.

The man who'd promised me a bright sunny future had effectively placed me in a position where I'd be known not for my accomplishments or intelligence, but for being ugly. Just another woman he had "therapy" sessions with. I would be laughed at, ridiculed, and criticized.

Then there was my own part in this. I'd agreed to this relationship. There'd been no gun to my head.

That's why I didn't need advice; I needed a strong shoulder to cry on.

I took a shower, dressed in my most comforting black yoga pants and white tee, and then went in my room and called my brother. It was about seven in the morning West Coast time.

"Lily?" he answered with a groggy voice.

"John, I've fucked up."

"It's about time."

"I'm serious. I've ruined my life with this one."

There was a moment of silence. "Okay. I'm listening."

When I got done telling John the entire story, even the part about sleeping with Mr. Cole—minus the unnecessary details—I expected my big brother to say something like "Wow. You're screwed."

But that's not what he said. "I'm going to fucking kill that guy."

I sighed. "I've got that covered on my to-do list already."

"No, I'm serious, Lily. That asshole needs to pay. You have to go public with the other women."

"What? Why the hell would I do that?"

"Because he took advantage of you. He used you. And now your life is going to be fucked because of him."

"Yeah, I know." Of course, I'd agreed to the using, just not the public scandal part. "But going against him doesn't help me."

"That man is about to become the most hated

guy on the planet. If you side with him, if you defend him, they'll take you down, too. The press will have a field day."

"They'll have it either way," I pointed out.

"If you come out as one of the injured parties, at least you'll have the sympathy of the public. You can move on. Eventually. But you can't defend that jackass, Lily. You can't do that. He deserves what's coming to him."

Wow. Okay. I wasn't expecting this reaction from John at all.

"He has a disorder, John. He can't help it."

"Lily, do you hear yourself? He put you in this position to save his own ass without you knowing."

"I know." It was the reason I felt so goddamned hurt. And pissed. "But I agreed to the arrangement. I don't think I can come out against him."

"You need to save yourself now, Lily. He made his bed, let him lie in it."

I ended the call with John, got on my running clothes and shoes, and did the only thing I could do in that moment. I ran. And I ran some more. And when I didn't think I could run any farther, I Forest Gumped myself and kept on running until I literally had no idea where I was. Some suburb with those little houses stacked next to each other in long rows.

I walked to a small playground next to an empty elementary school, found a drinking fountain, then dropped down under a tree. Running hadn't given me any answers. Not one. Because while my brain and logic said I needed to distance myself from Mr. Cole and possibly follow John's advice, my heart didn't want that. I didn't want to hurt him. Or anyone, for that matter.

The fact was, I realized that I liked the person I was. No, I didn't like everything, but the kind, genuine, and caring parts of me were good. I didn't want to "get my hands dirty" or be a cutthroat bitch. So if that meant I wasn't cut out for a future in the corporate world, then so be it. But I also realized I wasn't a quitter. So wherever this thing landed, I had to trust that I'd make it through this. But I had to do it with a clear conscience.

The other thing I thought about was my looks. The situation was absolutely forcing me to confront the one thing I'd been trying to ignore my entire life. Yes, that had been my way of "accepting" things—*just pretend it's not really there. Just pretend I'm okay with everything.* But this one aspect of my life and body that I didn't want to face would soon be under a huge, glaring public spotlight. It was as if karma was finally having it out with me. *You can run, Lily, but you can't hide.*

So fine. My face was a problem for me.

There, I'd said it.

But what did it matter now? The issue was in my head, and it didn't matter if I had this face or another. If I got into a car accident and ended up with scars all over my body, I'd still be me. Lily

Snow. It wouldn't change my insecurities at this point—the damage was done—and it wouldn't make me more or less smart or more or less loved by my friends and family.

On the other hand, as long as I had this face, people would never see past it. And now the world would only be looking at it.

So if my face really didn't matter, then why was I holding onto it so tightly? And why was I so afraid to trust the one person who truly understood me?

Because he's the only person who really understands you.

I was afraid, because he made me feel so vulnerable. I couldn't trust my judgement around him.

※

From my red Mini, I buzzed Mr. Cole's gate at around seven p.m. and a woman answered the intercom. "Hi, I'm here to see Mr. Cole? My name is Lily Snow."

"Yes, of course. Come in."

The gate buzzed, and I drove up to his door. There were several cars already in his circular brick driveway, including a limo. I didn't know why, but I'd been expecting him to be alone.

When I got out of my car, a nice middle-aged woman in a black dress opened the door. "Mr. Cole has asked you to wait in his study." She gestured to the left.

"Thanks." I entered, hearing several voices and one in particular I would never forget. Adeline Taylor, the model slash actress Mr. Cole had been getting friendly with at the after party in Milan.

My blood began to sizzle. Why the hell was she here? Had he asked her to live with him, too? Maybe we could all be a happy threesome, drowning in scandal together. How wonderful.

I entered the study, just off the foyer, and stood in the middle of the room, inhaling the scent of his sweet, masculine cologne that permeated the entire space. Looking around, his study reminded me of his office downtown—clean, lots of awards on glass shelves behind a black cherry desk—but here he had stacks of magazines piled in one corner. We had the same "fashion junky" magazine-hoarding habit.

"Miss Snow, I'm pleased to see you." He wore a beautiful tuxedo and looked like the most handsome bastard on the planet.

More of that scent, so delicious, so him, filled the room. I wanted to roll around in it.

"Sorry to interrupt your dinner party," I said.

"We're actually going to a fund-raiser. But, as always, I'm happy to see you."

So while I was falling apart, he was business as usual.

He added, "Had I known you were coming, I would've invited you along."

I obviously wasn't dressed in my formal wear—just black yoga pants and a white sports tank, in case I needed to run right after having this conversation.

"I'm not staying, Mr. Cole. I just came to say that I'm accepting your offer."

"To live with me?"

"No. I want out. I want that surgery," I said.

He jerked back his head, frowning.

"Don't look at me like that," I fumed.

"May I ask why you changed your mind?"

"Because the future that you've so kindly thrust onto my shoulders isn't one I can live with."

"Lily, like I said, I never intended for you to get dragged into this."

Okay, I knew he wasn't alone in the blame, but I had to say this. I had to confront him with his part in all this, because things were going to get very bumpy and I needed to know if I could really trust him.

"You knew the book was coming," I said.

"Yes. But Nancy had already written it. I had no idea she'd approach you when she had all the ammo she needs to wage her little war."

I looked down at my feet, panting with livid anger. "Well, I guess you were wrong."

"Lily." He approached and gripped my shoulders. "I can't tell you how sorry I am. But I'm the injured party here. And so are you."

"That doesn't fix anything."

"I know. And neither does having surgery." Why was he changing the subject back to me?

"That's not your choice, Mr. Cole. And you're not the one who will have to go through the rest of life being known as that fucking ugly woman Maxwell Cole hired just for his 'therapy.'"

"Fuck them. There's nothing wrong with you, Lily."

I scoffed. "Says the man who can't even look at my face."

He looked up at the ceiling. "There's nothing wrong with you," he said, with a frustrated irate tone. "The problem is me. Me, Lily." He looked at my face, trying his best to hold his gaze there. "I think by now, you would've come to realize that."

"We made a deal. I want the surgery. I don't want to talk about it."

He blew out a breath. "Fine. I'll make the arrangements, but you can't have the surgery until after the book comes out."

"What? Why?"

"Because everyone will think you were trying to cover something up or, worse, that I made you do it for a twisted reason."

So he was afraid it would make him look bad. "So all you care about is yourself."

He shook his head. "I'm looking after you, Lily. I don't want this to be any worse than it already is. Let the book come out. I'll refute it with an army of publicists, experts in the field, lawyers—I'm prepared for this, I promise. Then you can quietly go have your surgery. You can tell anyone who asks that you did it for your own reasons. Besides, you just started working at C.C. If you take time away now, it will look bad with the clients."

"That doesn't matter, Max—I mean, Mr. Cole."

He grabbed my hand, and it was warm and soothing on my skin. "You can call me Max," he said with a tone that made it sound like I was being ridiculous for maintaining the formality between us.

I looked up at him, knowing he was right. I was being ridiculous. Using his last name wasn't going to insulate me from getting hurt. Not anymore.

I took a quick breath, crossing over that invisible threshold. "*Max*, I told you I want out. I can't stay at C.C. and face the people who work there or the clients. I can't do anything but get surgery, move back to California, and find a way to move on with my life quietly. After I've filed for bankruptcy because my student loans will eat me alive. But if I'm lucky, people will forget about me in a few years."

"So you're giving up. You're going to run away."

"You left me no choice, *Max*," I spat his name. Truthfully, he should've been honest with me from the beginning. Knowing about that book would've changed everything.

"I left you the choice to trust that I know what I'm doing and that I would not hurt you, Lily."

"I want the surgery. I'm doing it now. And I'm leaving C.C. This is what's best for me. Not you, but me."

Frustrated, he shook his head. "No."

"What?"

"No. I'm not letting you throw it all away, Lily."

"Seriously? You're going to tell me how I should deal with this mess you've left me with?" How dare he.

"Yes. Because you're making a mistake. And you do have backbone. You can stand up to anything anyone throws at you, Lily. And you have a promising career ahead of you. This issue will blow over, people will move on, and they'll see what I see in you after you give them a chance."

"What do you see in me?"

He cupped my cheek and stared into my eyes. "A very intelligent, feisty, beautiful woman, whose only mistake was getting involved with me." He bent his head and gave me a soft kiss.

I blinked at him, completely shocked, my body going tingly and nearly limp from the feel of his lips. "Why did you do that?"

There was a knock on the door. "Max, you in there?" It was Adeline. "We're already running late and the limo is waiting."

"Your girlfriend is waiting," I said bitterly.

"She's not my girlfriend, and she decided to surprise me by showing up here, instead of at the venue."

Frowning, I gave him a "whatever" shrug.

He gave me a look, walked over to the door and opened it. Adeline instantly noted me standing there.

"Who's she?" Adeline asked.

Of course, Adeline wouldn't remember me.

"Lily," he replied. "A very close friend. And I'm afraid I won't be joining you tonight because something important has come up."

Adeline's jaw dropped. "You can't make me go alone. What will the press say?"

He shrugged. "Tell them that Maxwell Cole stood you up."

"Nobody stands me up." She rolled her eyes.

"Then tell them anything you like, but I'm afraid I've got to stay here with Lily to work out a few things."

"What could possibly be so important that you'd flake on me for…" Her disgusted gaze completed the sentence.

"That's between Lily and me, but if you really want to know," he leaned down a little, "I'm hoping to convince her to be more than friends."

Adeline looked like she was about to implode with shock. "But…but…"

"Let me walk you out," he said.

As for me, I stood there trying to make sense of his words. *What the hell?*

He left the room, and I sat down in a leather armchair wedged into the corner near his bookshelf. *Wait.* This couldn't be right.

"Adeline is gone. And I sent my maid home." Max stood in the doorway, still in that beautiful tux, his freshly shaved face looking like he'd never been more serious in his life.

I stared at him. Speechless.

"Say something," he demanded.

"I can't."

"It's fairly simple. It's either yes or no."

"What about my…"

"You have no idea how much I like you, Lily. Do you?"

"No."

But…my face and my…well, face.

"I knew the moment you walked into my office there was something different about you."

"So why didn't you say anything sooner?" I asked.

"I'd planned to, but you ran me out of your hotel room in Milan. What was I to think?"

Made sense, I supposed. "But you and I…we can't work."

He shook his head. "So you mean, simply because I have this issue I'm not in control of, you wouldn't consider me."

"Don't put it like that—it doesn't make any sense." It really didn't. He was my boss. He had issues. There was a huge shit storm of scandal coming our way, too.

He stepped closer, reached down to grab my

hand, and yanked me up. "You honestly can't see how hard I'm trying to fix myself? And did it ever occur to you that you're the only reason it's working this time?"

He pulled my body against him, and as much as I wanted to push him away, I really couldn't. He felt too…too…perfect. Every nerve ending lit up with pulses, especially between my legs.

"Give me a few weeks, Lily. I'm close to breaking through this. I can feel it."

I wanted to. I did, but it felt like he was asking me to walk through a minefield with him, and frankly, my mind couldn't accept he really wanted me.

He went on, "I'll work through this issue with the press, and the fact you're my employee. The only thing you need to do is trust me and give me a chance. What do you have to lose?"

"Getting hurt by you."

He dropped his hand. "So you believe Nancy Little? You really think I misled those women and then tossed them aside or that I'm responsible for her sister's death."

I didn't know what to believe, but it was time to answer that question. He needed to know how vulnerable I felt around him.

"I kicked you out of my hotel room because I knew the moment you touched me, I wanted more. And I don't want to fall in love with someone who can never love me back."

He nodded. "You really believe I couldn't possibly be interested in you?"

"Not a man like you with the world's Adelines throwing themselves at your feet."

He shook his head. Then something snapped, and that side of Maxwell Cole, the side with a temper, showed itself.

"Fucking hell, Lily. You really are fucked up." He grabbed my wrist and yanked me along.

"What are you doing?" I said, digging my heels into the blond hardwood floor, my tennis shoes squeaking as he dragged me.

"I'm taking you upstairs."

"Why?"

"Because I'm going to spend the rest of the weekend fucking some sense into you." He whipped me over his shoulder, and I grunted with the impact. "Max, we're not in the Stone Age."

He slapped my ass really hard.

"Ouch!" *What the hell?*

"Shut up. I have had enough of your crap," he said.

My crap?

He got to the top of the stairs and turned the corner.

"What crap? Put me down."

"Your constant undermining and self-deprecation. You're hot, Lily. Really hot. Especially that mouth of yours. And your fucking little attitude especially gets my dick hard." We got to his immaculate bedroom—at least, I think it was his with the bright white walls, light gray curtains, and minimal decorations—where he slid me down and pushed me back. I landed on my ass on his king-sized bed.

He undid his bow tie and went to work on his shirt. "But obviously your hang-up is getting in your way. So as one fucked-up person to another, I owe you a little therapy of your own."

He pulled off his shirt and tux jacket in one swoop, revealing the perfection of his chiseled torso—ripped pecs and abs with those black tribal tats on his upper arms.

God, he's breathtaking.

Obviously, if I'd really been against what he was doing, I would've said so. But the fact was, having this man "fuck some sense" into me wasn't something I wanted to turn away from. I wanted nothing more, and he probably knew it.

He kicked off his shoes, slid down his pants and black boxer briefs and stood before me, naked, rippling, hard.

"Now, tell me, Lily. Does this look like the cock of a man who doesn't find you attractive?"

I gulped. "No."

"Good." He pushed me back on the soft light gray comforter, covering me with his body, and began kissing me. What I couldn't understand was how two entirely conflicting sets of emotions occupied this one man's body.

He wanted me and yet he didn't?

Maybe it's the same way you want him, but he terrifies the hell out of you.

That thought was an epiphany.

Remember when I said that sometimes there were two sides? Love and Lust. Rational and irrational. The two sides sometimes existed together, but in a state of tug-o-war until one side won or dominated. So just like I could want him, despite my fears, he could want me despite his own. His desire superseded his fear—no different than me.

He pulled up my tank and slid it over my head, diving straight for my breasts with that sensual mouth of his. The tip of his tongue swirled over my nipple, the suction tugging those erotic pulses right out of me, making me moan. Meanwhile, his other hand massaged and cupped and caressed the other breast. "I'm going to fuck those beautiful breasts of yours one day, Lily. But not today."

He then ran his tongue over every inch of my breast until I was slick with his kisses. He then began trailing his mouth down my stomach until he reached the waistband of my yoga pants. He gave them a tug, and I lifted my hips, watching as his powerful arms peeled away the last remaining barrier between us.

"You haven't been with anyone else, have you?" He looked up at me from between my thighs.

"God no. Have you?"

"No. And I'm always careful. Do you want me to use a condom?"

He hadn't asked the first time. I guessed he realized that was not the smartest move.

"I'm still on the pill," I replied to put the question behind us.

"Good." He pulled apart my thighs and stared at the sensitive flesh between my legs. "God, I've been fantasizing about this for over a month." He lightly floated his hand over my throbbing, aching bud. "I can't believe no one's ever touched you before, Lily."

Panting with hard anticipation, I threw back my head and grabbed fistfuls of sheets. "Just you, Mr. Cole."

He chuckled, and I felt his breath on my entrance. "I've got my face two inches from your pussy. Can't you call me Max?"

"Sorry. Old habits, Mr. Co—"

He thrust his finger inside me, and I reacted with a wince. I still wasn't used to anything going inside me, but it felt so, so good.

"Max." He pulled his finger out and thrust it in again, causing me to moan. "You'll call me Max." He thrust another finger into my slick entrance.

"Even when we're at work?" The sensation of his sensual strokes was making me lose my mind.

"Yes." He placed his mouth over my c-spot and slid his tongue over the tip. "Especially at work."

Oh, God. He'd barely touched me, and I was

already so close.

"Max…" I panted. "I really want…"

"Yes?" He pumped his hand and fingers between my legs, igniting every nerve. "Tell me what you want."

"You…I want you…" Forever. Like this. Him and me, our bodies touching, and no one else.

He moved over me and settled between my legs, every inch of bare naked skin-to-skin contact igniting every inch of desire contained inside my body.

And then he kissed me.

It wasn't like any of the other times—those rough hot kisses in Milan that only touched my lips for passing moments before vacating to my neck or breasts, or how he kissed me softly earlier in his study. This was the kind of kiss I'd dreamed of my entire life—filled with the sort of passion that only exists when two people pour themselves into one another. It was the open, sensual expression of a desire that could never be articulated with words. There was no premeditation or thinking involved—just feeling and giving and absorbing and wanting. It was everything, fulfilling and euphoric at the cellular level, and nothing all at once, because it left me with a hollowness, knowing it couldn't last forever. The best I could do was try to remember it, and hope I wouldn't go insane once it left me.

For the moment, however, that kiss was my world—free of negative emotions or impending scandals. And when he thrust his cock deep inside me, I fought hard not to come instantly from the overwhelming sensations and emotions. His lips were the emotional connection, his cock the physical one. As he pumped, I moaned into his mouth, holding his lips to mine with my hands on his cheeks. I didn't want one side to win—emotion versus physical. I wanted them both. I wanted all of him.

He fucked me hard, and I kissed him harder. Our bodies writhed in a sexual dance while our hearts pounded in unison.

His hands slid under my body, cupping my ass to increase the thrusting power. My hips slammed into him, my lips sucked and kissed and pushed to his.

The friction of his large cock sliding in and out, filling me over and over again, felt so different this time. There was only the intimate sensation of him deep inside my body and the delicious pressure I didn't want to end. I just wanted to get him deeper.

I tipped my hips, allowing him to angle the head of his cock toward that spot inside me I instinctively craved. When he hit it, I exploded with a hard orgasm that radiated outward in a blinding sinful light that sent my body somewhere else.

I moaned into his mouth, and he broke the kiss. Then our eyes met as he thrust hard and came, his gravelly groans mixing with my sounds. I felt his hard flesh twitch inside me, pouring his cum, the walls of my core milking him for every drop of pleasure.

Still, he never looked away.

People say that beauty is in the eye of the beholder. And in that moment, I knew—with every drop of blood flowing through my heart—that what we were together was so much more. It wasn't subjective or up for debate. It was the purest form of beauty that existed in the world.

Still inside me, Max relaxed into my body, resting his mouth on that little spot between my neck and shoulder. His hot breath tickled my neck, and the lazy kisses he applied were better than any dessert I'd ever tasted, any song I'd ever heard.

I stopped breathing for a second. Maybe two. How in the world could he make me feel like this? So wanted, so beautiful.

I was definitely falling in love with this man. We were two perfect halves who'd found each other and made something more.

But what would we do with the ugly halves?

I'd soon come to realize that they'd come after us with a vengeance, looking to destroy us.

chapter seventeen

"Tell me, Lily, when did you realize you wanted to be a goddess?"

I laughed, gazing into his hazel eyes, the dim light from the hallway casting light over one wall.

"A goddess?" Now separated, but our bodies still touching, Max looked at me—really looked at me—and his expression was full of affection. It humbled me.

"Yes. A goddess in my bed. In my life," he said.

"Don't be so corny, Max. It undermines your alpha-male mystique."

He smiled, brushing his thumb over my bottom lip. "I can't help it. I've been struggling for so fucking long, and now I have to wonder if it wasn't all for you."

"Oh, come on. Don't tell me you're some closet romantic."

"Closet romantic, no. But I believe in manifest destiny—you being the occupier, of course."

I smiled. "Oh, Mr. Cole, do talk historical terms to me. It makes me feel so dirty," I said jokingly.

He grinned, and it literally filled me, bathed me, permeated me in the deepest joy.

"All I can say is that sometimes things happen for a reason. And I can't explain the fact that I haven't been able to make any progress with my disorder until you came along. My only explanation is that I really wanted it to happen."

"That is the corniest bullshit any guy has ever said to get in my pants." I smiled. "Okay. It's the only corny thing anyone's said to get into my pants; nevertheless, I won't tolerate these cheesy lines from you. So either put up or shut up."

He laughed toward the ceiling. "My, my. Aren't we the greedy little woman?"

"Greedy?" I pointed to myself. "You promised me a weekend of fucking some sense into me. I'm still waiting." I was going out of my frigging mind. For him.

"Just giving my giant cock a little rest. But I promise there's more."

I laughed. "You call that giant? No wonder you didn't show it in that lip-gloss campaign. Us ladies would've mistaken it for the product."

His jaw dropped.

"Did I go too far?" I asked.

"You just called my dick 'lip gloss.'"

The thing was huge. Porn star huge. But did this man seriously need me to say that? He knew what he had. His ego was proof of that.

"I guess I could take another look and reevaluate?" I shrugged innocently. After all, I had really, really been dying to have another up close and personal experience with his penis in my mouth. It was a serious ego boost of my own.

"If you must, Miss Snow," he said with an exaggeratedly silly deep voice, "but why don't we take it to the shower? I've been fantasizing about lathering you from head to toe in soap and then getting you dirty again."

I liked that plan. A lot.

I jumped from the bed and bolted across his big open bedroom, heading for his enormous, scary-clean, shiny man bathroom—no frills whatsoever—for the shower. Yes, this man wasn't a clean freak, but he definitely needed a little more "dirty" in his life. I was there to help.

⁂

Sunday morning, I awoke to two things. One incredibly good. The second not so great.

"Max." I gave him a shake, his strong, heavy legs intertwined with mine, his head resting on my chest. I hated to break up this moment of waking up in a man's arms for the first time, but..."There's someone ringing the doorbell." *Over and over again.*

He groaned and rolled off, giving me his back.

Boy, this man was a heavy sleeper. "Max, wake up."

He wasn't having it, and after a night of animalistic, sensual fucking that resulted in me actually losing my mind in orgasmic pleasure, I couldn't blame him for wanting his rest.

I slipped from the bed, giving a longing glance at his tanned, hard, bare ass, and grabbed his tux shirt from the floor, closing it with my hands. Max was a big guy, so his shirt on my body looked like a very short dress.

I shuffled down the stairs and opened the front door, using it as a body shield and assuming the person would be his driver waiting to whisk him away.

I threw open the door. "Sorry, but Mr. Cole is mine for..." My voice trailed off as I took in the woman standing before me. Her dark hair and hazel eyes told me all I needed to know. This had to be his mother. He had the exact same scowl when he was angry. Other than that, however, her face was abnormally...perfect. You know when you see those people on TV who are addicted to plastic surgery and their noses are so straight and their lips are so full that they look imperfect? Nature doesn't make anyone that symmetric. Just like it doesn't make fifty-year-olds with tight skin and zero wrinkles.

"Lily Snow..." She looked me up and down like a turd that landed in her way.

"Yes, I'm Lily," I said weakly, not sure what to make of her tone. "How do you know me?"

"I'm his mother. I make it my business to know who's trying to slum their way into my son's life.

And I assume from the lack of clothing, you spent the night fucking my Maxwell. So now that he's had his fun," she lifted her chin, "I suggest you go back to whatever rock you crawled out from."

Had she really just said that to me? Had Maxwell Cole's mother treated me like a piece of shit?

Yep.

Staring at her familiar hazel eyes, I unclenched my fist. "I've got a really great idea. Why don't you go fuck yourself?" I slammed the door in her face and marched upstairs, giving Max a little jiggle. "Max, your mother is here. And I think I finally understand everything about you."

He cracked open one eye and looked at me. "My mother is here?"

I nodded. "Yeah. And Jesus, Max, what a bitch. No wonder you're so fucked up."

He blew out a breath and ran his hands over the top of his thick head of brown hair. "You don't know the half of it." He slowly moved to his feet and slid on his discarded black tux pants. "I'll be right back. You stay here."

Should I mention that I just told her to go fuck herself and slammed the door in her face?

I heard screaming, like a banshee with PMS, erupt from downstairs.

Nah, I think he just figured it out.

Then I heard every bitter, degrading, vicious word from her mouth—he was disgusting, stupid, a loser. How dare he tarnish their lives with the ugly filth he'd brought to his bed—and my pity factor elevated tenfold.

God, Max.

After several minutes, I heard the front door close and Max's heavy steps approach up the stairs.

Sitting on the edge of the bed, I dug my nails into the mattress, and his eyes met mine. He looked apologetic.

"That was awkward," he said.

"Max, she's so toxic. Why is she even in your life?"

"She and my father own fifty-one percent of my company—well, the family trust does. But she controls it."

I hadn't known that. "How did that happen?"

"She fronted the money when I started. We kept growing, so I could never buy her out."

I scratched my head. "How have you put up with that for so long?"

This man was...fearless. He took shit from no one. And compared to her, he was a saint.

He sat next to me on the edge of the unmade bed, but didn't look at me. "I've tried to get through to her—she is, after all, my mother—but she doesn't believe there's anything wrong with the way she behaves. Not even the fact that my sister disowned her and won't speak with anyone who has a connection with her has swayed my mother's opinion."

That was such a sad thing to hear. His own sister had chosen to leave her entire family behind rather than have even indirect contact with that evil woman. I understood why, but couldn't she have found a way? On the other hand, who knew how damaged his sister was. Maybe just looking at Max, who had his own issues to deal with, reminded her of her pain.

"It's the reason I decided to take C.C. public," he explained. "Once that happens, my mother will own stock—so will I—but we'll have a board of trusties and shareholders. She won't hold any real power."

I bit my lip.

So C.C. was really a family company and the IPO wasn't just a move to grow. It was Maxwell Cole's passage to freedom. Everything he'd been doing wasn't for greed or power, but to escape.

"Does she accept any blame for your disorder?" I asked.

"No. And she doesn't acknowledge her own."

What a great mom.

"And the book?" I asked. "Does she know?"

"Yes." He rubbed his unshaven jaw. "She's not pleased. She stands to lose a lot of money if the company goes under, but that's my issue to deal with, not yours."

Not exactly true. It was my issue too, but I understood what he meant. The problem was that I cared. And I wanted to know how he ever expected to truly get over his issue if this vile, cruel woman remained in his life.

"Max, will there ever be a point that she'll be completely gone?" I couldn't begin to articulate what being in her presence had felt like. There wasn't an ounce of compassion or niceness in her body. She was simply evil.

"Not unless I follow in my sister's footsteps and disown my entire family, including my father," he responded.

I couldn't imagine being put in that position. Having to choose between your family and your sanity. Especially since he'd already lost his sister.

"So your father's still with your mother?"

He nodded. "Yes. He's terrified of her, which is another reason I find it hard to cut them out of my life." I didn't have to ask if that meant his father never stood up for him. I pretty much guessed he hadn't.

Wow. I suddenly felt so grateful for my insanely loving parents. They would never allow anyone, let alone someone in our family, to hurt us like that.

"Let's get some breakfast," he said, giving my bare thigh a loving stroke. "Then I can take you to your thrift-store debacle to collect some clothes."

He didn't want to talk about it anymore, and I understood why. Still, my heart genuinely went out to this beautiful man, and strangely, it didn't make him lesser in my eyes. It made him more—more human, more admirable. He'd built his dream despite having to deal with some rather daunting emotional obstacles.

"Max, don't go insulting my woman cave. And why would I need clothes?" I stood in front of him and stripped off his tux shirt, letting it fall to the floor.

His eyes traveled up and down the length of my naked body.

He cleared his throat. "Well, I didn't say you needed them right away. But you can't go to work like that tomorrow. I mean, yes, you could...but then I wouldn't get any work done."

"I'll go home tonight."

"Not to stay." He folded his arms over his bare chest.

"Max, I can't live here. It's too weird. And that Nancy woman is probably watching your house."

"You're not living here; you're staying for a few weeks. To start. And that Nancy woman can screw herself." He stood and grabbed me around the waist. "And if you don't mind, Lily, I'd like to get on with some screwing of my own."

I couldn't resist that charming smile. Not when it was so genuinely seductive and those little smile grooves had made an appearance. "Fine. You can screw me." My sore body demanded it now that I felt the heat of his hard cock pressing against me through his pants. "But we're not done with this conversation." He kissed me and backed me up until my ass ran into the narrow table against the wall.

I reached for the button of his pants and opened them up. The moment they fell around his ankles, he stepped out and spun me around. Before I realized what he was doing, he pushed me forward and stroked me from behind, letting his fingers slide between my folds, instantly drawing a soft moan from my lips.

"God, Lily, you're already wet for me." His tone indicated how much that pleased him. He suddenly gripped my hips and thrust into me in one smooth, hard stroke, stealing my breath.

He pulled out and thrust his hips forward again.

I let out a sharp gasp. He felt so good inside me, but there was no doubt that the three rounds of sex from last night had left me raw and overly tense. He wasn't getting very deep.

"You're so fucking tight, Lily." Holding me firmly, he withdrew and eased in again. "Try to relax." This time he stayed there, not moving for several moments, allowing me to enjoy the sensation of his thick cock inside me. I felt my muscles relax around his hard flesh and then the throbbing, buzzing euphoric pressure building on my c-spot. I wanted him to touch me there, but knew if he did, it would all be over too quickly.

"That's right," he said in a husky voice. "Just like that." He slowly pulled out and eased back in again, applying pressure to that sweet, sweet spot deep inside me. "Try to stay relaxed."

The sensual sound of his deep voice and the coaxing, smooth motions of his hips and shaft felt like a blissful massage of my aching inner walls. They molded around him, allowing him to deepen the penetration.

I could tell he liked it and was close already because as he pushed forward again, burying himself fully inside me, his grip on my hips tightened. "God, you feel so good, Lily."

Now that I'd warmed up a little, I wanted him to show me exactly how good. "Don't hold back."

He didn't need me to twist his arm, because the force of his next thrust jarred my body forward, forcing me to press my palms to the wall. With the entire weight of his body, he pounded into me, his hips slapping against my ass. With the stamina of a wild beast, he went on and on and I never wanted it to end.

"Fucking hell, Lily, you feel so goddamned good. I can't get enough of you."

The sound of his deep husky voice pushed me closer to my own release. And when he bowed his large body over me, digging his forehead between my shoulder blades and cupping my breast, I couldn't wait anymore. I reached down with one hand and stroked myself, immediately feeling the hard waves of sinful contractions paralyze me. *God, what you do to me Max.*

Max's head fell back, his face tilted toward the

ceiling, as he came inside me with sharp little thrusts. "Fuck, Lily. Oh fuck." His tense body ground against me while my mind floated away.

After several moments, he dropped his head between my shoulder blades again, and I felt his panting chest matching my own vigorous breaths.

"I could do this all day with you, Lily."

Still panting, I said, "Fine by me, but you'll have to feed me eventually. Or I won't be able to keep up with you." He was an animal. Completely insatiable. I loved it.

"I'll feed you anything you want," he said. "Just don't leave."

It felt like a sincere plea from his heart. Or maybe it was his sexy afterglow talking. I wasn't sure, but I knew I wanted to stay with him, too. It was the fear of what was to come that had me wanting to run.

He withdrew, and I turned around, reaching for his neck to pull his lips to mine. His mouth moved in lazy, sated strokes.

Then a thought struck me, and I pulled back, staring him in the eyes. "Max?"

"Yes?" His tone indicated he thought I was up to something.

"You do realize you haven't looked away from me since yesterday." Not once.

He made a little blink, perhaps surprised. "I think it's because when I look at you, I see us. And we're beautiful together."

I slid my hands to his cheek. "Now that's the sweetest, corniest thing I've ever heard." And it genuinely melted my heart. "Please say it again."

chapter eighteen

It turned out that Max was just as bad of a cook as I was. Nevertheless, between the two of us, we managed to whip up some banana pancakes in his huge chef's kitchen with gleaming white-speckled granite countertops, stainless steel indoor grill, and a panoramic window with a view of the lake that bathed the space in warm, cheery light. My favorite part of the morning, however, wasn't the view of the lake. It was his unstoppable smile. Okay. That, and he wore absolutely nothing underneath his apron and every time he turned around, his adorable, perfectly round ass cheeks peeked out below that broad, muscled, smooth back.

After we ate on the patio, just outside the kitchen—and no, he did not put on clothes (so hot)—I borrowed some mouthwash and a spare toothbrush and we took yet another shower. I honestly felt like I couldn't get enough of him—his body pressed against mine, his hot kisses, his strong hands holding me to him.

After another slow session of long drawn-out orgasms, we lay in his bed again, facing each other. He didn't take his eyes off me.

"You're really enjoying this, aren't you?" I asked.

"Yes, Miss Snow, I am."

"Good."

"And I'll enjoy it even more once the drama is put behind us," he said.

That got me thinking. "You seem so confident that this will all shake out in your favor." And in mine.

He ran his finger from that hollow at the base of my neck and trailed it down between my breasts. "That's because I am."

"What if you're wrong?" I asked.

"I'm never wrong. And the moment she publishes that book, I'll prove *her* wrong."

I didn't like this one bit. "How?"

He looked away.

"Uhhh...what was that?" I said, sitting up.

"What?"

"You looked away. What are you planning?"

I looked down, and the worst possible thoughts trickled through my head. "Are you planning to use me?"

"What? Fuck no. Lily, I would never..." He sat up, gripped my shoulder, and gave it a squeeze. "I'm an asshole, but not a heartless one. I would never hurt you like that."

I released a mental sigh. Okay, it had been a completely ridiculous thought. Shame on me for even thinking it. "Then tell me."

He didn't want to. I could see it in his eyes. "I

don't know if I can at the moment; I'm too busy focusing on not spanking the hell out of you for that last comment."

I narrowed my eyes at him. "Don't be a barbarian."

"I thought you liked the alpha male in me," he countered.

I glared.

"Fine. No spanking," he conceded. "But do you honestly believe I built a multibillion-dollar company by winging it? Or not knowing how to manage the media?"

Well, when he put it like that. "No. I guess not."

"Then trust that I've got it covered. I've got a team of people ready to deal with this. Not only will that book be laughed at, but it will be used to sell millions of dollars of product."

I didn't like the feel of this. He was going to lie. Of course, he'd been backed into a corner and the truth was something very personal. Nancy Little intended to violate his privacy for revenge. An unjustified revenge. But how could this possibly end well? I didn't see it.

"I know that look," he said. "You're judging me and about to say something negative."

How did he know? "I just don't want you—us—to get hurt." Because at the end of the day, he was a good person. And I certainly didn't deserve this either.

"I will protect you. Your career will be fine.

Everything will work out. Now, can I take you to collect some clothes?"

"Why? You're cured now. Intensive therapy is over."

"Because I want you. Here. In my bed."

I liked the sound of that. "Fine. Twist my arm. But can we go for a run when we get back?"

"Are you going to jog topless again?" he asked.

"Do you want me to?"

"Do you have any idea how badly that image tortured me? I couldn't stop seeing your bouncing breasts in my head for weeks."

I gave him a sly look. The idea of him pining away for me was too much. "I'll run topless if you do."

He laughed. "Deal."

⁂

Monday morning at the office was sexual torture. No frigging way would we be maintaining a professional relationship at work, which meant something had to give.

I should've known.

For starters, on Sunday, we had gone back to my place for some clothes, fucked in my room, and then returned to his house to go at it again until we were spent, but not sated. When we left his house exhausted in the morning, and he'd insisted on driving in together in his new black Porsche

Panamera, I was unable to resist his uncharacteristic, dopy grin.

"I can drive myself. I promise," I'd said.

"You slept one hour. Let me drive," he'd argued.

"You, too."

"Yes, however, I run a global company. I'm used to it." He gave me his first puppy-dog look.

Yes, I melted.

"Fine. You drive," I said. My first mistake.

Then I told him to drop me off two blocks from the building before parking in the garage next door. He refused, kissed me at a stoplight until I couldn't think straight, and proceeded to do what the hell he pleased: parking where he always parked.

Okay. No big deal. No one from the office has seen us together. But it felt like he wanted us to be seen.

Or didn't give a rat's ass.

Walking to our building, I frowned at the beautiful man, awestruck by his extreme happiness, and knowing how long he'd waited for this moment—to finally feel free. Which made me happy, too. He could basically ask anything of me, and I would agree.

On the elevator ride up to our offices, we were alone, and he mauled me for twenty blissful seconds—tongue, hands, grinding action—the works—until we got to my floor.

"For lunch, I'm going to fuck you in my office so hard," he'd whispered, "you'll forget your name."

I staggered out of the elevator with red lips, my hair half fallen from the bun I'd carefully put into place, and my white fitted blouse half untucked.

Yes, I got plenty of looks from my coworkers, most assuming I'd just staggered in from a night of partying and getting laid. They were only half right.

Then came the monthly staff meeting. When I was supposed to be paying attention, all I could do was stare at my boss and think about the multitude of ways he'd licked me, sucked me, and penetrated me over the past two days. I'd counted fourteen orgasms. Fourteen. And I had the sore body to show for it. I'd literally zoned out through a thirty-minute marketing presentation on their new tropical-color trends because I was too busy fantasizing about Max—who, by the way, made it no secret that he did not approve of my blatant ogling and drooling.

Okay, so now he wanted to draw a line?

But if looks could talk, his said "I'm not a piece of meat. Stop staring at me like that." To which I replied, "Yeah, you are. And no, I won't."

When it was my and Mike's turn to present our recommendation for the new tween line of makeup, Max's sharp hazel eyes stuck to my face, creating even more of a distraction. To the world, he was merely paying attention. To me, he was showing me how much he really wanted me.

In summary, we both failed the "keeping work and personal life" separate. And for anyone who thought that I'd been an ass to even attempt such a feat, I'll simply say...

Yep!

Sure, there were plenty of examples of spouses or couples being coworkers, but this situation was wholly different, excluding the fact that he was my boss and ran the company. The truth was, we'd both been starving for this—whatever "this" was—and now that we had it, it felt like a drug.

After the monthly meeting, I left as quickly as I could, feeling an overwhelming panic wash over me. Nothing about this situation felt right, but everything about it felt good. I couldn't control myself.

"Lily?" There was a light knock on the doorjamb of my open office door.

Mike's blue, blue eyes and charming smile glowed in my direction.

"Mike, hi. How was your weekend?"

"Great." He approached with all the confidence in the world and partially sat on my desk. "Nursed a nasty hangover on Saturday and got in a few rounds of golf on Sunday. What about you?"

"Same." *Why had I said that?*

"You didn't seem drunk."

"After. I got drunk when I got home." *No, that didn't sound trashy at all. It was also a complete lie. What's the matter with me?*

"Oh. And how was golf? I didn't know you played."

"Did I say golf? I meant shopping. Same thing." *I'm an idiot. Need sleep.*

He raised his brows. "I suppose both involve a lot of walking."

"Exactly."

"So," he bobbed his head, "I was wondering if you were free tonight? I know Monday isn't a typical dinner-date night, but—"

"Mike," said a serious voice from just outside the doorway, "would you mind giving Miss Snow and me a moment?"

Mike looked at Max in his black power suit with his hazel eyes throwing off some serious angry tones.

"Yeah, sure, Mr. Cole," Mike said uncomfortably and then looked straight at me. "Let me know what you think."

"Lily is busy tonight, I'm afraid," Mr. Cole said. "She's behind on a special project."

I pasted on a polite smile, trying not to stampede Max with my womanly self-righteousness. "He's right, Mike. I can't tonight. But I'll check my calendar."

Mike left, obviously sensing something was off.

Max shut the door behind him. "You'll check your calendar?"

I gave him a look. "What did you expect me to say? Let me check with Mr. Cole's cock, and I'll let you know?"

"Would've worked for me," he said in a pissy tone.

I tilted my head. "You can't seriously be jealous."

He leaned over my desk. "Of course I can be, Lily. You're mine. And I don't like other men looking at what's mine."

I'd never experienced this feeling before—a guy getting territorial over me. Part of me really liked it. The other part didn't. "But I'm not really yours. Not as far as everyone else is concerned, which leads me to the point—"

"We're leaving for a few days. I'll have my driver, Callahan, take you home to pack the appropriate attire."

I blinked at him. "Sorry?"

"I can't focus on work. Not knowing you're here, suffering and in need of a good fucking."

My jaw dropped. "Well—okay…that's ta-ta-true, but I really have stuff to do."

"And it can wait for two days."

"It can't," I argued, feeling like he was the bad boy trying to convince me to skip class. "People are depending on me."

"I need this, Lily. And I think you do as well." He paused for a long moment. "What if I ask your boss for permission?"

I folded my hands neatly on top of my desk. "Max—"

"Liiily?" he warned.

"Max?"

"Liiily?"

I grunted at him and then smiled. I couldn't help it. He was too sexy to deny.

He folded his arms over his broad chest, flashing a bit of shiny silver cuff link. "If I can blow off a few days of work for you, and it's my company, I'm sure you can accommodate."

I sighed. He totally won me over. "Fine. Where are we going?"

"I have a little house in Kauai. It's very private."

That sinful, mischievous look in his eyes did me in. The thought of the things he would do to me…

"All right."

"Good. I'll have Keri reschedule your meetings to next week. Callahan is waiting in the lobby."

"You knew I'd say yes?" I asked.

"I can sell ice to an Eskimo, remember?"

Yes, I did. He'd "sold me" on doing all sorts of things last night, and I'd loved every minute of it.

"I'll go pack," I said.

He leaned toward me for a quick kiss. "Bring your running shoes, Miss Snow."

"A marathon, I hope?"

"Absolutely," he replied.

But why did I feel like we were really running away?

※

His "little house" in Kauai was a two-story, modern glass rectangle on stilts with a private beach, views of the ocean from almost every room, and thick jungle on all three sides. Automatic blinds and tinted windows provided privacy when wanted. Otherwise, I felt like we were outside, enjoying the breathtaking, natural surroundings. But with air-conditioning.

That first night—Monday—we arrived just before midnight in his private jet, and we swam naked in the ocean, kissing and touching and grinding away in the warm water, feeling like the only two people on earth. We concluded under the dark moonless sky with sex on the beach. No, not the drink. Real sex. In the soft warm, night sand. Aside from the piles of grit left in my hair, it was fucking raw and sexual in a way I couldn't have imagined.

After we showered, ate sandwiches, and covered ourselves in bug spray, we headed back outside (clothed in shorts and tees) to sit around a gas fireplace on the patio, where we fell asleep in each other's arms on a lounge chair.

The sunrise that next morning, snuggled in his arms, was more beautiful than anything I could dream up. I kept thinking that it was too perfect. This couldn't be real. Him, me, us. We were too happy and too ready to let go of everything that had ever mattered to us for a few precious days of living in this dream.

Yet, knowing it couldn't last, I convinced myself we had to take this chance. We weren't simply in paradise, snorkeling in the crystal clear blue waters, stealing kisses every chance we got, or enjoying the isolation, we were hiding in heaven.

Tuesday night, as I sat staring at the fire outside, slathered in a thick coating of mosquito repellent, still wearing my white bikini from our early swim in the ocean that seemed too beautiful to be a real place on earth, I felt reality seeping through the cracks, its darkness creeping into our safe haven and threatening to poison our paradise.

"What's the matter?" he asked, handing me a chilled glass of white wine. He wore a white shirt and white linen shorts that made his skin look even darker than it was. That man knew how to tan. I looked more like a strawberry milkshake.

Staring into the fire, I shrugged and then sipped my wine. "I don't want it to end." But it would.

"Lily, you know we can't stay on vacation forever."

"Says who?" I asked.

He gave me a look. "Says the people who depend on us."

Now who's being the responsible adult? "No one really depends on me."

"I do. And there are thousands depending on me."

I nodded, the quiet crackle of the fire mixing with the sound of the evening waves. "I wish it was different."

"You'd never be happy sitting on a beach the rest of your life."

"How do you know?" I could give it a try.

"Because you're like me; you have something to prove to the world."

"But what happens when we prove it?" I asked.

He looked at me, genuinely thinking. "I don't know. Maybe we find peace."

"Let's hope." Because after everything was said and done, finding a quiet corner of the world might be the only way for us to live.

"Max?"

He slid his arm around me. "Yes?"

"I want you to set up that doctor's appointment for Friday."

"Liiily?" he warned, not needing an explanation. He knew I meant the surgeon.

"Max, for the first time in my life, I'm really afraid."

"You don't need to be."

"Well, I am, and I just need to know I've given myself every opportunity to get through this."

He looked at me and cupped my cheek. "I'll do it, but you need to know that it's not what I want. I want you exactly as you are."

I placed my hand over his. "You've let go of your ugly. I need to let go of mine. There's no reason to hold on to it."

I could see him trying to digest what I was saying, that strong jaw tensing.

"Max, you can't pretend or lie to me. I'll never forget the moment you saw me for the first time. My face was the only thing you saw."

"And if not for that, I would have tossed you aside—just another beautiful woman who could never understand me."

"I'm tired, Max. I'm tired of fighting. I'm tired of struggling. I just want to move on." He of all people had to understand that.

He smiled softly. "If it's really what you want, but I'll still want you either way."

There were no words, so I kissed him. "I'll still want you either way, too."

He laughed. "Fine. Just promise me you won't change who you are."

"Why would it change me?" Except for the better.

He didn't answer at first. "I'll make the appointment, but all I ask is that you take some time before doing anything. Really think about this."

I had. And I was done thinking. "Sure. If you want."

He kissed me and pulled back. "If anything happened to you, it would kill me, Lily."

He was worried. Genuinely worried. Yes, it made me feel all gooey inside. "I'll be fine, I promise. What could possibly go wrong?"

chapter nineteen

Max and I returned to the office Thursday afternoon, and it was comical and absurd, but I genuinely think no one suspected I wasn't in Houston or that Max hadn't gone on one of his usual business trips to wherever, despite our matching tans. Because, of course, why would a man like that be interested in me?

Whether they suspected or not, however, everyone would likely know we had a special relationship in a few weeks. What would they say? That he'd been using me? Yes. That's exactly what they'd say. The book would come out, Nancy Little would probably out me, and if she didn't, people would still suspect. I really needed to stop pretending this wasn't going to happen.

My only question was: What did Max really intend to do about it? It wasn't that I didn't trust him or his abilities to handle the situation, but I didn't see a way through this. And my IQ wasn't exactly in the "bucket of rocks" category.

I had to pin him down, which I'd planned to do tonight after work. But, just as I was packing up, my cell rang. It was Max.

"Hello?"

"Hi there," he said, his voice totally charming.

"Where are you?" I asked.

"A dispute came up with the contractor in New Jersey. I'm getting on the plane to go hammer it out. I should be back tomorrow night. Callahan can take you back to my house if you'd like to stay there."

"Oh." I really wanted to talk to him tonight. Face to face, though. "No, I think I'll just grab my car from your house and head over to my place. It's not the same being there without you."

"Just as long as you're waiting in my bed when I get back—oh, by the way, I wanted to let you know I called Dr. Bloomfield. He can see you tomorrow morning first thing if you can make it."

I really appreciated Max supporting my wishes like this. "Thank you. I really mean that."

"Just remember, you promised to think this over."

"I already have."

"Think it over again," he said. "Because you don't really need to do this."

I already knew what I wanted to do, but to be honest, Max's repeated insistence that I rethink this was beginning to make me wonder. Why was he really so against this? It didn't make sense.

"I promise to think it over again," I said.

"Good," he said. "Now, I know you'll be missing my giant cock, and I want you to know that it will be thinking of you, too, tonight."

I laughed. "Yeah. Well, tell your friend there not to worry. My vibrator's been really neglected lately. We're due for some good snuggle time."

"Uh-uh. You throw that thing away. Nothing goes down there that isn't attached to my body."

"My, my. Aren't we territorial?"

"You better fucking believe it," he replied. "And I've already made out detailed plans in my head regarding how I intend to show you the many ways I take care of my territory."

I heard a loud roar in the background.

"Plane's taking off," he yelled.

"Bye. See you soon," I said into my phone.

"Bye, you fucking delicious piece of dirty woman."

The call ended, and I tried not to smile.

Honestly, I'd been looking forward to seeing him and having our talk, but we'd been in this whirlwind, and I needed to catch my breath. Everything was happening so fast.

Yeah, I can wait one day to have that conversation. Besides, I should trust him. He had this situation handled. *Right?*

"Hey, Lily. There you are."

I looked up at Mike, who had his laptop bag slung over his shoulder, looking ready to head out.

I cleared my throat. "Hi, Mike." I hoped to dear God he hadn't overheard what I'd just said about my vibrator. My door had been open.

"How was Houston?" he asked.

I shrugged casually, hoping I wouldn't blush. "You know Texas in September: hot." Okay, another lie. But my trip had been hot, especially the man between my thighs.

"Yeah, you look like you got some sun," he said.

You should see my ass from naked sunbathing while Mr. Cole tried to read the morning paper. "I burn pretty easily. It's very annoying." I looked down at my sleeveless white blouse and white skirt. I really did look like strawberry ice cream with vanilla swirls.

We stared at each other for an awkward moment, and then I realized what he was likely thinking: I forgot about him. "Hey, Mike. I know that you asked me to—"

He held up his hand. "It's okay. I know when I'm being blown off. I never should've asked you to begin with, us being coworkers and all."

"No. It's not that, it's just...I'm seeing someone, and it's getting serious." God, this felt so awkward. And I hoped he didn't put the pieces together, but the cat would be out of the bag soon anyway.

"Oh. I didn't know that. You never mentioned him." Mike bobbed his head.

"We haven't known each other long—just sort of happened."

"Completely understandable," he said.

"Great. Thanks for understanding."

"Yeah, of course. I actually came by to invite you

to grab a beer. A couple of us are going around the corner to the pub to talk about the news. No one can get any work done like this."

"What news?" I asked.

"I guess you were really busy in Houston."

"Yeah. I was."

"The rumor mill says B&H is going to do a hostile takeover the minute C.C. goes public."

"How could anyone know that?" I asked.

"They're raising cash. A lot of cash. That means they're getting ready to buy someone."

It didn't make any sense. C.C. was four or five times larger than B&H. Little companies didn't go around buying up larger ones. It was the other way around.

It had to be a rumor, but hey, if people wanted to use it as an excuse to go drink some beer, who was I to get in their way?

"Thanks for the invite, but I've got some work to finish up and have a doctor's appointment early in the morning."

"Sure. Next time, then?" Mike said with a friendly tone.

I didn't want him to think I was completely blowing him off. "Absolutely."

He left, and I felt relieved that was over. Honestly, I liked Mike, but I was falling hard for Maxwell Cole, leaning strongly toward the "L" word, and I couldn't see myself with anyone else. Not now. Not ever.

Friday morning.

Dr. Bloomfield was the best of the best plastic surgeons in the country, according to my research (aka web surfing), and after meeting with him, I had only one question: When could I have the surgery?

The consultation took all of thirty minutes, but with his computer graphics program he was able to show me exactly what I would look like after six hours of surgery—rhinoplasty, chin reshaping, and an eye lift. Three simple procedures. Three.

Staring at the screen, I could hardly believe that was all it would take to make me look normal and, dare I say, beautiful. It felt like I'd been living in a prison, deprived of sunlight, food, and water my entire life, when right there, all along the key sat on the floor inches from my face. No, I hadn't had the money to do surgery before, but had I known how easy it was to fix this, I would've found a way.

But you wouldn't be the same person, now would you?

True.

However, like I'd told Mr. Cole, I was ready to move on. More importantly, I really needed to start confronting the deeper issues in my head—those years of buried insecurities I'd hidden away.

"How long would I be out from work, and when can we do it?" I asked, sitting on the exam table.

Dr. Bloomfield, a fit-looking man in his fifties with glasses and a sprinkle of silver hair, stood up from his little rolling stool. "Normally, people need about a week to be functional—depending on the pain—but you should expect a full recovery from the bruising in about a month. As for when, I'm booked six months to a year in advance; however, the Coles are good customers and personal friends. I'll see when I can fit you in."

Good customers? Had Max had surgery? *No. Way.*

"Oh. Is that *your* work?" I said, taking a stab in the dark. "Max's nose is perfect."

Dr. Bloomfield smiled proudly. "Yes, he and his sister were two of my first rhinoplasties."

*Uh. But...*Dr. Bloomfield had been a plastic surgeon for over twenty years. *Maybe he only started doing nose jobs a few years ago?*

"Well, it's gorgeous," I said, shocked that I'd gotten that out of him.

He gave me a pat on the back. "And you will be, too, after I'm done."

I stood and stuck out my hand but really wanted to hug him. "I'm looking forward to it. Really, really looking forward to it."

"Excellent. I'll see you back here in a few months." He reached for my hand and when he took it, he stopped smiling. "Lily, I just want to caution you, though—as I do with all my patients—this isn't minor surgery. There are risks."

"I know," I said, wondering if Max had told him to hammer the message home. "Infections, scarring, and—"

"And people do die," he added, dropping his hand away.

"Aren't you supposed to be encouraging me to do this?" I asked.

"It's a normal part of the screening process. I need to make sure my patients are fully informed and are here for the right reasons. I take this seriously, and they should, too."

"Okay." I understood that I wasn't getting my hair colored. "How many people die?"

"Approximately one out of every two hundred and fifty thousand."

"Oh." I smiled. "Those odds are good."

"I lost a patient last week, Lily. She was forty-five. Cardiac arrest during lipo. It's nothing to smile about."

Okay, I got the point. And I had to admit his little dose of reality was effective. I had to be sure I really wanted to do this. "I'll give it some thought." And this time I really meant it. Was this worth dying for, even if the risks were low?

"Now that is the answer I wanted to hear," he said.

Why? Because of Max? Or because he really wanted to shoo people away who thought this was like getting their nails done?

He continued, "We'll start the ball rolling while

you think it over." He shook my hand again and instructed me to the nurse, who took blood samples for the lab work and made me sign a bunch of release forms. Now I felt unsure again. Part of me really wanted to do this, and it felt exciting, but the other kept telling me this wasn't necessary.

I laughed at myself, walking to my car.

At first I didn't want to have surgery, because I was too proud to admit that maybe I wasn't comfortable with my looks. Then I wanted to have it because I realized I wasn't. And now, I wasn't sure. Things in my life felt like they were in a good place—scary, but good. Maybe I would wait.

And wow. Max had his nose done, I thought, getting into my car to head to the office. I'd have to ask him about that later. Not that it was a big deal, but it just struck me as odd he hadn't said anything.

⋦∞⋧

The rest of Friday was a rush of emergency meetings and calls with customers who were upset that their orders hadn't shipped. Someone had leaked the alleged takeover to the press, driving up B&H's stock and turning the rumor mill into a full-blown media frenzy.

Add to that, Max had not answered anyone's calls, including mine, and I felt like the world was about to collapse. Something was definitely going down.

And we have no captain.

I spent two hours in a supply-chain triage meeting, arguing with Production and the other sales managers about allocation to customers with the sudden influx of orders. Not one person said a word about the elephant in the room: customers were stocking up, getting ready for something major.

Around three p.m. my desk phone rang, and I braced for yet another irate customer demanding more product, but it was not a customer.

"Miss Snow, it's Nancy Little."

I swallowed the lump in my throat and then decided to hang up. I had nothing to say to her.

She spoke before I had the chance. "Miss Snow, I'm calling to give you one last opportunity to come out publically and tell your story after the book releases."

"And I'd like to give you one last chance to do the right thing. You're going to hurt a lot of people. Good people."

"You're fooling yourself," she said bitterly, "if you think for one minute that Mr. Cole is a good person. He's a selfish, sadistic bastard. All he cares about is his money."

I could see how she might think that. Once upon a time, so did I. "You've misjudged him. But I'm talking about the people who work at C.C. and will lose their jobs. I'm talking about myself and the humiliation you'll put me and my family through. I don't deserve to have my life ruined for your vindictive bullcrap."

"Mr. Cole is responsible for this. Not me. So I suggest you talk to him."

I shook my head. There was no getting through to this crazy woman. "He's not a bad man, Nancy. And as much as I feel for you and the loss you've been through, I can't believe for one moment that this will make you feel any better." This book, hurting me, none of it would bring her sister back. "Why can't you just let it go and move on?"

"You lose your sister like I did, then tell me all about moving on."

I sighed. What she really wanted was the rest of the world to suffer with her. That's what she wanted. "Then good luck to you, Nancy. I hope the damage you'll do to thousands of people is worth it."

"Fifty thousand dollars, Lily. That's what it's worth to you."

"You're trying to bribe me?" I seriously couldn't believe it. And I had to wonder if she'd made the same offer to those other women. After all, Max had said he couldn't understand why those women had turned on him.

"I'm giving you a chance to do what's right and some money to start over," she said. "Because he's using you, Lily. He's going to toss you aside when he's done. That man is sick. A fucking evil bastard."

Whatever. "Goodbye, Nancy." I hung up the phone and dialed Max again. I couldn't lie; my conversation with this woman had shaken me hard, and I needed to hear his reassuring voice.

My call went into voice mail again for the fifth or sixth time, which only deepened my worry. Where was he? Why wasn't he answering my calls?

Regardless, I had a phone call of my own to return from my brother, John, who I'd now seen had left two messages on my phone and a text. I scrubbed my hands over my face, probably smearing my mascara all to hell.

"Okay," I picked up my phone, "let's do this."

I dialed and John answered right away. "What the hell is going on over at C.C.?"

He'd probably seen the news. "I honestly don't know, but I need you to help me tell Mom and Dad about the book." It was coming out soon and they needed to be prepared. "You have to keep them out of my hair, John. I can't deal with everything else and them."

"Fuck. You're not coming out against him, are you?"

"No."

"Don't do this to yourself, Lily. The guy is using you."

Why is everyone saying that? "You don't know him like I do."

"You're right. I don't know him at all. But what

sort of fucked-up asshole would ask my sister to hang out with him when he finds her—and excuse me for saying this—but revolting? Does this make any sense to you?"

No, it didn't. It didn't make any sense that Max wanted to be with me. But he did.

"He's your boss, Lily. He has no business fucking around with you in the first place."

Oh, my God. "I know. I know it looks bad. I know you think he's a monster, but you'll just have to trust me. He's not. And I know what I'm doing." Didn't I? "And right now, I've got to go and deal with hordes of angry customers. So will you help me or not?"

"Fine. I'll talk to them, but don't blame me when your life falls to shit."

Why would I blame him? "I'll be fine. Now go play with your stupid porn."

I hung up the phone, fuming. I knew John loved me, but why couldn't anyone believe me that Maxwell Cole wasn't going to screw me over.

Lily, do you really even believe it yourself?

Shit. I shoved my hands through my hair. *I don't know anymore. I don't know.*

chapter twenty

Danny was in our apartment when I got there just before eight o'clock, and I couldn't have been happier to see her. If anyone would know what was going on at C.C., she would.

"I don't have a clue," she said, standing with me in the kitchen, wearing a cute little white summery dress, mixing up a batch of powdered vitamin water, which meant she was expecting to have some fun tonight with her boyfriend. I'd finally figured it out. Sex hydration. "That doesn't make sense."

Great. "But something is definitely happening." I kicked off my heels and stood barefoot on the kitchen floor. My feet ached as badly as my head. "The customers are freaking out. Everyone's talking about jumping ship." At least, that's what I'd overheard at the water cooler. "And Max is nowhere to be found."

Danny looked at me. "Maybe the rumors are only half true—they're getting ready to sell, but not to B&H. Maybe Max knows about the hostile takeover, decided to scrap the IPO, and is going in another direction. But that doesn't make sense either. Because why would they sell? They're number one." She shook her large water bottle, turning the liquid blue. "Unless something big is going to happen and...the company is going to tank and they know it? They're saving what they can." She shook her head. "Nope. You know what? I don't have a fucking clue. And I know you don't want to hear this, Lily, but you might want to get your résumé tidied up."

Dammit. This really sucked. And I couldn't believe Max would just sit idly back and let his company self-destruct.

Unless, he's the one who's behind all this. After all, Danny had been right about something coming that might "tank" the company.

No. He wouldn't sell out. And he would've told me something was coming.

Would he really? He hadn't bothered to tell me anything so far.

Saturday morning, an insistent buzzing at the door woke me up. I staggered to answer it since Danny hadn't come home from her boyfriend's yet.

"Miss Snow?" said the man, shoving a giant bouquet of red roses at me.

"Uh. Yeah." I took them and held up my finger. "One minute."

"No need for a tip, ma'am. It's already been taken care of."

I thanked him and closed the door, going into the sad little beige kitchen to set the flowers down.

I took out the card, which read:

I'm sorry. I know this has ruined our plans. But it has to be dealt with. – M

I stared at the card, wondering what the hell it meant. Our plans for the weekend? Our plans not to have everything explode in our faces and ruin our lives? What?

I wouldn't have to wonder for very long.

After the flower delivery, I went for a stress-relieving run, only to return to seven news vans parked outside my building. The moment I came around the corner, I was mobbed by intrusive cameras shoved in my face and screaming reporters.

"Is it true you're dating your boss, Maxwell Cole?" "Has he ever called you ugly?" "How does it feel to date a man with such an unusual fetish?"

I was speechless. Utterly speechless.

Panicked and sweaty from my run, I pushed my way inside my apartment, closed all the curtains and got on my laptop. The front-page news was my deepest fears times ten. It was something I couldn't have fathomed. Not in a million years.

Pictures of Maxwell Cole and me leaving his house together, in his car, eating breakfast on his deck, making out in front of the fire at his beach house in Hawaii. Worst of all, there were multiple shots of him and me having sex on the beach.

No. No. No. Someone had taken great care to photograph us together and knew exactly where we'd be.

The headline read, *Soon to Publish Book About Billionaire Maxwell Cole—Fiction or Truth?*

I went on to read all about Nancy Little's upcoming tell-all and the claims it brought against him. But then the article went on to talk about me. My degree from Stanford, my hometown of Santa Barbara, how I'd recently been hired in a senior position without any experience—a lie—and how I was Max's lover—not a lie. The article included the photo from my C.C. employee badge, and the closing sentence spared nothing... *Suffice it to say that if allegations are true, Mr. Cole's definition of ugly would have to be grossly distorted. His current romantic interest, in this reporter's opinion, is no beauty.*

The words were extremely hurtful, but they were tame compared to the two online tabloids I'd checked. Words like "ugly creature" and "a face that could frighten small children" were used.

There were no words or enough space in my heart to contain the devastation and humiliation I felt.

I closed my laptop, reeling with anger and hurt. The only explanation I could come up with was that Maxwell Cole had done this to me. Him. He'd used me to create irrefutable evidence that the book was a lie.

My heart shattered into a thousand little fucking ugly shards of hate. How could I have been so blind? Yet, the signs had been there all along, and I simply refused to see them. Mr. Cole's sudden interest in me. His insistence in hiring me for a position higher than the one I applied for, giving me an office, and promises of the perfect future. The way he'd taken me to Milan, bought me a nice dress and put me up in an expensive hotel room. He blinded me with all that glamour and the dazzle. Then, he pushed back against my having surgery—would look bad for him—meanwhile he tried to flaunt our relationship.

I had been his plan all along, and I'd fallen for it hook, line, and sinker. He knew exactly what a woman like me wanted to hear—after all, he was the master at selling things to my gender.

You're a fucking idiot, Lily. A stupid, fucking idiot. I would bet that those first pictures that came out about me in the tabloids were no coincidence either.

I went over to the wastepaper basket—Danny never emptied shit around here, and I'd been gone most of the time—and there it was. I dialed and put my cell to my ear.

"Nancy? It's Lily Snow. What do you want to know?"

It took forty minutes, on the record, to tell Nancy everything. This time, I told the truth, except for one thing: I did not tell her that I loved him. I knew that I did because there was no possible way I could be hurting this badly if I didn't.

I sent a text to my mother, guessing from the lack of texts and calls that she hadn't seen or heard anything yet...

Me: *When you see the news, please don't worry. I'm coming home. Be there soon.*

I knew she and my father would freak the hell out. And for a mother to have to hear the world call her child an "ugly creature" or accuse me of being some sort of slut because I'd slept with my boss—one man, whom I loved...

Loved. Past tense.

I hung my head and gathered myself as best I could. This was not going to blow over—not for me, anyway. And Mr. Cole would come out looking like a champion for women and sell a ton of makeup with the free press. Just like he'd said. He'd turn this into a million dollars of sales. He was now, and officially, the most desirable man in the world who only dated women whose "souls turned him on," because unlike the other PR stunts of him merely being seen in public with unattractive women, the press couldn't poke holes through claims that he was really dating me. The nude photos, though taken at night, of him fucking me senseless on his private beach said it all. Add up all of the other photos, and it told a story of a man who didn't seem to have any phobia whatsoever.

You're a fucking genius, Mr. Cole. A marketing genius. And he was a coldhearted, greedy fucking bastard. I never thought him capable of such cruelty.

I grabbed my suitcase from the closet and packed up all of my essentials. I'd call Danny later to fill her in and work something out on the rent so she wouldn't be left high and dry.

Before I left the building, I left a quick goodbye note for Mrs. Jackson, telling her I'd miss our little chats, and then took one final breath. I couldn't stand the thought of facing all of those reporters outside, but if I had to go through this, I needed to be with my family.

The moment I emerged from my building, they hit me like a swarm of stinging bees, shouting horrible insults posed as questions.

I pushed my way to the car, trying not to bawl, but the tears were there. And these heartless assholes wouldn't let me get to my car.

"Get the fuck out of my face!" I yelled. I finally lost it and pushed some guy with a camera out of my way. He fell back and lost his grip.

Bastard deserved it. Why were they being so aggressive? I was a nobody.

Finally in my car, my suitcase shoved into the passenger seat, I got out of the parking lot, thinking they'd let me go. They didn't. Several vans with satellite dishes followed me onto the highway.

I can't fucking believe it. Were they going to get on the plane with me, too? Should I keep on driving all the way to California? I didn't know what to do, and the only thing I wanted was to get away.

My phone rang, and when I saw the caller ID pop up on my car's console, I flipped. *Max...*

"You fucking sonofabitch! How could you?" I yelled.

"Lily, calm the hell down. I'm at your apartment; where are you?"

I whisked away the tears from my face. "Where am I? Where am *I*?" I yelled. "Where the hell have *you* been?"

"I was trying to keep you out of this while I tried to—"

"Fuck you, Mr. Cole. Fuck you to hell." I was so, so in this, and he'd put me there!

"Lily, please listen to me. I would never—"

"Don't ever call me again. Do you hear me? Don't come near me or so help me I will kill you."

Words of anger, surely, but I meant them in that moment. I honestly envisioned wrapping my hands around his neck and squeezing the life out of him. How could he? How?

"Lily, you need to—"

I hung up the phone, my entire body shaking with rage. I couldn't think or breathe or—

I looked over my shoulder at the news camera in the fast lane to my left, filming me have an epic breakdown while driving eighty miles an hour.

What is wrong with these people? Why was my life falling apart so fascinating?

When I turned my head to change lanes and move away from them, I almost hit another car passing me like an idiot on the right. I overcorrected, jerking the car left, and then it just kept on going. I plowed my car into the center divider.

chapter twenty-one

The moments after the accident were a blur, mostly seen through a sheet of blood that poured into my eyes. I remembered screaming voices, sirens, and pain. Lots of pain. In my back, my arm, and my face.

When I came to, the drug-induced fog wasn't enough to kill the agony, and I knew there was major damage all over my body.

I groaned and lifted my hand to my face. It was covered in bandages, and I couldn't help but laugh. If I'd been ugly before, I was hideous now.

"Lily?" said a kind-sounding female voice. "Can you hear me?"

"Yes," I mumbled.

"I'm Haley, your nurse. Do you know where you are?"

"In the hospital." *And I need more drugs...*

"That's right. You've been in an accident. The doctor will be here in a moment to check on you, but you've just come out of surgery, and I want to ask you a few questions."

She went on to ask my name, age, and where I'd been when the accident occurred. I could only assume they wanted to check for brain damage.

After I passed her test, I asked her the only thing on my mind. "How bad is it?"

She looked at me. "You broke your arm, hairline fractured your skull, and you have a deep cut on your forehead. But you'll survive."

"What about the rest of my face?"

"The airbag spared you from the worst of it, but you hit the divider at an angle. Your side mirror broke off and hit your nose, but the doctor will explain everything that was done and possible follow-up surgeries."

I wanted to laugh. I'd be getting my face rebuilt anyway. Only this time, I'd probably be lucky to look as good as I once had. I could feel the throbbing in my nose, cheeks and jaw, and my head felt like someone had taken a hammer to it.

"Just hang tight, Lily," she added. "The doctor will go through everything with you and then you can see your parents."

"They're here?" I asked.

"Yes. So is Maxwell Cole."

How dare he? How dare he come here? What a heartless prick. I was sure, that out of everyone in the world, his was the last face on earth my poor parents wanted to see. "Send him away."

"I can't make him leave, but you don't have to see him if you don't want to."

The doctor, a tall woman with short brown hair and wearing scrubs, came in holding a clipboard.

Her tag read *Dr. Meyers*.

"How are you feeling, Lily?" she said, flashing a little light in my eyes.

"Awesome," I replied, trying to move my jaw as little as possible.

"Well," she pulled up a chair and sat, "I saw the accident on TV, and considering how fast you were going, you're very lucky."

"When do I get to see my face?"

"I think the bandages can come off next week. Dr. Bloomfield will take a look, make sure everything's draining properly and re-bandage you."

"Dr. Bloomfield?"

"He handled your facial trauma."

"I had plastic surgery?" I asked.

"You had all of the paperwork signed and since you were stable, I approved. It's generally better to make the patient have to go through healing once—when possible. And your nose was shattered. He's taken some rib cartilage and rebuilt it."

Ohmygod. I moved just a little and did feel some bandages on my side, but the pain was everywhere.

"You had another laceration above your eye, right under the brow, so he repaired that and did the lift. The chin has been reformed, too, since we needed to go in and dig out a lot of debris from the mirror that embedded into your face."

I was speechless.

She went on, "We won't know about the extent of the scarring, but Dr. Bloomfield is an excellent surgeon. He'll be around later to give you instructions to minimize scarring."

"So am I going to look normal after this?"

"You'll have some scars. Some will fade over time." She smiled. "But you're alive. Try focusing on that." She stood up.

"Thank you. Thank you so much for taking care of me."

"You can thank Maxwell Cole."

"Why would I do that?" I was in this mess because of him.

"I was off today, at my daughter's soccer tournament in Detroit for the weekend—but that man wouldn't take no for an answer. He made sure Dr. Bloomfield was called in, too."

"I'm so sorry. Thank you, Dr. Meyer." I would later learn that she was one of the best surgeons in the state with three medical degrees. Her specialty was treating trauma patients—broken bones, internal injuries, that kind of stuff.

"Don't mention it, Lily."

As I lay there, feeling my body ache and throb, I felt grateful for what Max had done, but did he really believe he could buy me off or absolve himself with this? And why the hell did he even care?

Maybe he hoped I'd retract my story.

When my mother and father came into the room, wearing their wrinkled khaki shorts and old T-shirts they normally gardened in, the stress was all over their tear-stained faces. They must've dropped everything and jumped on a flight to Chicago and slept in the waiting room. If my heart wasn't already broken, it would be cracking into two right now.

"Don't even pretend to be upset," I groaned my words, trying to crack a joke. "I know how happy you are to finally have a reason to worry."

My mother sat next to me, her brown eyes beet red from crying. "What were you thinking?" She took my hand, careful not to tangle the IV.

I wasn't. "I wanted to get away from those reporters." *Assholes.*

"Well, Max is going to make sure they pay for what they did to you. They had no right."

I had a feeling the press wasn't even close to being done with me yet. Nevertheless… "I don't want his help, Mom. That man is just as responsible as they are."

She shook her head, making her messy lopsided ponytail flop around against her shoulder. "You've been out for a while, so you haven't seen the news, but you might want to give him a chance, Lily. He really, really cares about you."

I looked away, the tears stinging my eyes.

"Honey," my father said to my mother, "let's not upset her. She's been through enough and this other stuff can wait."

She looked up at him. "You're right." He leaned down and kissed the top of my hand. "I'm glad you're okay, sweetie. That's all that matters."

"Tell Max to leave," I said. "I really don't want him here."

She sighed in that special way when something bothered her. "I'll let him know."

Asshole had fucked up my life, and now he snowed one over on my parents. Was there no limit to how low he would go?

⁂

Over the next several days, I received flowers from a few coworkers, including Keri (a shocker given the scandal); friends back in California; my brother, who'd also called to chew me out; and even Danny had brought some along when she came to visit. Thankfully, my parents had instructed her not to mention you-know-who, but I could tell he'd gotten to her, too. The look in her big brown eyes was pure angst and worry, but I just didn't want to hear it. Anything she had to say would be tainted with more of his lies.

Anyway, after three days in the hospital, I was stable, with a few weeks of healing ahead for my cuts and face, and months for my arm. Regardless, I'd be going back to California just as soon as I saw Dr. Bloomfield in a few weeks for my checkup.

My father wheeled me out of the hospital with my mother at my side, and we were again mobbed by the press. Standing off in the distance behind them, I spotted Maxwell Cole, his dark sunglasses covering his eyes as he leaned against his Porsche. Just seeing him sent me into a tailspin of emotions and made my heart feel like it had been filled with cement.

I pretended not to see him.

That night, my parents flew out—my dad needed to get back to work and I begged my mother to go with him. I needed time alone, and Danny had graciously agreed to take me to my follow-up appointments, help me pack, and then get me onto a plane in a few weeks. Everything would soon be behind me. If I could just let go...

But that same night, I found myself on Danny's laptop, mine having been totaled in the crash, surfing the news sites for...well, I didn't know. I just wanted answers, I guess. But I wasn't ready for what I found. Pages and pages about the crash. But the bigger story was what Maxwell Cole had done immediately following. I couldn't stop crying.

What did I do? What did I do?

The answer: I had just fucked my life. And his.

I was possibly the ugliest person on the planet. And I'd hurt him. I'd put him in the worst position ever.

I'd destroyed his life. The man I loved.

chapter twenty-two

Two Weeks Later

"Are you going to be okay?" Danny asked from her idling black Jetta standing at the curb just outside the C.C. headquarters.

With my two black eyes, very bruised face, and large bandages covering my nose, forehead, and chin, I tried not to smile. It still hurt way too much, but Drs. Bloomfield and Meyers had both said I was good to go and could do any follow-up with my family doctor back in California.

"Yeah, I'll just be a few minutes," I said. She'd be taking me to O'Hare right after and then going back to our apartment to pack up her own stuff. She was going to move in with her boyfriend—finally!—and give their relationship a serious go. I planned to send her a case of vitamin water as soon as I got to California. With the way those two went at it, I was sure I'd be sending diapers and formula soon, too. Honestly, though, I couldn't be happier for her.

I got out of the car and entered the lobby, passing men hauling boxes and furniture on dollies.

There was no security at the desk, but why

would there be? C.C. no longer existed.

I rode to the top floor, exiting into an office space stripped of any personal items. All evidence of the life that once breathed here was gone, and I wondered what would happen to Keri and all of the others who once worked here. With luck, they'd all find other positions, but there was no doubt this had become a major speed bump in their lives.

The guilt I felt for the part I'd played was overwhelming.

I walked into Mr. Cole's office and found him staring out the window at the Chicago skyline. He wore his usual black suit, but his silhouette lacked that rigid posture I'd become so accustomed to. I wouldn't call him relaxed or sad, but simply…different.

"Hi," I said, trying not to startle him. He was expecting me after my text this morning—our first communication since the world turned upside down—but he looked deep in thought.

Hands shoved into his pockets, he slowly turned and looked at my face. I pretended not to feel anything from the gesture, but I couldn't suppress the hope he might forgive me and still want me. Despite everything. Despite my having made an epic cluster fuck out of his life.

"So," I said, unsure where to start.

"How are you healing?" he asked.

I shrugged. "Okay, I guess. They had to put pins in my arms, so that will take longer, but you already know that." He'd hired Dr. Meyer to ensure I was put back together nicely.

"Glad to hear it."

There was a long, long awkward moment of silence. "I don't know what to say. Somehow, I'm sorry doesn't seem to cut it." He'd lost everything because of me.

"I'm not sure you're entirely to blame. Nancy Little and my mother had a hand in all this, too."

I knew that was true, but he hadn't been counting on them to trust him. Still, I had to ask, "So at what point did your mother decide to throw me under the bus?" She'd had us followed by a photographer and then leaked the images to the press.

How'd I know?

Because I'd watched the press conference he'd held to clear the air. For me. And I believed him. Every damned word.

He replied, "I'm guessing my mother decided after you and I went to Milan. That little tabloid episode probably gave her the idea."

"I'm so sorry I blamed you," I said. "I should've known you wouldn't do something like that."

"Yes, you should've, and why didn't you trust me?" I could see the hurt in his eyes.

The truth wasn't an easy thing to say, but I felt he deserved it.

I cleared my throat, trying to push out the words. "Because I honestly didn't believe someone like you could really ever love someone like me. It's just like you'd said; I didn't feel I deserved it. I wasn't good enough. Not for you or anything." But that didn't mean I didn't want him or the life I'd dreamed of.

"You should've trusted me," he fumed.

Every single woman who'd been part of that book had come forward, saying they'd been paid off by B&H, arranged through Nancy Little, to severely exaggerate their stories. At what point she'd decided to approach C.C.'s competitor, no one knew, but all that would come out in litigation. Likely. But she had to have lost her marbles to go after him with such a vengeance, and what better way to do it than blow up C.C.'s reputation and devalue his company completely. B&H could then make a play to buy up all of their assets, including their factory and patents, for pennies on the dollar. It was such a deal, baby.

Only Max had a plan to blow it all up and get the truth out there. He'd been armed and ready, already knowing everything B&H and Nancy Little were up to. His mother, however, seemed like a curveball. Still, he'd had it all handled. And then I ruined everything by telling Nancy how he'd lied and only pretended to care about me. I hadn't accepted the money from her, so that created enough public doubt. Me against two women who'd put their stories into a book, only to suspiciously recant in the eleventh hour. It made it look like they'd been threatened by Maxwell Cole to recant, and I was the only one telling the truth. But I hadn't. I had assumed the worst, erroneously.

Max had no choice but to come out with his very, very private truth, because once the ball started rolling, he couldn't fix the damage I'd created. He could only hope to lessen it.

"So why did you sell C.C.?" I asked.

He shrugged. "It was the only rational choice."

"I read the articles and blog posts and...there was no reason to fold, Max."

He'd come out to the public right after my accident, and he'd told the truth. About me, about his phobia, and about everything. He held nothing back, including pointing out the fact that I was right to have believed he'd betrayed me. He literally cried on TV, not a sob or a bawl, but a very touching manly sort of teary-eyed speech apologizing to me, to his customers for hiding his painful truth, and to his employees for letting them down. I'd never seen anything so heart wrenching and inspiring than this man standing in front of the world, telling women not to listen to anyone who tells them they're not good enough because they weren't born airbrushed. He closed with saying that he truly loved me and that the press's behavior was a new low for humanity. "A woman is worth so much more than her looks, and Lily Snow is proof of that. She put her pride aside to help me because she cared. And I find that truly beautiful."

I had cried my eyes out watching that video on the Internet, but knowing he announced the sale of his company to some Canadian corporation with an office across town, that he would be giving it all up, broke what was left of my heart.

"I had one very good reason to sell C.C., Lily. You were right; my mother is toxic, and her willingness to hurt you was proof there could be no good in maintaining any connection with her."

"I thought going public would solve that," I said.

"I was fooling myself. She'd still be a major shareholder. She'd still be in my life. I want nothing to do with her. She's done enough damage to you, me, my family—especially my sister, who I am now searching for."

So...was he saying he would've sold either way? I suppose I should've felt some sort of relief from knowing that, but I didn't. At the end of the day, I hadn't put my trust in him when I should've. I made a huge mess. The only silver lining out of the whole thing was that he might get his sister back.

He continued, "I never should've traded ambition for what was right: being there for my sister and getting the hell away from my mother."

God, I couldn't argue with that. If not for his sister's sake, then for his own. He probably would never be quite right, but he'd get better if he put some distance between himself and the problem.

"Did she really make you have plastic surgery when you were thirteen?" I asked. In his press conference, he didn't give much detail other than to say his "obstacles stemmed from some extreme circumstances growing up." Of course, I knew his mother had the same phobia as he did, and I also knew from Dr. Bloomfield how long ago he'd done Max's nose—that perfect, straight beautiful nose. It had been twenty years ago and that would've put Max at thirteen. His sister had gotten hers done, too, at fourteen.

"Her quest for perfection was a very big part of my childhood, but I've moved past it now. And I want to keep it that way." Meaning, he didn't want to talk about it.

"I'm sorry, Max. I'm really, really sorry." I'd already retracted everything publically, but it didn't matter. The press seemed more focused on the B&H part of the story now. The executives were probably going to be indicted for fraud. "I can't say it enough."

"None of it matters now," he said. "C.C. is sold—all essential personnel are being moved over to their new home and the others are enjoying generous severance packages—I can let my mother fight in the courts with B&H, and you're alive. It's over. And I'm out."

"What will you do?" Not that he was broke. The press said he'd gotten a tidy sum for the company, shared with his mother of course, but now I knew the truth: This was never about the money for him. He was a man who loved living and wasn't afraid of challenges. He loved to push people to their fullest potential and believed in being genuine. What you saw was what you got. No bullshit. Just...beautiful. Inside and out.

"I haven't decided yet," he said.

"Max, I know you have no reason to forgive me or want to let me back in your life—not after you trusted me so implicitly—but you have to recognize that I was right about one thing: I am absolutely not and never will be good enough for you. You are completely amazing and strong and such an ass and you should've told me what you were doing or called me when the shit hit the fan, but nevertheless, I'm sure you had your reasons, which now, knowing you as I do, had to have been because you didn't want to drag me into all this and you were trying to insulate me because that's just the sort of guy you are." I drew a sharp breath, pausing my rushed words. "But I am begging you to give me another chance. I'll do whatever you want, go anywhere you want, say anything you need to hear, but please, please forgive me, Max. I honestly love you. And I have since the moment you looked at me. Really looked at me."

I waited for his reply, but all I got was a view of that pulsing jaw, that large hand running through his messy hair, and the other hand parked on his waist.

God, how could I have let that fucking ugly voice inside my head tell me so many lies about him?

How had I allowed myself to ignore my heart?

"Thanks for coming by," he finally said, giving nothing away and glancing at his watch, "but I've got to meet with my lawyers to settle a few remaining loose ends."

Body language says a lot, more than words ever could, and his said he didn't want anything to do with me. *Full circle.*

We ended exactly where we started: Maxwell Cole was repulsed by me. Only this time, it wasn't because of my face and I couldn't argue.

I held back my tears—not for my pride, but for him. He didn't deserve to feel bad for rejecting me. He really didn't.

"Goodbye, Max. And thank you for everything." *Thank you for being the only person to ever really take the time to see me.*

chapter twenty-three

My name is Maxwell Cole. I am now thirty-four years old. I am six foot three, and I was once the man millions of women longingly stroked themselves to each night, wishing for a taste. I am also fucking ugly.

Yes, they say that beauty is in the eye of the beholder, but so is ugly. And if anyone's picture were to be posted in the dictionary, surely my photo would deserve the spot beside the word.

No, I am not lacking when it comes to looks—a face that can stop any woman's heart with a subtle twitch of my lips, and a body I've dedicated the last twenty years, several hours each day, to sculpting and perfecting, right down to the diagonal ridges that run below my six-pack and end right at my large dick.

My bank account is nothing to sneeze at either. I am, by most people's definitions, fucking handsome as hell and a great catch.

Yet, there is a part of me, buried deep inside, that thinks so many ugly thoughts that sometimes I wonder if I'm human. How can anyone with a heart or a soul think such despicable things about women?

Because I do.

Those who fail to meet my standards of beauty have revolted me as long as I can remember.

My mother beat those thoughts into me. She nearly drove my sister mad, too.

But knowing those toxic thoughts weren't my own, yet feeling them anyway, triggered a lifelong obsession. Ironically, I also found inspiration in these women who cause such deep emotional conflict inside me.

Short, tall, small tits, big asses—didn't matter. I found a certain fascination in these people who, despite their superficial imperfections, clearly loved themselves. *I can learn from them*, I'd thought. *And I can be that voice that tells them not to listen to the Mrs. Coles of the world.*

That was why I founded C.C.—to prove to myself that I did not have to be a product of my mother's illness. There was a sweet, twisted, vengeful beauty making billions by preaching to the masses how wrong her ideals were.

But everything I had was built on lies. My lies. Because I shared her same sickness.

Then I met Lily.

It's difficult for a man, especially one like me, to articulate how someone like her affects you. But the moment she refused to accept my disgusting, afflicted ways, the belief inside her that a person was more than what my eyes saw, I knew; I'd never seen a more beautiful woman. And that moment in Milan when I couldn't stop smiling? That was when I saw her beginning to realize it also. If there was hope for her, there was hope for me.

Unfortunately, too many assholes like me had gotten to her. She wasn't a lost cause, but it would take some work to get her to see herself through my eyes.

Only I'd failed. I'd failed to get through to her.

She said that she didn't deserve me, but it's only because she had no clue what I'd been before I'd met her. And now, I needed to tell her everything, including how I had never planned to keep her as my employee. I'd planned to have her work by my side. Forever. Only, I hadn't had the balls to come clean before it all went to shit.

A fucking coward.

Yet, here I was, standing outside her little store with daisies painted on the window that she'd created with her own two hands. Those soft, loving, sensual hands.

I stepped inside her small clothing boutique, just a block from the main street in downtown Santa Barbara. I knew she had no employees—yet—worked twelve hours a day, if not more, and had paid off her loans from the settlement with those fucking news vultures who'd stalked her. She would never have full strength in her left arm again, the scar on her forehead would never fade, and despite the surgeries, her nose would always lean slightly to the right, according to Dr. Bloomfield.

But I knew I would love every imperfection more than ever, because despite six months of separation, I couldn't move on. And I had finally forgiven myself just like I'd forgiven her. Like me, she'd been blinded by that ugly voice in her head. But she'd also given me back my life. Lily was everything to me.

"Hello, Lily."

She turned, and her beautiful brown eyes went from a warm friendly glow to trepidation.

"Max? What are you doing here?"

Looking at her face, now healed, took me by surprise. It still looked like her, but the bulbous nose was replaced with a thinner more delicate shape. That large square chin had been sculpted down into a rounded point. And those eyes that once had lids sagging over the sides were wide open and round. The scar on her forehead left a little mark that ran into her hairline, but other than that, I couldn't see much evidence of the meat grinder her face had gone through during the accident.

However, as I stood there staring at her, the beauty of her new face was completely lost on me. All I could see when I gazed into her eyes was us.

"I heard you're hiring a part-time assistant." I pointed to the sign in the window.

With a stern expression, she placed that petite hand on her sexy little hip in that feisty way I so adored.

"I also heard you might be looking for a husband," I added. "But I don't have any experience. Think you might consider me anyway?"

She smiled, and it was the most beautiful thing I'd ever seen.

THE END

note from author

Hi All,

Usually, I have a note at the end of every book telling you about what comes next or swag or some other fun stuff. But I felt like this story deserved something different. A little backstory.

While it is perfectly okay to enjoy this book as entertainment, the underlying piece of this comes from a recent realization in my life.

It's insane, but despite my beautiful children, loving husband, triumphs, and degrees, I realized that there is something broken in the way I think. And I'm not alone.

Getting older, grayer, and larger has made me question my self-worth. But here's the kicker: When I was 15, 19, 22, 28, 35 and 42, the face staring back at me in the mirror has always been the same: Not good enough. 110 pounds or 190, I've despised aspects of my body equally.

This book was never about a young woman looking for acceptance, but about that derailing inner voice determined to sabotage our best intentions and potential. It tells us women that we don't deserve to love ourselves because we're not perfect. And it's toxic. (Just like Mr. Cole's mother.)

But we all know that beauty fades. And true love does not. And that includes self-love. So I hope if you're like me—constantly struggling to keep your fugly voice from taking you down—this story will inspire you to never give up and trust those who love you. There is a reason they love you: because you deserve it. And when those moments come when you doubt yourself, just take a moment and try to see yourself through their eyes.

With Love,

Mimi

P.S. Yeah...I've still got some swag made up. ☺ Send a note to mimi@mimijean.net with your address. Be sure to mention if you POSTED a review so I can include something extra as a "thank you."

PLAYLIST:

"Written In The Water" by Gin Wigmore

"Respect" by Aretha Frankllin

"Between Love & Hate" by The Strokes

"The Blower's Daughter" by Damien Rice

"Spanish Sahara " by the Foals

"Be Together (feat. Wild Belle)" by Major Lazer

"Lean On (feat. MØ & DJ Snake)" by Major Lazer

"Come On Closer" by Jem

"Ask Yourself" by Foster The People

"Can't Pretend" by Tom Odell

"Together (Lost Kings Remix Radio Edit)" by Cazzette

"That's How Strong My Love Is" by Otis Redding

"All of Me" by Billie Holiday

"Beautiful World" by Carolina Liar

acknowledgements

I wanted to come up with something cute to say to everyone, like thank you for being so "f-abulous" or "f-antastic," but I just couldn't find a good antonym for the word fugly. Falluring? Fawesome? See. It doesn't work!

So I'll just give a heartfelt thank you to everyone who's always there to help me make these books!

To my hubby and kids who never stop showing their love and support and who bring me coffee in the morning.

To my critique partner, Kylie Gilmore, who always drops what she's doing to take a read when I'm under the gun.

To my beta-beauties, Dali, Ally, and Bridget, for making time in their busy lives to provide wonderful, and sometimes very entertaining, feedback!

And one final thanks to Team Mimi: Su (another fabulous cover, woman!), Latoya, Pauline, Stef, and Jan!

From my heart, I thank you!

Mimi

MerCiless

Coming November 30th, 2015!
Book #3, The Mermen Trilogy

This Guy Messed with the Wrong Woman...

There's a funny thing about luck. One day it runs out. And when it does you'd better be ready to answer for your sins. Especially if you are a merman.

BUY LINKS:
www.mimijean.net/merciless-book-3.html

MACK (from the King Trilogy)

Coming February, 2016

He won't break you. But his story will tear your heart to pieces...

BUY LINKS:
www.mimijean.net/mack.html

about the author

Mimi Jean Pamfiloff is a *New York Times* & *USA Today* best-selling author of Paranormal and Contemporary Romance. Her books have been #1 genre sellers around the world. Both traditionally and independently published, Mimi has sold over 600,000 books since publishing her first title in 2012, and she plans to spontaneously combust once she hits the one million mark. Although she obtained her international MBA and worked for over 15 years in the corporate world, she believes that it's never too late to come out of the romance closet and follow your dream.

When not screaming at her computer or hosting her very inappropriate radio show (*Man Candy Show* on Radioslot.com), Mimi spends time with her two pirates in training, her loco-for-the-chili-pepper hubby, and her rat terrier, DJ Princess Snowflake, in the San Francisco Bay Area.

She continues to hope that her books will inspire a leather pants comeback (for men) and that she might make you laugh when you need it most.

Sign up for Mimi's mailing list
for giveaways and new release news!

LEARN MORE:

mailto: mimi@mimijean.net

www.mimijean.net

twitter.com/MimiJeanRomance

http://radioslot.com/show/mancandyshow/

www.facebook.com/MimiJeanPamfiloff